MORE PRAISE FOR
PLAINSONG

"This dreamlike tale can be read and enjoyed on several levels. . . . A deceptively simple but haunting tale that interweaves mythology with the religions of the world."

Booklist

"Grabien weaves Christian, Greek and Hindu myth into an alternative vision of life and a remarkable understanding of faith. . . . Her imaginative story makes the fantastic seem possible."

Publishers Weekly

"A charming fantasy."

The Kirkus Reviews

Also by Deborah Grabien:

EYES IN THE FIRE
FIRE QUEEN

PLAINSONG

Deborah Grabien

FAWCETT CREST • NEW YORK

A Fawcett Crest Book
Published by Ballantine Books
 Published in the United States by Ballantine Books, a division of Random House, Inc., New York, and simultaneously in Canada by Random House of Canada Limited, Toronto.

Library of Congress Catalog Card Number: 89-77955

ISBN 0-449-21985-2

This edition published by arrangement with St. Martin's Press, Inc.

Printed in Canada

First Ballantine Books Edition: December 1991

In Memoriam:
Professor Joseph Campbell,
for the seeds of myth perfectly sown.

Prologue

ONE DAY, WHEN the Son of God had been long wandering through the halls of heaven, he stopped to rest beside an aged man on a bench of alabaster.

"You look weary, my son," said the old man.

"I am weary indeed," the Son answered. "So many days have I wandered, seeking him that was my earthly father."

"Strange," said the old man, "but I, too, have grown weary, seeking him that was my earthly son."

A gleam of hope shot into the Son's eyes. "My father was a carpenter."

"I was a carpenter," said the old man, surprised.

"He was not my father in flesh, yet he treated me as his son all the days of his life."

"My son was not the son of my loins, either."

Hope burned bright now in the Son's eyes. "My father's name was Joseph."

"My name, in your tongue, would be Joseph," said the old man, and great joy came up in his face.

The Son threw wide his arms and embraced the old man. "Father!" he cried with delight, and the old man hugged the Son to his breast and, through his tears of joy, said,

"Pinocchio!"

1

Painters and Big Sisters

A MAN STOOD IN a meadow, painting.

To anyone passing, to any curious eye that might have chanced to fall across this green strip of land, the scene would have appeared both pastoral and strange. A large man in a tattered bathrobe, an easel, a palette on which the brilliant colors had run together in places, like Joseph's coat; the air above his head seemed full of light, an exquisitely golden translucency with a voice all its own.

Counterpointing the light was the quiet. At the end of the twentieth century, one might have expected the low-frequency hum that had been omnipresent since the invention of the automobile, a familiar rumble of engines, footsteps, machinery, a sound whose threatening overtones had long since passed into the contempt of acceptance. Yet the quiet was absolute, not broken but enhanced by the few audible noises: birds, insects, flowing water, the voice of the wind as it soughed through cloud and tree.

No cars hurried down the highways, no planes moved

through the skies leaving contrails in their wake. With the voices of modern life silent, the voice of the life beneath had somehow come into its own.

The painter paused, standing immobile for a moment. His fingers, knobbly and oddly beautiful, clutched a long, stained brush whose fine hairs were matted with ancient paint left to dry on the tips. The canvas that rested on the wooden easel was a swirl of unearthly images, disturbing conglomerations of small geometric squares unaccountably married to loose shapes.

He dipped the brush in a brilliant pool of alizarin crimson, covering the tiny flecks of old paint, and brought his arm down in a parabola. The wet brush hit the canvas with a satisfying smack; beneath the thin blotch of red, a curious glitter of old, dried paint shone.

A man, an easel, a vivid sky.

There were also ravens.

One of them, small by the standards of its species, sat calmly atop the easel. Three others, enormous black birds of omen, perambulated around the man's feet with a sense of purpose that was both obvious and incomprehensible to human understanding. Every few minutes, one of the birds would break into a series of croaks and clicks, lifting an impressive set of wings as if to emphasize whatever arcane point of philosophy it was trying to communicate. Then the croaks would stop, the wings would drop, and the brush would move again, circling and turning, dancing its way to its properly ordained destination.

It was a scene of summer. The green of grass and tree looked not quite real in its density, the sky overhead was gold and blue, the wide meadow was dotted with scarlet flowers so brightly perfect that they might well have been touched with the paintbrush themselves. Even the ravens shone, enormous square exclamation points of ebony gloss, glinting against the day.

The man was smiling, a faint, abstracted, close-mouthed smile that showed no teeth and gave nothing away. His eyes were very wide and very blue and seemed, on the surface, to hold not very much of anything. A second look, however, revealed one thing: a faint expression of happy surprise.

The brush executed a perfect square, vermilion, edged in a paler scarlet. The raven on the easel arched his back delicately, and peered straight down. "That's not half bad, if I do say so myself. But why red? Those tiny bubbles in the house stream, they're blue. *Blue.* Not red."

Something, perhaps a fleeting look of patience too often tried and renewed, moved across the blankly happy face. "I don't see them that way, John. Actually, they're white, not blue. But white's boring." The brush moved again, leaving the canvas to show another square shining bubble. "Scarlet and more scarlet, that's the ticket."

The raven snorted, a peculiar noise indeed to come from a bird's throat. "Ben, you'll drive me to molting, you really will. Scarlet, indeed. White, rubbish! They're blue, I tell you."

"Blue yourself. You want them blue, you paint the bloody picture, that's what."

The raven, whose beak had not once opened during this silent interchange between bird and biped, gave an irritable shake and croaked loudly. "Matthew, Mark, will you listen to the man? Paint it myself! Is this the thanks we get? Luke, did you hear him? Hark at the pride of the wingless!"

The man laid his brush down and ran one hand through his hair. Since he had brushed that same hand against his palette not a moment before, this activity left his pale hair wildly streaked with color. He looked, in fact, rather like a bird himself; not a raven, but something exotic, something that would perch in the green canopy of the rain forest, craning its neck toward the sun.

"Sorry, John. Didn't mean to ruffle your feathers." The pun, a traditional apology when one of the flock had been outraged by some aspect of human perversity, brought forth the usual sigh from the bird on the easel. The other three paused in their purposeful strolling about the lawn to listen expectantly.

"All right, all right, all right. You say scarlet, scarlet it is. What color do you mean to make Old Trout? Pink? Fuchsia, maybe?" He shook his head. "Humans."

"Of course not. Deep smoky gray, with a purple tint to him." Ben aimed the thought quickly, as if to forestall another outbreak of irritation from the raven. "He looks that way, especially in stormy weather. Well, doesn't he?"

"True." The raven lifted his head and settled; the effect was unnervingly like a yawn. "Lord, I'm hungry. How about something to eat, then?"

The man gave this mild question serious consideration. The brush, by this time, had been absently deposited behind one ear, and now he had a blotch of crimson high on one cheekbone, like a Regency beauty patch. "Um. Yes. Yes, I do believe I am hungry. Food?"

"Right. You go on painting, Ben. Matthew! Teatime, mate. Let's go forage, shall we? Mark and Luke, stay here and mind the store."

Two ravens lifted their bodies to meet the wind and flapped away to the south. The other two came up, close behind the painter. He stood a moment, staring after the black shapes diminishing now into the soft cloud bank, and then glanced down at the two birds, sitting solemn and improbable at his feet.

"Arg," he said sympathetically. Taking brush in hand once more, he went happily back to his picture.

"One pie, two pie, they'll do for me till the day I die. Three pies, four pies, time to bake some more pies."

Dilly Wren stood in the spacious kitchen and caroled, happy and off-key, at the top of her lungs. The sunlit room was redolent with the mysterious and joyful smell of pastry straight out of the oven; apple mingled with apricot, drifting through the open windows and out into the orchard, uniting with the summery scent of fruit still on the tree.

"Pies, pies, how I love you pies," she sang, and fed more wood into the massive antique stove. In an ancient highchair at the scarred kitchen table, a small child watched Dilly, her fat poppy cheeks puffed with concentration. After a moment, she gurgled and banged, once, on the tray of her chair.

Dilly pushed a strand of brown hair, erratically streaked with flour, behind one ear. "Now then, my Maddy, eat your eggs. The pie's for afters. You know that."

The baby, perhaps two years old, puckered her face as if in protest. In an abrupt reversal, she suddenly chuckled, a fat, thick sound, and delicately lifted a lump of scrambled eggs between her fingers. Dilly nodded, approving this action, and set one of the pies in its heavy iron dish on the window ledge to cool.

"Apple and peach, apple and cherry, pie is for Maddy as brown as a berry," she half-sang, half-chortled, and another pie followed the first. As if in agreement with this primal song of happiness, a streak of sun found her, leaving her standing in light like a stained-glass madonna.

So Dilly Wren, twelve years old, sang in her bright kitchen. Behind her, two-year-old Maddy chewed with the loving intensity of young childhood, massaging the soft egg between her eleven teeth, worrying about nothing at all. A third pie, and then a fourth, moved from oven to mitted hands to windowsill and, as the pies moved in their assembly-line dance, Dilly was free to think.

At the moment, she was thinking about birds. They had come twice already, the large black birds, and they would come again; it never crossed her mind, edged with the absolutes of adolescence, that the birds might not return.

Ravens, she thought, they must be ravens.

Twice, now.

She had missed them, that first time. She had taken a small ham from its tin and baked it in honey, leaving it on the doorstep to cool properly, and found it gone. It was only after they had come back, returned to her garden to steal her food once again, that she had seen and understood.

She had gone to sit Maddy on her little plastic pot, curling herself up at the baby's side and crooning as her sister sat, grunting and straining, doing her business proper. She had heard a rustle of wings, sensed rather than heard a muttered conversation with a hint of disagreement, and come back to the kitchen to find one of the pies gone from the ledge.

Dilly had run out into the orchard, to stand staring and amazed at the sight of two black birds, each clutching a side of one of her precious pie pans in its talons, flapping for all they were worth in their effort to gain height and speed. As she had stood, mouth agape, the larger of the two had glanced back in her direction; this oddly disconcerting and intelligent look had been immediately followed by a wild chittering and a sudden effort from both creatures. There was nothing to be done but watch them, two moving black shades disappearing into the blue distance.

She had felt fury, amusement, and something deeper and more moving; a kind of empathy, a *frisson* of understanding that left her wondering if she had, in fact, overheard some kind of logical, sensible speech between the two birds.

It was possible, that was the thing she had to remember. It was certainly possible. Ever since the Big One had ripped through the world, taking most of the adults in its wake, the children and the few adults that remained had all noticed one thing: animals and insects, even things that grew, had changed. They were bolder, more assured; the very grass seemed to grow straighter and stronger. Sometimes, lying very still under a warm moon beneath the apple tree on a summer night, Dilly would close her eyes and open her ears and listen, simply listen, hearing the small rustlings of insects, the chatter of night wings on the open sky, in a way she had never before heard them.

Speech, it was speech. It wasn't just imagination, or wishful thinking. There was no room for doubt; they were talking to each other.

She poked the apple pie, massively impressive under its high arched crust, with one forefinger, and frowned. I think, she pondered, I think that maybe I wasn't imagining it, pretending it all. No. No, I wasn't. I wasn't. It was real. Talking, birds and bugs and things. Talking . . .

Words, sensate things unto themselves, came back to her, a memory of that first night, after tumbling her parents' bodies into the river. She had been uneasy indoors, claustrophobic, unused to the vast silence of a world now emptied of humanity. The night had been warm. She had checked on the sleeping Maddy and taken an old lawn sheet into the enormous garden to lie wakeful. A clicking, tiny but distinct on the air which was so quiet now that most of the world's noisemakers were gone; click, click, and then, astonishingly, words.

And she remembered them, remembered with perfect clarity what those tiny voices had said. Come on then, hurry it up, we've got to feed them bleeding grubs again. Who'd want to be a parent, anyway? Lord love me, William, don't they never do nothing but eat? Greedy little sods, the lot of them. Makes me tired, the appetites them little twisters has got . . .

Languid and accepting, she had rested, facing the lovely golden crescent that rode the horizon, remembering a misty time in her youth when her mother had read to her from the Alice books. The one about the looking glass, wasn't it, with a gnat sighing away in Alice's ear? But these weren't gnats—no, the clicking gave them away. Beetles, that's what they were, black beetles, and very likely the ones that Dilly herself had seen living at the edge of the small ornamental pool by the stone gates . . .

There was a banging behind her, followed by the soft pad of paws against the kitchen's stone floor. Maddy laughed, swallowing the rest of her eggs, and blew bubbles. Dilly knew what she would see, it would be the gray cat home from her hunting. She turned anyway, dropping to her knees, rubbing her fingers together, trilling under her breath.

Gadabout, called Gad, beautiful in the way of all cats, walked between her legs, rubbing her hindquarters against Dilly, marking the girl as her territory. This was a ritual she never neglected; Gad had a high respect for ritual and order, as did all cats. She banged Dilly's ankles, purring briefly, and then made the leap from floor to highchair. Maddy, oddly gentle with animals for so young a child, bent over and touched the cat between the ears.

"Gar," she said charmingly, "Gar, Gar," and looked up at her sister. Her great brown eyes were luminous with tears; even so young, she was as familiar with this rite as Dilly was, and she knew that the ankle bumping meant that Gad had gone successfully among the tall grasses by the riverbed, had found some small warm food there, brought it back, and secreted it by the kitchen door until she had, by her precise actions, informed the humans within that she would now drag it, bleeding and ready, across the clean floor.

Dilly nodded at the gray cat, and pushed the cat's ceramic food dish away from the hot stove. Gad tilted her slender head in perfect comprehension; for a moment, she actually seemed to nod, a motion part apology, part approval. She disappeared through the kitchen door with a lift of her tail and reappeared a few moments later with her lunch dangling from her teeth: a field mouse, limp and bloody. With the peculiar high-stepping gait she always used when carrying something, she carefully deposited the mouse in her dish.

"Oooooooh," said Maddy, wide-eyed and open-mouthed,

and Gad glanced up at her with a certain amusement in her amber eyes. Holding the mouse firmly in place with one paw—now, why does she need to do that, Dilly thought, it's dead, isn't it?—the gray cat washed her meal. Dainty and instructive, she settled on her haunches and began to eat.

Dilly reached for the apple pie, its warm crust covering a mass of hot fruit, and cut it carefully into large slices. She was momentarily disturbed by a fleeting memory—Mum rationing pie as though there might never be another pie to eat, explaining in her careful voice that too many sweets were bad for children—and shook the image away. Tense, Mum had been, tight as the old drum in the town museum, and what had she got to show for all that tension? She'd died, that's what, died with all the other grown people. If that's what being worried all the time and rationing sweet things brought you to, Dilly thought, me and Maddy'll eat ourselves sick, every day, forever.

She slid a huge slab of steaming apple and crust onto a dinner plate and dumped it ceremoniously down on the egg-littered tray in front of Maddy.

"Hot," she told her sister, "careful, now," and Maddy eyed the food with animal pleasure, sniffing at the cinnamon, her grief over the dead mouse forgotten.

Dilly cut herself a slice, putting it aside; she liked her baked goods completely cool, except for bread. For a moment she stood staring at the half-empty pie tin, thinking, considering, planning. Then, making her decision, she reached a hand into her apron's deep pocket and pulled out the note she had written. The bit of colored paper, folded up small, disappeared into a plastic sandwich bag, and the bag disappeared into the rest of the pie. She slid the pie onto a large paper plate and walked out into the garden with it, setting it down on the edge of the ornamental pond.

Twice, now. They would be back.

* * *

With his head lifted to face the singing breeze, the small raven called John twisted his body to the left and began to circle a garden filled with fruit trees.

Behind him, soaring easily despite his greater weight, Matthew spoke cautiously. "Any sign of her, mate?"

"No." John was a microcosm of confidence, a bird who had only to watch for marauding hawks and humans irate at having their food lifted from them while their backs were turned. "Not a glimmer. There's some of that pie, though."

"*Is* there, now." His beak half opened, Matthew glided upward for a better view. "You're right. Oh, lovely! Hot pie, what a nice child." He stiffened suddenly. "Johnny, my lad, what's it doing in the middle of the lawn?"

"Blessed if I know." John, too, had realized the difference; a fair amount of pie had been carefully, almost ceremonially it seemed to him, placed on a paper plate and set enticingly to wait for them. The age-old networks of warning sounded in both ravens.

"Peculiar," John muttered. "That's what it is, peculiar. Do you think she's expecting us?"

"Hmm," said Matthew. Though his head was as still as his hovering body, his eyes were darting the length of the garden with incredible rapidity. "Dunno. Could be. I don't see her. Maybe she knew we were coming and left us a little something. Civilized, that's what I call it."

John snorted. "What, a little present? Civilized indeed! You're wandering, my Matthew. What member of the wingless tribe was ever civilized?"

"Ben is," Matthew said, but he radiated uncertainty. "At least—isn't he?"

"No." John was scanning the grounds, gauging the best angle of approach, the safest and fastest line of retreat, in case, in case, in case . . . "Definitely not. Innocent, yes. Kindhearted and gentle, I'll give you those. But civilized? Matey, his whole tribe civilized itself into limbo. Them that's gone, they were civilized. I think it was only the civilized ones that went. Anyway, Ben's not civilized, Ben's just good." He added, with great irritation, "That's right, ignore me. Ask a question and then just ignore me. Where'd you learn your manners?"

Matthew, momentarily diverted by a dragonfly, turned his attention back to his companion. "Bloody bugs, what a racket they make. Sorry. You know, Johnny, I've been wondering . . ."

"Well?"

The larger raven turned his head; two pairs of yellow eyes locked brightly. "Maybe all the wingless ones that are left are all right. You know?"

"Humph." John, the acknowledged mental leader of his coven of ravens, always adhered to a firm policy of never showing immediate agreement. It was a lesson learned from clear example; be too lavish with the praise and you lost your handle. You had to seem smarter, if you wanted respect.

In fact, he had long been considering this very question. In the trees above the rural community of Killiford, he and his three disciples had watched as the muted everyday life of the township had tightened, first to worry and eventually to outright panic. The birds had gone about their business, hunting and sleeping, one ear tuned always to the pulse of the wingless who ran the world.

Run the world, right. Run themselves right out of the world, John thought sourly, that's what they'd done. What with their germs and their machines and their stupid sense of superiority, they'd managed to play with fire once too often. The ashes of that game, the plague known as the Big One, had been the final result.

"Them that plays with fire must expect to get burned. Better them than us," Matthew said cheerfully in his ear, and John jumped; as the others so often did now that the distractions were gone, Matthew had picked up on a stray thought and answered it. We all used to be able to do that, John remembered. It was a tale, a tale passed from parent to nestling for a hundred thousand generations.

Knowledge, pure concentration, once the birthright of all living things.

And then man had come, noisy, destructive, rapacious, usurping the privileges of the rest of the natural world until an honest bird could barely hear himself think over the clamor of trees falling, engines running, music playing . . .

"Could have been a lot worse," Matthew continued. He was still tuned into that bright line of awareness. "Least they didn't use those filthy things they'd got piled up all over the place. You know, the bombs. They would have taken all of us with them. This way, it's just them."

"True, true. And I think you're right, mate; you know, when they all started dying, I used to pop down to Kilford proper and listen to the radios going. Well, I was interested, who wouldn't be? They said . . ." John wrinkled his face in concentration. "They said it was all about something called stress. The way the Big One worked, see, it attacked part of their brains, and part of their blood." The word came back to him suddenly. "Adrenaline, that's what it was called. The Big One fed on this adrenaline stuff. The more stress you had, the more adrenaline you'd got. And the more adrenaline you'd got, the worse you got the disease. And of course the worse you got the disease, the more stress you had." He shook his head sadly. "Wages of sin."

Matthew made a rude noise. "Wages of stupidity, you mean. They did it to themselves. Not our problem. John, we've been up here nigh on fifteen minutes now, and I don't see hide nor hair of that small one. Ben's likely starving, poor old thing. Let's get that pie."

"Right. Seems safe enough. Anyway, she's a small one, hard to see what harm she could do us." Curling the strong black primaries under for a more accurate landing, the two black birds headed for the pie, shining like a welcoming beacon on its white plate.

They landed together, two gentle thumps of black on the green lawn. Matthew reached a talon out for the pie plate and an expression of delight crossed his face. "Well, bloody hell! Johnny, this plate is soft!"

"Oh, rot. Whoever heard of a soft plate?" John hopped sideways, his nose picking up faint traces of an old, beloved enemy. "There's a cat been in this garden," he whispered.

"Crikey, Johnny, will you forget the bloody cat and look at this? It's soft, I tell you. Look here!" And he lifted one side of the plate, feeling the thin paper curl soft and easy under his pull.

John blinked at him. "A soft plate? Whatever next! Well, and that's a bit of luck, anyway. Much easier to carry than that heavy thing we took last time." Something rustled in the undergrowth, and John ruffled his feathers unhappily. Every sense he possessed was vibrating. "Look now, I've got this feeling, see? Something's watching us. Come on, take your half and let's get the hell out of this garden."

The cat called Gad, enveloped in a glorious wall of greenery, sat with her head tilted and watched the birds on the lawn.

Her mind was scrupulously blank. This emptying of all rational thought, this banking down of understanding to the service of necessity or will, was a trick the birds had not yet recalled. They had it once, she knew, had it and lost it, watched it sink without a tremor under the raucous, omnipresent clamor of the bipedal world. Cats, on the other hand, had never lost it. And that, of course, was the difference between fur and feather . . .

With her own mind peacefully emptied, the thoughts of the ravens flowed in like water and filled her. She heard the discussion, the memories, the muttered clarion call of Up and bloody away, mate; she felt the nervous awareness of the smaller raven—John, was it? Yes. John. It was, in its own way, amusing.

Had the birds but known it, Gad had little interest in birds. Too much bother, the flesh stringy and tough, and none of it worth the inevitable mouthful of feathers. Chicken served by her kept humans was one thing, all nicely plucked and mixed with things to enhance the taste; raw bird she ate only in the direst necessity. She infinitely preferred the small country rodents, the mice and the voles, to anything that flew. And fish, of course. Lovely, lovely fish, the best of all foods.

Even if she had enjoyed the taste of bird, Gad would have left the ravens unmolested. She had eavesdropped to some purpose on Dilly's scattered thoughts, and understood that the girl wanted the ravens left alone. A curiosity was growing in Gad, a suspicion that perhaps these odd birds were not, after all, as fond of warm fruit pie as their recurrent thefts might indicate.

Stupid creatures, she thought vaguely; stupid, and slow with it. Gad was aware of a spasm of irritation; they were taking an unconscionably long time, out there in the garden. Time to move them. After all, however much her beloved Dilly might want them about, Dilly was not a cat and had very little understanding of the basic precepts of territorial imperative. This garden was Gad's, her patch, her hunting ground. It would simply not do to encourage these winged ninnies to hang about.

She moved. It was a very slight movement, the merest stretching of long legs and tail muscles, but on the taut awareness of the raven John it acted like a tonic. In a moment the birds were moving—Up and bloody away, mate—carefully toting the paper plate and its pulpy burden between them, uttering little grunting croaks of effort and self-encouragement. The plate wobbled madly as one of the ravens adjusted his back, then steadied. In a few minutes, they had become indistinct black specks and vanished from view.

Gad stretched, rippled, and stalked from her verdant cover into the molten sunlight of the day. As she nosed in the grass, taking in the lingering remnant of bird scent, she heard the kitchen door bang open and the soft fall of feet.

"Gone," Dilly said, and smiled. Her small body was tilted at an impossible angle under the weight of the baby. Maddy, squinting and beautiful, patted her sister's face very gently and made small wriggling movements, indicative of her desire to be put down.

"Now then, now then," Dilly said absently, and obliged. She looked down at Gad and spoke seriously.

"I've forgotten her blanket. Keep your eye on her, sweet Gadabout, will you? Don't let her wander off."

Two pairs of eyes, one yellow green and the other brown, regarded her. The cat lifted a paw and touched the baby's hand with it, a tender signal of agreement, her eyes never leaving Dilly's. Satisfied, the girl nodded and ran toward the house.

"Gar," said Maddy.

"Not Gar. Gad. You know my name, little one."

"I know it, but I can't say it properly. Not yet, anyway." Maddy rolled over on her stomach and stared into the cat's face. Unlike her incomplete baby's speech, her thoughts were clear and brilliantly easy to follow. To Gad, they shone like a beacon; unlike Dilly, who must be within a close radius to make herself heard, Maddy's thoughts could be easily followed at great distances.

"I love you, little one."

"And I love you, Gad my Gad. What was sister doing with that pie, then?"

"Giving it to the ravens." It was incredible, how quickly Maddy could read thoughts; you barely had time to smother something, even just a hint of an idea, and she was on to it like a rat with cheese.

"Do the ravens have people?"

Gad, dainty and purposeful, stretched her neck and began to wash Maddy's face. She relished the baby's giggling, finding it oddly moving; none of her kittens had ever been so charming or so cooperative. It was odd to wash skin, bare of fur, and the baby's flesh was indecently soft. "I haven't a clue, my angel. I think they might."

Maddy turned her face, allowing Gad access to the other cheek. The cat's tongue, scratchy and warm, felt fine. "Does Dilly know? Is that why she put that paper inside the pie? Because she wanted the ravens' people to find it?"

"Not know, Maddy. Not for certain, I don't think. I think she believes they might. After all, whoever heard of ravens eating pie?"

"Here's Dilly come back again," Maddy said, and rolled over to face the sun.

Dilly, dropping the knitted afghan on the grass, took note of the slightly reddened cheeks, the sheen of the cat's healing saliva on Maddy's face. Gad had been washing Maddy again. Good; the knowledge was warming and disturbing at the same time. Since the Big One, Dilly had been slowly succumbing to a peculiar feeling; conversation, a ceaseless dance of pure communication that flowed like the tides, just out of her range of mental hearing.

She was not jealous, it was nothing as simple as jealousy. Eventually she would hear it, participate, take part; the knowledge sat just below her conscious awareness, a good feeling. She only regretted the time it was taking to come clear. Maddy and Gad, now. They had something going . . .

Maddy, as if on cue, gave her a look compounded of sympathy and encouragement. It was unsettling, the way the baby seemed able to tune in.

"Proper little transmitter. Little Radio One, that's what you are," she told her sister, and Maddy, under Gad's approving eye, promptly held her arms out for a hug. "Durry," she said, the closest she could come to her sister's name, "Durry," and Dilly picked her up quickly, holding her for a moment in a suffocating grip.

Together they sat on the afghan as the afternoon moved languidly past them, Dilly alternating between her tattered book of nursery rhymes and absently tickling Maddy's bare stomach. As the baby giggled, as Dilly read, as Gad watched, all three of them thought, in their own fashion, of ravens.

2

At The Shops

WHEETABIX, CHOCOLATE DIGESTIVE biscuits, tinned milk.

Julia Reynard, mentally consulting a nonexistent shopping list, shifted the plastic basket on her arm and moved down the deserted aisles of Geo. Congreve, Purveyor of Fine Groceries. This weekly activity, strolling through an empty shop and helping herself to food and drink and toiletries that, before the Big One, she had never been able to afford, had become one of the most comforting things in Julia's life.

On a bad day, a day when the weather and her mood screamed at each other, a day when memory and the realization of her own stunning loneliness swelled in her like her own unborn child, she would close her eyes as she laid one hand on the brass doorknob of the glass-fronted store. Behind the darkness of her lids poetry would move, slipping through nerve and bone and heart, and suddenly Congreve's would be peopled, alive once more.

Today was a bad day.

It had not started out that way. She had woken early, before the sun was up, into the soft pearly gray of a room that would shortly fill with the dawn. For a moment, as happened every morning, she was disoriented and bewildered, not knowing where she was or why the world was so quiet. Then The Bump moved, perhaps in acknowledgment of the increased placental flow that accompanied its mother's return to full consciousness. Julia came fully awake, rubbing her eyes, remembering, staring around the luxurious room with its flocked wallpaper, its elegant rose-patterned rugs, the ornate antique tester bed she lay in.

She lay, relaxed and quiescent, and The Bump moved again. A good hearty kick this time, cheering her.

She got out of bed and walked through the absolute quiet, across the lush rugs, through the oak-paneled hallway, down the curving staircase that had been carved by Grinling Gibbons centuries ago, when the world echoed with life.

In the enormous kitchen, she stood over the refectory table and, carefully lighting her butane-powered portable stove, made herself a pot of tea. The cups were Sèvres china, the willow pattern, beautiful and delicate; against the blue trees etched so perfectly, so delicately into the white porcelain, fragrant steam rose in lazy clouds.

Out of the kitchen, into the dining room with its framed Gainsborough, across to the drawing room with its tall French doors. Balancing the cup and saucer with extreme care, she unlatched the doors and stepped out onto a lovely little terrace, into the first touch of the morning sun.

For a few moments she simply stood, basking in her own langour and the soft summer air. It would be warm again, a warm gentle day, as all the days seemed to have been since the Big One. She closed her eyes, sniffing; the air was full of mingled beauty, tea rose and wisteria.

"Lapsang souchong for you, Bump," Julia told her swollen stomach, and the baby shifted. With one hand on her belly and the other holding her cup, she opened her eyes and stared out across the vale, across the green fields that, day by day, grew ever riper, ever deeper, ever more beautiful. She was visited by a sensation that had become as much of a ritual as her morning forgetfulness: a feeling that was partly disturbance and partly profound gratitude that she, Julia Reynard, had survived the end of the world.

And The Bump had survived too. Another straw to clutch in the inexorable wind of complete change, another blessing to count, another small thing to remember in the face of a universe that had given a single roaring hiccup before settling into itself once again; settled, this time, denuded of people, though certainly not of life.

There were sheep on the hills. Julia, the breeze lifting her red hair from her face in teasing little waves, squinted into the blaze of sunrise to stare at them. Once the property of all those dead farmers, they now roamed wild, helping themselves to whatever seemed good to eat, growing fatter, seeming even healthier than they had when the men who had tended them had allotted the precise, correct amount of nourishment. Even at this distance, appearing as small gray specks, their fleece seemed thicker, denser.

The poetry moved in her again, turning her back toward the house, sending her in search of pen and paper. The formal library of Sparrow House had, among its first editions of Pope and its expensive reprints of Dryden and Swinburne, all three volumes of her own work. The discovery, made the first night she had decided to appropriate as her own the house she had coveted since childhood, had delighted her. She had since ceased to take any pleasure in the presence of this bit of herself among the greats, however; like so many things since the moment she realized that she was alone in the world, her own books, those slim and expensively bound mementos of another time, had joined most of the manmade world as sources of disturbance.

In the end, the poem would not come; it dangled, as incomplete as The Bump, an amorphous shape of texture and color behind her eyes. She sat and stared at the blank paper on the desk before her, her eyes wide and straining and edged with frustrated tears, and around her Sparrow House warmed itself to the rhythm of the morning sun.

Finally, denied and miserable, Julia threw the pen across the room. It struck the wall and spun away, leaving a tiny smear of blue ink on the velvet flocking. She looked at this minimal damage and felt a mixture of spite and guilt.

"Damn," she said aloud, and the echoes rang in the empty house. "Blast, blast, *damn*," she repeated, pitching her voice—oh, such a lovely voice, the way it had rung like a cathedral bell on all those ridiculous nights, standing to recite her own work to small college theaters and smoke-filled folk clubs—to carry, and carry well. Then, suddenly claustrophobic, she went hurriedly upstairs to dress. When the words refused to come, only a long stroll through Congreve's would do.

"When the going gets tough, the tough go shopping." Had she heard that somewhere, or invented it? Never mind; it was apposite to her mood, and that was enough. Perched precariously on the edge of the tester bed, Julia talked out loud to nothing, and struggled with her deck shoes; really, it was too much, her stomach simply must not get any larger. "Alice in Wonderland," she muttered, "that's what I am. Alice, drinking all those odd things, shrinking and growing. I've forgotten what my feet look like."

She managed, albeit clumsily, to tie both shoes. Ah, a motive, something else to give shape to her day. The shoe shop for a new pair of shoes, comfortable flat slippers, espadrilles perhaps, with nothing to tie and no reason to bend over . . . Her dress, a plain maternity smock of lightest cotton madras, was already sticking to her back; not a warm day, but a hot one to come. "Oh, wonderful. Precisely what I don't require." Suddenly the warmth of the day hit her in full; dizzy and off balance, she clung limply to the banister and stumbled back downstairs and into the morning.

Congreve's, here it was. Years ago, as the badly dressed only daughter of a working-class family, she had learned every color, every shape, every aspect of the marvels that waited behind Congreve's leaded storefront windows. Lord knew, she had spent enough time staring longingly into the dim interior, at the brightly colored jars of penny candy, the sachets of lavender and potpourri, the scented bubble bath and tins of caviar.

Occasionally, she had been fortunate. At Christmas, birthdays, some distant relative in Scotland or Germany or Cleveland might send her a special gift, the best gift of all, money. Not much money, it was true; the family was large, spread out across the Western world, and the children tended to receive the tokens of such a situation: a pound here, a few francs there. One glorious birthday, an uncle she had never met had gotten lucky at a racetrack in Florida and sent her a ten-dollar bill. She could still summon her sense of awe, the painful gratitude she had felt as she opened the envelope and saw the single green bill flutter onto her narrow bed . . .

Julia stood in the empty street. Congreve's and Sparrow House, the two beacons of childhood; she had coveted them both as a woman might covet a man, yearning after the exotic delicacies of one, the tapestries and china and huge glorious comfort of the other. They were both hers now, the store of wonders and the shelter of luxury, triumphs she had never thought to achieve. Of course, she had never thought she would finish up as the last woman alive, either.

She turned the brass doorknob, cool and heavy in her hand, and walked in.

Ritual can be an incredible blessing. She took up one of the store's wire-handled plastic carrier baskets—red today, since last week it had been a blue one—and stood a moment, simply relishing the feel of it in her hand.

These baskets had not been the least of Congreve's attractions to a raggedy little girl; red, blue, green, and yellow, stacked in a neat pile by the door, the vivid colors and slim handles had seemed like shadows of utopia, lovely, brilliant, totally out of reach.

Well, she thought, the meek, such as they are, have inherited with a vengeance. A pity they didn't really want the inheritance. She slipped the basket over one arm and began her shopping.

Tins of milk—best check the smell when she got them home—and coffee. Flour, baking chocolate, oil. What was this, then, a tin of Portuguese sardines? Saliva rose in Julia's throat, for she loved sardines. The tin fell, plop, into the red basket.

People, people. That was all Congreve's was missing. In her youthful longings, she had seen herself as a rich, respected member of Sparrowdene, strolling every Monday and Thursday through these very aisles, chatting with the deacon, the matron in her furs, the young barrister who had moved into the ramshackle shell of Dills Cottage and renovated it at stupendous cost. But they were dead now, butcher and baker and candlestick maker; still, there was no reason that she, the successful young poet with three books, two television appearances, and a lecture tour of French universities under her expanded belt, could not hold the witty conversations she had always dreamed about.

She paused between the shampoo and the diapers, closed her eyes, and began the laborious process of conjuring up Mrs. Lufton-Hall, that imposing demon of good works. So intent was she that she never heard the tiny tinkle of the front door as it opened.

And here, in her mind, was Mrs. Eulalie Lufton-Hall, fifteen stone if she weighed an ounce, her ever-present fox stole—she had slain the creature herself at a hunt and was never seen without it—lying limply across the vast shelf of her bosom. In Julia's vision the narrow eyes twinkled, the pinched ungenerous mouth stretched into a simper. Odd, how vivid this unpleasant woman seemed; it was harder by far to summon up her own mother's face. Now the matron nodded to her, commented on the weather, asked when the baby—dear little thing!—was expected?

"Oh, in about a month," Julia told her.

"In about a month, what?"

Julia's eyes popped open and were caught by a dazzle of sunlight. When she stopped blinking, she found herself staring at a little girl.

For a single moment, time altered. It ceased its constant flow and contracted, hard and taut; Julia could feel the ball of it in her stomach, a tangible thing. The Bump stirred briefly, as if in protest at this sudden necessity to share its chosen space with such surprise, then settled.

The child, stringy-haired, slender, as leggy as a young colt, held a basket too. Yellow. Long brown eyes regarded Julia from a thin pointed face, aware and somehow foxlike. The girl spoke again, in the accents of the county, the accents of Sparrowdene. "What was that about a month? Were you talking about your baby, then?"

"Yes." Astonishing, absolutely absurd; Julia, half convinced that she had suddenly died or was suffering from some esoteric hallucination that would float off into the air with the dancing dust motes, heard the normalcy of her own voice with a mixture of annoyance and dazed disbelief. "The Bump. In about a month." What in the world?

The child nodded approvingly. "Good. That's quite nice, in fact. After everybody *dies*"—she sounded pedantic and hilarious, a wizened old professor instructing callow youth in the shape of a pregnant woman—"after everybody dies, there should be some things born. For balance."

"Balance." Congreve's was coming back into focus; the dimness and shadows were lengthening, sharpening, and Julia suddenly realized that she must have been mildly in shock. She swallowed hard.

"Look here," she demanded, "are you alive?"

The girl blinked once, and then stepped back from her. "Alive? Well, what do you think? Are you—are you quite all right?" The girl tapped her forehead once, gently, a horribly graphic gesture. "You know. All right?"

Julia's voice was suddenly joyous, suddenly sure. "If you're really here, and I'm not hallucinating because of The Bump, then I'm all right. In fact, never better."

The child regarded her for a moment. Then, swiftly, she reached out and pinched Julia's arm. "I'm really here."

Julia was unaware of her own sudden tears, of her hand automatically reaching to rub the red shadow of Dilly's pinch, of anything in the world but the access of totally unexpected delight that was threatening to drown her. "Oh God," she said, "oh God, oh dear lord, another person. I thought I was the only one, I thought everyone was dead, oh sweet Jesus." She reached out blindly and Dilly, no longer cautious, seeming to understand, stepped up to meet her and was gathered into a bone-crushing embrace. "A person, a person, another person, oh lord oh God oh all the angels in heaven if there is a heaven, I'm not alone in the whole world. There's more of me."

"More of you," the child agreed solemnly. "Don't you think we ought to finish our shopping? I've left Maddy outside in her pram."

"I never realized before just how beautiful this house is. I thought I did, but I was wrong."

Julia, with fat-cheeked Maddy in her arms, stood beside Dilly on the deck of Sparrow House. Sunlight, fluid and laughing, fell around them in a blaze; on Julia's feet the new shoes, soft flat espadrilles, expanded imperceptibly to take the shape of her feet. The intense heat was made bearable by a soft breeze, and Maddy touched her face and her hair and smiled joyously. Why was I worrying, Julia thought, loving the baby and her sister and the distant sheep; how could I feel so bad, everything looks fine, so fine.

"It is pretty," Dilly agreed. "The house, I mean. The world too, of course, it does look very fine. But the house, especially. Roomy, too."

What? Julia turned her head to regard the girl, who had seemed to be answering her unspoken thought, rather than the spoken one. As she moved she caught the baby's eye; something moved between them, a faint shudder of thought, and Julia tightened her hold, unsettled. Dilly, seeming not to notice either Julia's narrowed eyes or start of confusion, scrutinized the sweep of the garden with a critical eye, and spoke with some severity.

"Empty, though. Where are your animals?"

"Animals?" Maddy had begun to wriggle and Julia set her down on the silk quilt she had spread there. "Pets, you mean? I haven't any."

What? What? It was almost pain this time, that flash of pure thought, bright and dizzying. They were both staring at her, both, though surely to heaven Maddy couldn't have understood her. Inside, The Bump moved abruptly.

"No animals." Dilly stood rigid, watchful. "That's not good. Not even a bird? A cat, a dog? None?" Julia shook her head. "Oh, that's bad. That's very bad."

On the far hills, a woolly ram suddenly paused in its slow grazing. He was the largest of the flock; now he stood with his head slanted, grave and stately, listening intently to the summer, his long wise silly face stained green around the muzzle. Nearly a mile away, Julia looked in bewilderment at Dilly, whose face, had she known it, bore an almost identical expression.

"Why? Why is it bad?" she asked, uneasily aware that both comment and question should have sounded nonsensical when, in fact, neither had. Unsettled even further, she heard herself repeat it. "Why is it so bad?"

The ram had begun to move, picking his way magisterially through the flock. Unlike the ravens, the sheep were neither excitable nor talkative; he answered a few placid questions and began to walk toward the enormous sandstone house that shimmered in the distance, a high castle on an alien shore, in the heat of the day.

Dilly was looking down at Maddy. Julia, too large, too full of The Bump to kneel properly, leaned her suddenly trembling body against the terrace and followed Dilly's gaze. The baby's brown eyes were brightly wet, tears rimming the hollows and points of cheek and nose; they met Julia's and then, suddenly, jerked away. Maddy began to smile.

"What?" This time the word was spoken, whispered aloud instead of in her mind. Dilly was regarding Maddy with an urgent concentration she had not displayed before. "What?"

"Gar," said the baby, and clapped her hands. "Gar."

"Gar?"

Dilly was smiling now. "She means Gad, Gadabout, our gray cat. You can't be alone, Julia, truly. It wouldn't be good for you. Not safe. Maddy's right, you know."

"I don't understand." Yet, even as she spoke, she did understand, something passing like a kiss between her and the baby and the girl beside her, and suddenly she loved them as she had loved nothing in her whole life, a real love that was totally unrelated to the wild gratitude she had felt for their mere existence.

Yet the oddly electric feeling was gone almost at once, leaving her momentarily empty. Mute, she turned her face to the hills, just as a beautiful gray cat jumped up from the garden and landed on the terrace's edge.

"Oh good," Dilly said. "Here's Gad."

Julia was fond of cats. She had never been permitted a pet during her childhood years—a mother with mild asthma and never enough money to properly feed the human young, much less pets—but she had always loved the look of cats, their sleek economical ease of motion, their cleanliness, their unwillingness to compromise with humans, with predators, with each other, with themselves.

Independent, that's what they were. Different cultures, loving and intimidated, had worshiped them as gods or condemned them as creatures of the devil, and, in truth, the mixture of fire and ice that seemed their hallmark could send a superstitious mind in either direction. Now she looked at the cat, who had briefly bumped Dilly's legs and then gone immediately to the baby, and knew a sudden longing to touch it.

"Go ahead," said a quiet voice. "I understand that you know little of my kind, very little, but go ahead anyway."

What? What? The quiet voice, the lightest, clearest possible echo in her mind, went on.

"It will do you good, and you should get used to it. There is a ram, a woolly ram, wise and old. He has left his flock, poor one, and is coming here. Don't worry anymore; you will have a creature. He will tend you."

The voice had been neither Dilly's nor her own. Julia made a small noise in her throat and felt the calm gaze of the cat on her. Her hands wove together and lay, protective, across her stomach.

"What is it? Why are you looking like that, what's the matter, did the baby move, does it hurt?"

"No." She answered Dilly's question, unable to take her eyes from Gadabout. One hand, seemingly of its own volition, moved, a pale freckled thing, until it was touching the fur that was so impossibly soft. Gad arched under her fingers. "I—it—didn't you hear?"

"Hear what?" But Dilly's voice was a little sad, the voice of one who understood but could not hear, and even as Julia began to stroke the cat her head snapped sideways to look at the girl. "Did Gad talk to you, then?"

The cat rose, stretched, and vaulted lightly into Julia's arms. A day of miracles, a day of roses and summer that might never end, never.

"I won't be alone now," she said, and the tears began again, moving down her cheeks, refreshing and unnoticed. "There's a sheep coming to care for me."

The cat was purring. "As I told you, a sheep. His name is Peter, I think. Would you happen to have any fish?"

"Tell me about your baby's father."

Julia, lying naked in the sun on a Victorian chaise longue, turned her head to regard Gad. She had dragged the chaise from drawing room to terrace, with Dilly to help her, something she had wanted to do for weeks but had been afraid, in her condition, to attempt unaided. On the broad lawn outside, a woolly ram placidly grazed; he was, he insisted, unwilling to interrupt their conversation at this time and, besides, he was hungry. Gad, in fact, had been wrong; his name was actually Simon.

The gray cat was lying on the marble beside her; her lids, half-opened at an odd angle, did not quite obscure the bright eyes. Julia saw the sun reflect off the opaque color, and smiled to herself.

But the command, phrased in Gad's high, passionless tone of thought, had brought memory too close to the surface and she was momentarily disturbed. Pictures, short and fragmented, moved and were gone. Max had been strange—strange and worrying—in life; it was interesting to know that he had not lost that power, even after presumed death . . .

"Was he that peculiar?"

Gad had caught the line of thought. Although their conversation was completely unspoken, Julia nodded. "Yes. Oh, yes, he was, definitely. Max . . ."

Gad, who had been lying on her side and frankly panting in the sun, curled herself up in the classic couchant position of cats paying attention. "Now then, not to worry. No need to get into a fret. But I wouldn't ask you if I didn't want to know."

"I know." In the brief hours since Dilly had excused

herself and gone home with Maddy—there was a batch of cookies, she explained with grave significance, waiting to be put in the oven—Julia had learned something of Gad and the strange, timeless species to which she belonged. Aloof, self-possessed and self-contained, everything the books said about them, but more, much more. The single thing that stood out most clearly about Gad was the clarity of the feline mind, a wondrous thing, pure and direct, totally unwilling to waste time on trivialities.

So Gad had asked about Max with a purpose, however obscure that purpose might have been, and it was incumbent upon Julia to answer. She closed her eyes, feeling the sticky heat against her face that much more strongly for the lack of visual distraction, and began, for the first time since the world had died around her, to think about Max.

Memory, even the darker edges of it, can be a dangerously easy road to travel. Time bowed, grave and courtly, and moved aside like water parting to give her passage; a club, smoke-filled and crowded with students from the Sorbonne, serious and pompous.

Literature students, most of them. They had been to her lecture class earlier in the day, and had come to her reading here tonight, all of them wanting the extra credit and the points of prestige that introducing themselves to a famous English poet would give them among their compatriots. There were blond Germans, exquisite Scandinavian students with their astonishing cheekbones and strong brows, and a large number of indecently beautiful young French women students, mostly wearing black leather.

The study group had been mixed, of every nationality in Europe and even a few ethnic groups from outside—African and Chinese. What coalesced these students was their extreme youth; none of them looked older than twenty.

With one exception . . .

He had been sitting alone, at a small table next to the tiny stage. Julia had noticed him at once; he had the air of a wolf among the lambs, and yet, somehow, he was not predatory, simply different, strange, completely by himself. The students, chattering, drinking, discussing things of great weight in the solemn voices that are such an endearing feature of youth, had not even seemed to see him. Their conversation washed over him like moonlight, and his eyes never moved to their faces. He simply sat there, a man in a nondescript suit, drinking from a glass that, in the chancy light of the club, seemed full of clouds.

She had been annoyed to find her eyes returning to him over and over again during the recital. As far as she could tell, he had never once looked up at her. Yet he was aware of her, paying attention; after one or two lines of poetry especially potent to Julia herself, she saw him nod down at his tablecloth as if in somber agreement. Once she caught a fleeting smile, sharp as a knife's edge, on the averted face.

She finished her reading with the poem that had made her famous, "The Liar's Game," and, as always, she lost herself in it; of anything she had ever written this was the deepest, the darkest, the easiest entry into her own eternal shadowland.

Her audience was silent now, chilled by it and by her concentration. She gave them the long poem with her eyes closed, because it was a story about the heart of darkness; in some obscure fashion, it made her feel guilty, speaking it, to look at the light.

(Mystery, daughters of mystery)

White hair, almost too thick, a streak of smoke drifting across it as his body tensed toward her voice. Eyes shut, she could still envision him. It brought the poem closer.

(And I will consider the fall of the moon and the words of my people)

Students smoking pipes, small briarwood ovens, eyes intent on her, she could feel those eyes through her lids.

(And I move through cloud and cold, slow and sure)

The chink of glasses, the feel of smoke against her throbbing skin.

(And the mother has abandoned the child
and the child runs laughing through the
shadowed dark
        that is her gift
her gift and her birthright
to lie, and then to lie again . . .)

When she opened her eyes to the thunderous applause, the man was gone. The table was empty, virginally clean; no empty glass, no ashtray, not even a wrinkle disturbed the smooth tablecloth. She saw no sign that anyone had sat there, not tonight, not ever. Gone like an incubus, a ghost conjured up from her poetry. Nothing more.

That was the first time, in Paris. Two weeks later, visiting a cousin who taught at the University of Edinburgh, she had gotten a phone call from the Poetry Department; they hated to bother her, knew it was an imposition, but their guest lecturer, the dramatist Martin Still, had come down with the flu and, knowing she was in town, had suggested her. Please would she consider . . . ?

So Julia had gone to the university with her two bound volumes under her arm, to take her old school friend Martin's lecture hour. And there he was, the man from the little café off the Rue Saint-Jacques, sitting on a low wall at the University of Edinburgh.

Even now, months later and in a different world, the shock of that was still with her. Julia could still summon up the tightening in her belly, the sudden constriction in her chest as if her lungs were suddenly too small to hold their proper allotment of air. No staring down at the green turf this time, no hiding of the flying bird's face, no, not this time. This time he had been looking straight at her, the sharp vagrant smile that she remembered set across his face as if by a sculptor's thumb in wet clay, and she had looked into that face and known it, wanted it, understood without understanding why that of any face in all the world, this would be the one that mattered.

His name was Max, just Max; she was never to learn any more than that and she did not learn even that in Edinburgh. Throughout recorded time, men and women alike have fallen immediately in love with each other's bodies; Julia, who had never loved a body or anything else, fell into a bottomless pit of adoration, not for his body, not for his mind about which she knew nothing, but for his face. She had only once seen anything like Max's face, and it was not until this day, lying seven months pregnant with Max's child on a terrace in an empty world, that she remembered where and how.

"A statue?"

Julia, unaware of the slow tears trickling down her face, jumped galvanically. So Gad had been there all the time, following the twisting path of memory from the Rive Gauche to the stately hills of Scotland, listening to the unspoken poetry, seeing the invisible smoke, hearing the shadowy laughter and chatter of the Tower of Babel that was now gone, lost forever. Julia lifted a hand to dash the tears away, and turned her face to the cat.

"It was in a villa in Tuscany, that's in Italy, a lovely old villa in the hills. On a sarcophagus, a coffin, of a Byzantine knight. That face. The same one. It was the smile, the smile . . ."

The cat's voice was soothing, almost hypnotic. "Tell me about the smile." As Julia groped in her head for words, Gad's tone sharpened. "No. Don't try, only tell. You're a poet. Tell me in those words."

It was suddenly easy. "Lively, beautiful, merciless, pitiless without malice. A thin mouth, the most sensual thing I ever saw, it hooked downward at the corners. The face on the sarcophagus was identical, just the same; I swear, he might have posed for the bloody thing. A smile that had been everywhere, seen everything. It had shadow, sun, cold water in it, everything—oh God it was a beautiful face, Gad, simply beautiful. He had black eyes, really black, the kind you see on very old Orientals; they were sunk so deep in his head they seemed to go down through him, as if they linked him to the earth below. I couldn't look into his eyes for more than few seconds at a time. It was too scary."

Julia laughed suddenly. "I had a fancy about them, that they were pipelines, that all the world where he put his feet traveled up through those pipelines and made his eyes a little blacker every time. All compact of time, somehow. He had white hair, thick and fine, cut short. Incredible bones. He might have been any age; I never knew much about him."

"You knew enough."

And that was a strange thing to say, even for Gad. Yet she had no time to probe or question, for the gray cat had shuttered the thought and returned to the point, telling her to continue.

Back through the winds and the drifting smoke. London, Bloomsbury, the tiny comfortable flat. A month after the Edinburgh meeting, she had not seen him or heard from him; she had no way of finding him, knew nothing of him except for the fact, the reality, the simple basic fact that she had looked across a wide green lawn into a face out of time and had toppled totally, helplessly, into thrall.

And they had never exchanged a word, touched—nothing at all. There was only the reality of him, only that he existed and by his existence had robbed her of the capacity to think clearly, to consider anything else in the world. And that was the true liar's game.

Coming back from the off-license with a bag of groceries, including two heavy bottles of the Israel apricot wine she occasionally treated herself to. Setting the bag down on the front steps of the old house that had been divided up into little flats. Dark, the new moon a razor against a black patch of sky, dark against dark, suddenly disappearing as the first few drops of sudden rain blew against her face, moved up and down the street shuddering windows, splotched the dirty pavement.

Rummaging for her key. And the voice that she knew at once, though she had never before heard it.

Let me help you, Julia.

"So that was how it happened." Gad's voice was softer now, gentler; perhaps the memory had affected her, perhaps the sudden choking emotion she felt in Julia had touched her. Yet even this new gentleness held deliberation. "You saw him in one place, then in another place far from the first, and then he came to your home. You never realized that he had sought you out for a purpose, a reason? You never asked him how he found you, or even why?"

But Julia could not answer. The memory was full now, complete; the spiritual had given way to the flesh, and as her mind's eye remembered the two bodies that night, in their only dance, she was suddenly drowning in it, wanting him again, knowing he must be dead.

"No, I don't think so."

That penetrated; this time Gad was like a knife, so clear and so urgent was the thought. It fell like a lifeline through the terrible want that was threatening to swamp her. "What? What don't you think?"

"Not dead. Not dead at all."

Julia closed her eyes, drained, too exhausted to even question the strangeness behind Gad's words. "He must be. The rest of the world is."

"No." The cat's voice held knowledge, knowledge with something underneath; a tint of sorrow, a tinge of gladness. And then she said something so strange, so out of place, that Julia could find no reply. "I know of him; he was forbidden to die. He's still alive, Max is. Trust me for it."

There were children in the street below, as there had been children, night and day, since the dying began.

Sometimes they played, sometimes not; often they

would come, the little bands, to stare in silence up at his window or whisper among themselves. They never approached him or set their hands against his door; on the rare occasions he went out into the street they moved back from him, standing in silent ranks, watching him with eyes at the stretch. He had never heard a true sound from any of them.

Today he ignored their presence entirely; there were other things on his mind, and his attention was elsewhere.

He sat with the thin muslin curtains drawn against the clear London sky, not bothering to notice the little streaks of dusty sun that broke their way in through the woven fabric. He eased himself back against the sofa that had been Julia's, the sofa where, shy and inexperienced, she had laid her head against his waiting shoulder. He held a glass in one hand. Rotating it gently, so that the liquid inside swirled nearly to the top but did not spill, he began to talk to the ceiling.

"I know you're there; what use, to hide from me?"

The ceiling made no reply. But around the bare bulb that dangled from the white plaster, something moved. It was neither light nor darkness, while holding something of both; a patch of shadow that was not shadow, small, mobile, vaguely anthropomorphic.

The bottomless black eyes fixed on this conundrum. Max was used to this battle of wills; he had been doing it for two thousand years, doing it ever since he had made the mistake of spitefully teasing a man with a cross, a man who was yet more spiteful than he himself was and had, most unfairly, the power to back up his malice. Well, the Son had had a long time to learn one simple lesson, that the pleasure of spite was not restricted to gods.

"Come out, lord."

He wouldn't, of course, not willingly. Max had been doing this for so long—battling him on this level that was part hate and part love and part the simple familiarity of two old geezers locked into a disagreement that had carried over the rise and fall of the empires of man—that he knew every possible twist of the game. In the end, they would speak to each other; two millennia is a long time over which to hone one's willpower, even when that willpower is directed against a deity. The simple fact was that Max's dislike and his will to use it had grown, while the Son's had grown weaker. It would be precisely as Max wished.

"The children are out there again. I think they sense something, don't you? It won't be long now, a few months perhaps, no more than that. And whatever will you do then?"

The man with the Byzantine smile spoke in a casual voice, a flicker of amusement running just below the surface. Ah. The darkness around the bulb flexed itself, shimmered, became a momentary flash of light, and died again. Max stared at the bare bulb, wondering; a bare bulb seemed unlike Julia. Why was there no shade? As if responding to this random thought, the cloud above him grew fractionally lighter, pulling away, and immediately all of Max's attention was riveted, repeating the question that had drawn the cloud to him in the first place.

The cloud darkened, thickened. So, the old man was irritated, was he? Good. It never failed, never; Max had never known a fish who would rise to the bait faster than the Son. Whatever attributes were purely his own, he had certainly inherited his Father's temper and impatience.

The Voice, when it came, was thin and querulous. "I don't give a damn about those benighted children. I'm damned if I'll waste a moment worrying about them. And I never liked you. Never."

"You weren't precisely my cup of tea either, you know. Still, I shouldn't have poked fun at you; a cross is a heavy thing to bear." Max's voice was meditative. "Do you know what I regret the most? I wish I could have been there when you bumped into Satan in the desert. I'll bet he told you where to put it and how hard to put it there. Hard to argue with your big brother, especially when he's so much more successful at what he does than you are.'' Spite, spite, and such a lovely taste it had, after all this time; a cheap pleasure, perhaps, but what else was left? The thin voice took on more body, thickened, gained color.

''Shut up. Just shut up. You never learned the lesson I set for you, little man. And it will bring you down forever, in the end.''

''Do you know, I seriously doubt that? And in spite of your vanity and the vanity of the whole stinking Trinity, you've never had any real right to set anyone a lesson, not after those first early days. You weren't bad, but you began to slide toward the end. The cracks showed; even Judas knew that.'' Max, his eyes never leaving the ceiling, reached for a cigarette and lit it. ''You've had your time; two thousand years, the maximum for a god of men. Almost over, almost done. Pity you never learned to be a god for women, or children, or the world represented by anything that wasn't close enough to what you wanted it to be.'' Max laughed, and the sound rang loud and hollow around the comfortable room. Had he been paying attention, he might have felt the corresponding intensity of concentration from the street below. ''A god for demographics. Yes, it's a pity. You might have lasted longer, but you won't, you won't, you'll be following the others, the ones you drove out. You've had it, lord, had it. Your day is almost done.''

''Be damned to that! Liar! My day will never be done. Even as I died I rose, and I linger eternal.'' Yet there was a flicker of dull fear beneath the often repeated words, the first time Max had heard it, the first sign of the break in the overriding will that had kept Them on top for twenty centuries. Had the older gods, Max wondered briefly, reacted this way when the Trinity told them the same thing? Pan, Osiris, the Great Mother, all swept away in the anger of the patriarchal pantheon; had they faded gently, or burned out in rage? Or had they stepped aside with a grace unknown by the Holy Trinity, bowing with humor or sorrow to the inevitable?

"I say my day will never be done!" The Voice had risen to a high anger, reacting to Max's contemptuous silence, and the bulb momentarily disappeared beneath a swirl of motion. Furious now, was he? Was it fear of his own ending, sorrow at the impending death of his power or honest rage at Max's inattention? Max drew on the cigarette and grinned at the ceiling. His voice held mockery.

"Oh, it will. Isn't that amusing? You stuck me here out of pure spite, you so-called apostle of forgiveness. I've never been too sure whose sins you were supposed to have died for, but they sure as hell weren't mine." There was a note of savage amusement in Max's mimicry. " 'I go, but you remain.' Right, then. I remained. Well, the Second Coming's on its way. Pity you won't be there to see it."

The Voice had gone flat. "I shall never allow it to happen. Never. You are not free yet."

And with that flat statement, Max knew and understood what the Son had in mind. He got up, slow and dangerous.

"Oh, won't you? Mister High and Mister Pure, the One, the Son of the One, you're so threatened by your loss of power that you'd murder the innocent? Suffer all the little children to come unto me, is that the story? Not this time, *my lord*. You can't touch us, not mother, not child, not me. Not now."

But the cloud was gone, the bulb was clear. Max, alone in the quiet room once again, breathed heavily. After a moment, he opened the curtains and stared out over London.

She was out there somewhere. One night he had spent with her, one night in two thousand years of nights, the only night in all his protracted existence that meant anything. Every breath he had ever taken had led up to Julia's bed in Bloomsbury, to the planting of the seed, the sowing of the usurper, the final nail in the coffin of the unnatural world of humankind.

Over three billion people had died of the Big One, the plague that had begun at the precise moment of their coming together, the sacrifice that had been offered to the tiny egg being fertilized. Three billion people, the chaff from the wheat of two thousand years of Christianity. And Max did not regret a single one of them.

But the fear the Son had shown disturbed him, spurred him; it ran through him now, a consideration of that fear, and acted as a catalyst. There had been a threat implicit in the Son's final words; two or three months more in this wretched place and then free, free to be gone if he chose.

The child would deliver him from the burden of Jesus's spite, the sentence laid upon him at the foot of the skull-shaped hill, when he had made a fatal mistake and teased a man carrying a heavy piece of wood up a steep hill to his own crucifixion.

The child would free him. If it was born.

Something was happening down in the street. The children had gathered beneath his window, staring up at him, watching him. Now, for the first time since the plague had swept across the planet, he heard sound from them, a low hum, ragged and uneven. A few of them were touching; the rest stood apart, each one a small, self-contained unit of life.

They were singing.

And on the voices of the unborn child's first adoring choir, Max, the Wandering Jew, the conduit through which the supplanter of the Jehovans had been sown, closed his eyes and let himself go until he saw Julia Reynard, lying naked and gloriously pregnant in a chaise longue on a marble terrace, a large ram curled up on the green lawn beyond her.

She was talking, astonishingly, to a sleek gray cat. As Max strained and stared, the cat lifted her slender head and found him across whatever distance separated them, and Max looked into a pair of eyes he knew, the eyes of the protector, the guardian of the new life coming, a pair of eyes as old as his own.

3

Conversation and Vision

"MESSY, INNIT?"

By the time Ben's meadow and little house came into view, the two ravens had completely forgotten their delight with the new innovation of paper plates. Lighter than tin the plate certainly was, but there were drawbacks; the paper tended to wobble, and it had noticeably less ability to keep its shape as it moved. A few times they had nearly had to touch ground in order to keep the pie from spilling over the side and spattering on the ground so far below them. They were glad, both of them, when Matthew's sharp eyes spotted the easel and the tray of paints that meant home.

But Ben was not at the easel, and for a moment John knew a moment's unease, a tiny prickling between the shoulder blades that came with any departure from the norm. It was Ben's custom to wait by the easel, his five little plates set out on the grass, the bright red and white checked tablecloth set out with the berries he had picked while the birds were out foraging for him. The cloth, the little plates, the badly made tea, all of these things had the gently comforting feel of ritual. Besides, the regularity and continuity of the proceedings made Ben feel good. Though he could not find his own food, he could pick the berries for them. The fact that the ravens, ancient carnivores that they were, only nibbled the berries out of sensitivity to the painter's feelings took nothing away from the daily rite.

But today there was only the easel. No cloth and nothing on it; more than that, no other birds. The cold moved down John's spine, taunting and unpleasant. Mark and Luke, where were they?

"Down at the stream." The line was there, the pure gold and scarlet of thought between them; Matthew was recovering his species' old talents with a vengeance, John thought, and sometimes it wasn't half alarming. He stifled the unworthy thought and straightened his body for the gliding landing. It was only after they had set the plate by the foot of the wooden easel that he answered his companion's words.

"The stream, is it? Unusual."

Matthew opened his eyes at him. "No problem, matey, none in the world; I can see them. Not to worry. Ben's all right, the boys are with him. They're just standing there, looking at the stream—"

"Oh!" Suddenly the picture came clear to John, as it had so much sooner to his junior; what was more, there was knowledge in the vision, which Matthew, with his superior sight, had apparently been denied. John felt a little better. "You're dead right, chum, no problem. Ben got to thinking about Old Trout, what color he is, that's all. They forgot all about teatime and went down to see. Oh, look—Luke's caught a squirrel!"

For a moment the two birds were silent, each busy with his own image of Luke, far and away the best hunter of the group. Of all the four ravens, imposing predators that they were, Luke was the best designed for catching and killing his dinner. He was the lightest of the quartet, but had the longest talons; he also possessed surprising speed in the air, an instinctive knowledge of the best use to be made of the shifting currents that carried him, and a sharply defined curve to his beak.

It was common for him to kill two or three meals in a single hunt, a squirrel, a smaller bird, or a rat grown fat from living in the fields of rich grain, and bring them back for the others. If nothing else was available, he had even been known to bring down a dog, a species he despised on general principles anyway. There was an odd beauty to Luke on the hunt, and even Ben, who disliked seeing things killed, rather enjoyed watching him.

Now the two foragers stilled their wings to watch him. He had set the squirrel, its eyes open in a last look of surprise at the death that had come upon it so suddenly, on the ground at Ben's side and taken to the air again.

He was not hunting this time, but playing. The beautiful, ancient yew tree that shaded Ben's favorite spot on the stream bank was a perennial home to pigeons and Luke, a typical predator, was affectionately contemptuous of the noisy gray birds. His sharp eye picking up a clutch of some forty pigeons near the top of the tree, he had decided to throw a small fright into them.

John, his nerves tuned to the scene like antennae, could feel the yearning in Ben like pain, an unspeakable, voiceless desire to paint, to fly, to do something that would make him a part of this beauty. Above the stream Luke soared, slanting his body against the sun, casting a huge and ominous black shadow across the grass. Ben stood subsumed in this patch of darkness, every inch of him leaning toward the light, as the raven reached the top of the tree, hovered a moment as if striving for maximum visual effect, and pounced.

In Ben's garden, Matthew snorted. "Childish, really," he said with some amusement. "Luke wouldn't be caught dead eating one of those filthy things; he's just having them on."

John shook with strange and silent avian laughter. Luke, with a rusty croak that echoed across the meadow, had settled onto the uppermost branch of the yew. Predictably, the terrified pigeons had scattered in all directions, cooing and scrabbling and flapping madly off into the sky like snow shaken loose from a hilltop. Luke, now in sole possession of the tree, craned his neck to caw some derisive remarks after the hastily departing pigeons.

"He just does that to amuse Ben," John said. "Come on, Matt, let's go fetch them home. Playtime's over."

But when they reached the stream, they found that Ben's attention had shifted from sky to water. Just under the blue and gold of the water's surface, a large shape lay placid and still. Old Trout, eight pounds at the lowest possible estimation and reputedly as old as the stream itself, had deigned to show himself to the watchers on the shore.

He was impressive, certainly. In the time when men still lived to come to the stream with rod and bait, he had been the focus of lust for every would-be fisherman in the county. Young men came and went sadly away again, empty-handed or with smaller fry; older men shook their heads over it and kept to themselves the presence of the great creature in their dreams at night. Other, lesser fish had succumbed to the lure of the fly and gone to their deaths; Old Trout, the father, the patriarch of the moving waters of Sparrowdene, had lain in deep water for years beyond man's counting, contemptuous, cantankerous, as wise as time.

Knowing Ben for what he was and understanding that there would be no threat offered, he had felt the presence of an admirer and lifted his heavy body from the pebbled bottom. Now he lay, motionless except when he sensed Ben's desire to see another side of him; at those moments he would turn himself, knowing how the sun would catch the diamond scales through the water and send the color dancing into Ben's eye. The ravens he simply ignored.

And, John thought, Ben had been right after all. Old Trout was purple, a shimmering streak of gray and mauve. Only the darker gills and great flat eyes, open now and staring up at them in all their dark and liquid danger, were denied the breathless tones. Though the ravens quite enjoyed fish, Old Trout was sacrosanct; the natural order of things imposed respect, a certain formality, and Old Trout was wise, ancient, a repository of knowledge and a well of memory without bottom. Secure in nature's pantheon, he had never faced danger, except from man, and man was gone now. The ravens would no more have assaulted Old Trout than they would have tried to eat each other, for such a brand of stupidity was the concept and prerogative of walkers on two legs.

"Oooooooh," Matthew muttered, impressed despite himself by the sheer magnitude of Old Trout, and by the potency of his presence. "Lovely color he's got."

"Not bad." John, mindful of a leadership already mildly threatened by Matthew's burgeoning gifts of thought, refused to show awe. "For a bleeding fish, anyway; he'd look a proper nit if he had feathers." Matthew turned his head to regard him, and he added hastily, "But he's got a certain something, no doubt about it. For a fish, that is."

Luke and Mark had wheeled to greet them. Ben, on his knees before the water, paid them no mind. He sat gazing at Old Trout, his concentration rapt and complete.

"Good hunting, mate? Little bit of squirrel for teatime, then?"

Luke cocked his head, the evil beak half open. "No question, John, squirrel for tea. I got him for you and Matt; me and Mark had us a rabbit while you were gone. Did you find a bite for Ben? And what about that child?"

"Pie for Ben, as usual. And no great ruddy tin plate this time, either; she'd left it out on the green for us, on a soft plate. I didn't see her." A thrill of memory ran across his back, ruffling the feathers into points. "I smelled a cat, though. Wager it was watching us from all them bushes, too. Cor, I bloody hate cats."

"Didn't give you a hard time, though, did it?"

"No, it didn't." And, John realized suddenly, that was peculiar in itself. Whereas few cats would choose to tangle with a raven, to hover in the shrubbery with its eyes shining in patient amusement—and John had known, with absolute certainty, that this vivid picture was the truth of it—was very strange behavior for a feline. And he had sensed, as clear as the afternoon sky itself, power and control in that garden; whatever the cat's motivations in leaving the birds unmolested, it had not hung back out of fear. Interested now, he was prepared to opine, when their attention was suddenly and effectively distracted.

Old Trout had spoken.

The voice of the fish was the voice of the water. Unlike the birds, who spoke with their thoughts and paid no mind to the sky that carried them, the fish was of his element, totally and completely. Should they lose their wings and find the sky forever lost to them, the ravens would remain ravens, living their lives as ravens on the ground, however frustrated. This was not so of those who spun out their lives in the deep waters. Without water they ceased to be, and so, as the freedom of opinion returned to them, their deep voices came whole and alive, echoing in the tiny bubbles of movement they sent bursting along the surface: the voice of their element, their home.

"She means no harm to you."

Ben straightened up abruptly, and the birds saw his smile. However likable and worthy of their patronage they deemed him, however high their respect for his uniquely human genius with color and light, he remained a mystery to them in many vital ways: the working of his mind, his feelings, what passed with the idiot savant for thought. They saw this lack of comprehension, shamefacedly, as some failing in themselves, not realizing—and how could they realize, when Ben himself could not have found the words to tell them of their error?—that the lost ones of Ben's own kind had shared their ignorance. They had come to terms with this in the only way feasible, adopting, after the way of balanced cogs in the universal wheel, a kind of significant, heavy-handed tact.

So now they looked at each other briefly out of the corners of their eyes, nodding, shrugging, sensing that Ben in his serenity and innocence had understood Old Trout perfectly, where they had not. John felt a brush along his side and knew that Mark, simple little Mark, had nudged him to speech.

"No harm? And who is this 'she,' anyway?"

Ben tilted his head a moment, the lovely child's smile an imprint of pleasure across his face. Then he held out a hand to John, a rare gesture, for Ben mostly shied away from touch of any kind. John, oddly moved and surprised into a momentary abdication of dignity, hopped forward to land on Ben's paint-stained sleeve.

"The cat, Johnny, the cat. The old man says she doesn't care to harm you." Bubbles scattered, small jewels across the stream, as Old Trout spoke again; his body turned to face the sky, purple and gray, and once again incomprehensible Ben acted as translator, shaking his head at the world. "Bad language, fish; I've known lots of cats, and they are not all killers at heart." He spoke to John's head. "She'll watch you, that's all. She guards the two small ones who make the food, the way you guard me." The lush smile slackened, died, reappeared again; he had been listening to the water. "He says— what? I don't understand that, old man."

The bubbles themselves might have been all compact of an iron patience; seemingly Old Trout knew with whom he dealt, knew that his legendary bad temper would work no profit here. Ben listened, seeming not to notice the heavy bird who had moved, careful with his claws, from arm to shoulder. Suddenly he laughed, a delighted chuckle, honest and gay.

"Oh, I *see* . . . the cat is also guarding something else, something not born yet."

"Kittens?" Luke, who was growing hungry and poking at the stiffening squirrel, spoke randomly.

"No . . ." Ben's thought was hesitant, and the four birds all fixed their attention on him. "No, a baby, one of my kind. Important, Trout says."

For a moment they were all quiet, listening to the hum of insanely busy insects against the drowsy summer afternoon; the silence itself had substance, a deep, thick music that ran for half one turn of the world as a counterpoint to the chill lack of passion of the stars' movement at night.

Something, a knowledge or a premonition perhaps, stirred the birds into a sudden frenzy of activity. John fluttered into the air, the others immediately taking to the sky with croaks and caws, nervous now, wondering, afraid to wonder more, knowing that wonder too often meant change and that all change meant a violence of sorts. Thoughts sprayed from them like machine-gun fire, We must get back, it's teatime, come on, Ben, come on now, let the old one sleep . . .

Resonance followed them as they went, shadowy, plangent, the voice of the waters before Old Trout sank once more into the cool places where he slept the hours away—strange, nonspecific words.

She will be welcome here.

The ram whose name was not Peter but Simon came to Sparrowdene with a full heart and no more arduous a task before him than the provision of companionship.

The dominant male of his flock, he had left them knowing that, as soon as his shadow faded from the long grass, the strongest of the younger rams would go horn to horn for the attention of the females. A silly system, he had always known that; the ewes were actually amused by their male counterparts and frankly didn't give a flying damn whom they mated with. All they truly cared about were the lambs, wobbly and plaintive on their spindly legs. That they humored the rams in their exhibitionism, regarding them all the while as fit for nothing but stud purposes, had long since ceased to bother Simon, and the other rams were far too young and stupid to realize it.

Well, let them fight it out. The call had come, the call he had been waiting for since the last panicked screams had faded to silence, since the scattered corpses with their accelerated disease-ridden metabolism had decayed with the uncanny speed conferred by the Big One. It was coming, it was on its way; male, female? It didn't matter. All that mattered was the fact, the fact that a human woman, swollen with the protection of life on earth, awaited him.

So Simon had trotted toward Sparrow House, following the pulsing call from the gray cat who was even older than himself. He felt nothing and he felt everything; the sky seemed to stand beneath the black canopy of space for him alone, the sun was warm breath and light, favoring him. He had been chosen for this task uncounted years before the woman who carried the savior ever saw the darkness of her own mother's womb. He would watch her, cherish her, protect her from whatever last attempt at darkness might be thrown at her, in any way he possibly could.

As he approached the long meadow that culminated in the stone terrace of Sparrow House, he stopped. Something was watching him, eyes upon him, seeing him, knowing his purpose. The oily fur could not bristle as Gad's silken coat could, and yet it seemed to move, to thin with his electric tension. But no, it was all right, all was well; a gaze there was, it was true, a stare that came from outside, but it was not inimical, it carried no danger, only interest.

The eyes left him, dismissed him, as unexpectedly as they had found him. Suddenly exhausted, Simon stopped to graze, knowing that he had another mile to go yet before the great stone house was reached and the gray cat set him to his appointed task. Finally sated, he lifted his great head and sniffed the air for water; smell and sound reached him together, and he moved to the tiny stream, so charmingly hidden in the reeds, to drink. He dipped his muzzle into a still place between the rocks, and when he had finished and gone on once again, he had left a slick of green on the water behind him.

And there, at last, he was. The stone wall, a curve of amorphous gray in the distance, took shape and became solid; vague lines separated and became individual stones, set together into a serrated masterwork of design. A blob of color became a head of hair, a small dark splotch became a cat, gray and slender, designed to hunt, to think, to live. The cat stood and stretched, and the head of hair half rose from its recumbency and became a woman, startled, questioning, indecently beautiful in her nakedness and abundance, the great swollen stomach seeming to shine with a light from within.

"Welcome," said the cat, and the woman smiled; her face, though she had no way of knowing it, had the look of one of Ben's paintings. As Ben, exasperating the ravens with their linear vision, saw not only the green of the grass but every molecule of shade and shape that had gone into the green to create it, so Julia appeared to Simon, her face an infinity of colors, dots, tiny geometric shapes set precisely into the miracle that was the final product, Julia, the mother, the carrier, the hope of the time.

"Hullo," she said, and reached a hand out, letting it rest in infinite gentleness on the ram's face. He felt his eyes fill with sudden tears. Clumsily, stiffly—for a quadruped is ill designed for genuflection—he knelt before her on the soft lawn. To his astonishment, she sounded startled, and rather shy.

"What are you doing? Isn't that awfully uncomfortable? I'm—I'm afraid I don't know your name, Gad told me but I've forgotten, but welcome anyway, I'm so glad you're here . . ."

"Simon," he told her, "my name is Simon." Rising shakily to his feet, he looked into her eyes that were full of summer and saw that she had no idea of the treasure she carried, no idea in the world.

The children below his window had sensed his movement, heard his carping bitterness at the Son, seen his vision of Julia and her guardians. Something had certainly stirred them from their quiet vigil, for as Max, moving under the hard spur of urgency, quickly gathered the small essentials he would need in his search for Julia and the key to his freedom, they began to shift from their positions in the street.

Clean socks, the ancient flask of Damascene silver full of wine, the box of crackers, all were taken swiftly and pushed into the leather sack. From outside, the children's voices rose in a dense and shapeless hymn, seeming to cheer him on. Max, the reaction to the threat implicit in the Son's words setting in, had begun to tremble; the singing calmed him, steadied him, for surely the innocents out of doors would know if a threat were truly offered . . . ?

With the leather bag across his shoulders, as it had lain too many times since that cloudy day at the hill men called Golgotha, Max closed the door of Julia's flat behind him for the last time and set off on foot into another day.

As he came out among the children they moved, hands reaching out with the stealthy grace of children, to touch each other, to nudge, to point. The singing stilled and died; they had tasted something on the air, a feeling or a need that was carried across to them like poetry or pollen. They reacted in the only way they knew, with the wonder that, as Julia had said in the poem that had shown Max what her destiny was, was their birthright.

They made no attempt to stop him, nor yet to follow him. He came down the dirty stairs and stopped to smile at them, his small paladins, his guard of honor, and they stared back, their eyes wide and opaque. Then, as he reached the street, they parted before him and gave him passage.

He stood a moment, trying to fix on Julia, not really knowing which way to go. Though the vision had been clear enough, the directions—because of the jealous rage of the Son, or because of some other veil he could not yet put a name to?—had been oddly obscured. Threat, threat, he had sensed it, and the image of the child's breath cut off in the womb ran unbearably behind his eyes. All his needs, his desires, had crystallized into one simple driving necessity; he must find Julia.

She could be anywhere, anywhere in England; sequestered in this green and pleasant land she certainly was, he knew that much, for where the child grew Gad would be found, and Gad had sent him that much of a clear signal. England it was. But where?

He shrugged, and turned to the children; at the front of the crowd was a small boy, placid and clearly possessed of some intelligence. His face was dirty.

"Tell me," Max asked him, "tell me, where is the mother? Do you know?"

"In the west," said the child immediately, confidently, and then looked absurdly surprised at his own words. Max bit back laughter, not wanting the child to think himself mocked. Yet he felt no inclination to disbelieve the boy; the answer had come from inside and out, without thought, and as such was probably true.

"In the west, I see. Yes; the Son came out of the east, so that makes some sense." He moved one empty hand through the air toward the boy, and something sparkled as it took shape from nothing. "Catch!"

The boy held out both hands, palms cupped, to catch this fragment of brightness. It landed in his hands and lay there, bright and luscious: a sugar rose, perfect in every detail, vibrant red candy petals poised atop the lush green leaves and stem. With the world dead at the drop of his seed, it was somehow comforting to know that this small art of psychokinesis, developed over the millennia he had spent here, still had the power to delight someone. The child, however altered by the strangeness of the world around him, was nonetheless a little boy and, as such, open to clouds of wonder; his rosebud mouth rounded into a breathless "oooooh" of rapture. In a moment the others had crowded round him, silent but yearning.

Max smiled at them, feeling the boy's joy as a kiss against the heart, loving the ragged group while not caring that he might never see them again. Immortality's greatest sorrow is the lack of it among the rest of the world; to love is a brutal agony, for those we love fade and die while the immortal lingers, able only to watch.

He shook the thought off and spoke. "If you go into that house there, you'll see stairs that go up and up. If you go up to the top floor, you'll see a door. If you open the door, you'll see my flat. And if you go inside my flat, you'll find treats there, sweets and things, for all of you. Goodbye."

They were already moving as he turned to the west, jostling in their weird silence to be the first to see the wonders he had left behind him in the flat they had kept watch on for so many days. A light rain had begun to fall, a thin sorry drizzle that mounted the London twilight and held it. He reached the corner alone; as he turned, he heard the little boy's clear voice reaching out to him, calling him, finding him.

"Goodbye," the boy called, "goodbye, goodbye, thank you for the candy, and give the baby a kiss from us when it gets itself born, okay, okay? And remember, you must cross only on the *green* lights." When Max turned back the boy was gone, his flying heels just disappearing into the dim hallway, seeking magic and reward.

In the west, in the west. So the Wandering Jew set out on his final journey.

This was the only journey in a thousand, a million, for which his only feeling was impatient eagerness. He had wandered the centuries out of no desire of his own, but because he had been cursed with the wandering, forbidden from resting, until the time was right.

He walked with long easy strides, covering block after block of deserted London pavement. Bloomsbury became Soho, its tattered posters of naked women crumbling on the peeling doorways; Soho gave way to Chelsea, a Chelsea blank and featureless now that the great red buses no longer ran on busy wheels down the King's Road. Chelsea eventually became Fulham and Fulham ceded pride of place to Chiswick.

He passed through the drab streets of West London like a ghost, walked unseeingly by the ugly tower blocks, council housing that had once teemed with people, with wet laundry hung haphazardly along the mean balcony railings to dry as best it could in the dirty sunlight, with petulant babies howling for attention from the dominance of their prams.

Night came, and with it the colder air. Neither darkness nor chill meant anything to Max; though aware of it, he could ignore it. What, after all, could happen to one who was forbidden to die? He had come a goodly distance already, reached the western fringe of the city; his eyes functioned as well in the darkness as they did in the day, and the night shades held no terrors for him.

All through the night he walked, unerringly choosing the correct road when a choice presented itself; the boy had been right, Julia lay to the west, and Gad's signals were growing slightly stronger now. Intermittent images painted themselves against the blue-black sky: a sunlit meadow, a pair of small children, an empty shop with brightly colored baskets piled by the door. It made no difference; all the pictures led to Julia, and Julia led to the child. Through the touches of inner light, Gad's voice ran like a melody, beckoning, a siren's song whose only message was follow, follow . . .

Shortly before sunrise, he got a clear picture of a man, a man with wide child's eyes and big black birds to bear him company. The image was clear, joyous, incomprehensible in its very lack of Julia; for a moment he stopped walking, considering it. As the picture faded, the first touch of sun lit the horizon behind him and he began to sing.

"Now, Ben, don't be such a twit, right? You know there's no use asking us; we can't read your language, we weren't taught."

The exasperation in John's voice was the measure of his frustration. Who would have thought the little girl would be so clever, answering all the uneasy questions with a little bit of paper stuffed in a pie? Smart, yes, smart as a whip she was; it wasn't her fault, was it, that Ben couldn't read?

Now the painter's face, usually so blank and unlined, had creased into tears. He held Dilly's note between his hands, turning it this way and that, trying to make sense of something he had never made sense of before—words, the language itself in all its graphic glory, alien and strange. He was wretched, bereft as a baby, and the ravens who loved and nurtured him screwed into tight balls of protective sorrow in the face of his misery. The birds were so upset that they had only managed to pick at the squirrel, the lovely delectable squirrel Luke had caught for them; even Matthew, that greedy eater, found himself taking no pleasure in his food, so pervasive was Ben's sorrow.

It was Mark, surprising Mark, who solved the problem in the end. He hopped over to Ben's side, something he rarely did, and peered over the big man's shoulder. Something in his stance arrested the attention of the others; they turned to regard him hopefully as silence fell.

"Oh," Mark said, suddenly pleased. "This is simple."

"Simple, simple? What the hell do you mean, simple? You can read this muck, can you?" John, displeased at a sycophant seeing what a king did not, vented irritation.

Mark flapped and settled. "Course I can't read it. But it's *pictures*, isn't it? I mean, these are words, right? And words are just pictures that you draw different, right?"

John remained truculent. "So?"

"So, Ben sees pictures. He sees pictures better than anybody, he sees pictures all over the bleedin' shop. All he has to do is look at the pictures behind the words, and he'll get it then." He peered up at Ben, who was staring at him open-mouthed. "Go on, mate. Give it a pop."

Ben began to chuckle. "Mark, you're a pistol, good and proper. Right, then. Here goes."

It didn't take long, after all. Mark's instinct had been right, for words, after all, are merely condensed images, a kind of shorthand of the visual world, and every word ever created in every language was created to express something. The words were merely the skin that was stretched, for the sake of convenience, across the skull that was the eye. Had Ben known this simple fact earlier on, he might never have developed the searching eye that stripped the skin away, revealing the world of mystery beneath. When at last he had deciphered the hidden meaning, he put the note down on the grass and regarded his companions with triumph.

"She wants her pie plates back. Her name is Dilly Wren and she lives in a house called Dills Cottage and she has a cat called Gad and a sister called Maddy and she says she doesn't mind your taking her pies, but would you please bring her good pie plates back when you come next?" Though Ben's innocence left him incapable of real surprise, he understood pleasure better than most, and his delight in the new and marvelous technique of reading that Mark had discovered was tangible, covering the meadow.

John was stupefied. "That's all?"

"That's all," Ben said. "You know, I kind of get the feeling that she won't be able to bake any more pies if she hasn't any pie plates. That makes sense; I remember now, that Matron used that kind of thing for cooking, at the Home. Well, that's fine, I don't want the things, though I suppose they might be useful for mixing paints. You told me Dills Cottage wasn't far; we'll take them back to her tomorrow."

4

Innocents

WHILE MAX RESTED on the rain-washed steps of a Middlesex train station with his face turned toward a pale dawn sky, the cat Gad had taken herself out to hunt in the darkened fields that ringed Sparrowdene.

She was not, this time, in search of food; another, more primal need had come on her some hours before in the bright moonlight. No matter how urgent the need, however, there was a duty which must be performed first.

Slipping into Dills Cottage—a Georgian home bought by a rising young barrister and his wife not only because the cottage would be beautiful when restored, but because the likeness of the cottage's name to that of their elder daughter was too odd a coincidence to be ignored—she checked on the sleeping children. Dilly, in her faded Winnie the Pooh pajamas, lay in unconcerned perfection; she slept on her side, her face dim and untouched in the pale light. In the cot beside her, Maddy was a golden rose out of heaven, long-lashed and smiling, exquisite in the way of all babies at rest.

Safe, sleeping, untroubled by dreams. Her care taken

and duty done, Gad turned her face to the night and padded out of doors.

The heat in her loins seemed patterned, matching beat for beat the pulse of the warm air, the moving wings of bird and insect. It had a voice, high and insistent: Thump thump, it is a time for joining, thump, breeding, thump. She jumped for the stone wall that circled the garden and landed, silent and feral, in the open field to the south. Her scent, a banner of purpose, lay heavy on the air behind her.

The need, of course, was hardly a new sensation. Cats, that long-lived and matriarchal species, had a beautifully balanced season of unity; they mated when that mating would result in young and the best possible season for each individual cat. In her earliest memories, when she had been white and long-haired and the adored totem of the priestess of the sacred grove in Mesopotamia, she had mated at the time calculated to bear kittens in May, when the young king was ritually slaughtered; his blood, sprinkled on the ground for the continuation of prosperity, had seemed a fortuitous omen for her own race.

In the centuries since then, she had moved across the world, different toms, different seasons, a different brood, and the kittens had been born, a procession of lovely soft fur and pointed ears and feet that seemed too big for the bodies that must grow to match them. For some years now, gray and English, she had mated at the end of winter, so that the babies would be old enough to hunt before snow came.

Tonight, a search for procreation out of its proper season, was something beyond the normal; this need came differently, from a separate place. It was not a true heat, but something deeper and stranger.

She went light-footed across the fields, her instinct leading her on, stopping for a moment to sniff the breeze. In the distance she heard a howl, deep-throated, wild, irresistible: a tom, probably that enormous ginger tabby from the sheep farm. She had never much cared for orange cats—her one experience as a marmalade tiger had not been a happy one—but tonight the tom was unimportant, except for the function he provided. All that mattered were the kittens.

They would be, must be, born with Julia's child. Gad had not stopped to consider it until Max's long-seeing eye had found her, but the ritual was necessary, vital in fact. She had always been a guardian; sometimes with eagerness, sometimes unwillingly, she had kept watch over the birth of the great wheel's temporary crowns ever since human beings' earliest evolution had convinced them that, whatever their own place on the wheel, they would never feel secure unless there was someone to answer to.

She had counted the hours for Isis, supervised Athena's first faltering steps, taken a certain spiteful pleasure in swiping at Baal, rotten with a dark hunger from the moment of his conception, with a careless paw. All their beginnings, all their endings; she put her nose to the ground and sniffed for the tom's spoor, even as she shook with silent laughter.

Beginnings, endings. That last time, the Son staggering with his cross under the soft spring clouds to his death, his birth, the beginning of his reign. Would Max remember her, the long-haired, exotic, chocolate-pointed creature that had woven those comforting figure-eights between his ankles as the angry man with the cross laid a price upon his head? No, very likely not. It hardly mattered; their eyes had met and he had known her for who she was. He would come.

As it happened, it was the ginger tom, and Gad was able to achieve her purpose. As she hunkered down against the hard ground, ignoring with the ease of long custom the ivory teeth in her neck, she probed into him for the spark that gave him life. As she had expected, it was simple, savage, driven by a need untainted with knowledge; perfect, she thought grimly, for she had no room—no, no room and no time either—for unnecessary complications.

The tom saw her as a receptacle, nothing more, and it was best that way. She listened to the pleasurable growling behind her with an iron patience, waiting for the moment, knowing when it came.

When the kittens were planted, the tom showed an inclination to linger, but Gad drove him off. He had served his purpose, and his presence now was no more than an unnecessary irritation.

She turned into the woods in search of a post-coital meal. Toward morning, as she sat by the stream contentedly gnawing the remains of a hefty bat whose radar had somehow failed, she heard the deep voice of the water calling her name and, for the first time in their long mutual existence, went to have speech with Old Trout.

Even Ben's eye, tuned to miracles, could not have made out the great shape; in this light the water was black, a quilt of wet darkness to cover and protect. Gad, coming to the water's edge with the last of the bat dangling from between her teeth, had no trouble at all, for cats are night hunters, their eyes adapted to the hours of the chase. She dropped the bat, laying a cautious paw across the remains.

"Good morning, father. You called me, I think? A good thing, too; it's high time we spoke."

The water rippled. "Good morning to you, Guardian. Or should I say mother? You have had a busy night."

Gad moved her shoulders in a shrug, and the pearly fur rippled. "Out of season, but necessary. Things are coming close now, are they not?"

"They are." She felt a sudden suspicion in him, a stiffening. "What do you eat there, hunter?"

She thought she could understand his tension, and spoke soothingly. "A bat, father, a creature of the air." She chuckled wickedly. "No fish for me tonight, though I confess I'm fond of fish."

She felt his relief. "A bat. Ah. No ravens?"

So that was it, the source of his worry. But really, Old Trout to worry over a gaggle of birds! Things must indeed be moving. She spoke soothingly. "No ravens, old one.

Strange as it must seem, I don't really care for birds; too many feathers and claws, bits and bobs, and not enough meat on them. But even if I adored the stupid things, you'd have no cause for worry. The ravens are safe enough. I watch them, no more than that.'' She knew a curiosity in him, and rewarded it with confidence. ''I watch two small girls, trout, humankind and the barest children. Ravens are big birds, dangerous and fierce. If they don't touch my girls, they're safe enough.''

The tension had vanished, the water grown still. ''Good, good. Because, you see, I told them you meant them no harm, and I'd hate being proved a liar.'' His voice took on a deeper significance. ''Particularly at this juncture.''

''As who would not? No, they're safe enough.'' Now her own curiosity, that attribute which had reputedly gotten an early cat into grave difficulties, was peaking. ''Why the ravens, father? I've been watching them, reading them. They're not one of us, just a set of first-generation English ravens in their first and most likely their only lifetime. I can't fit them into anything. I can't see their purpose, except that they're obviously caring for a human—ravens have many faults, the thieving bastards, but I've never known one to sink to eating blackberry pie. Why the ravens, father? You must know.''

The water moved as Old Trout came closer to the surface. ''Oh, a fluke, nothing more; an accident of the wheel, if indeed the wheel contains any such thing as an accident. They are fit guardians; all ravens are, you know. Thieves they are, that's the truth, but think of it, mother Gad; they steal brightly colored bits of gold and silver and food, and watch them jealously, very jealously—they watch day and night. Marvelous protectors, they are. And they know humankind and can deal with them, at least this lot does; I know you don't much care for them, but even you must admit that their devotion to their chosen objects is patient, and their patience is complete.''

Gad had forgotten the bat. Some revelation lay under the surface, some piece of the puzzle that she did not have was about to be made clear. The curiosity was tangible now, an itch below the skin.

"And so? Everything you say is true, but I'm missing something. Guardians, you said, but I'm that myself, so why ravens? Why are they sacrosanct? Who are they guarding?"

The light above her head was golden now, shot with coral and amber, the morning falling and settling. There was bat's blood on her paws, dark and sticky. "Why? Tell me."

"Why, eyes, of course. Eyes and innocence. Vision for the child." There was a current of something in his voice that it took her a moment to identify. It was smugness. "I thought you knew that."

Thump, thump. Ben, who had not left his small area of security since the day he arrived there, heard the sound of his own feet smacking on the road that led to Dill's Cottage and knew wonder.

He had been born in this cottage and, in a way, might be said to have never left it. Memory was a confusing thing, a potential source of pain or danger, something to be avoided, so as he walked he thought of Old Trout and admired the grace of the four birds leading the way, John a little ahead of the others, Luke folding his wings now and then to drop like a stone, frightening the slender wits out of some small food that scurried, in a frenzy of self-preservation, to a safe haven. The past he thought about not at all, and the future was a concept well beyond the reach of his life.

They came to a stone wall with a wooden gate, and Ben, pushing the wooden door open, paused to listen to the sound of it, so sharp and clear, as it banged back against its moorings. Thump, it went, and thump again. He had never really considered sounds before; for a moment he stood, struggling with some fleeting thought. Had there been something about a thump, a rhythm during the night, soft feet pattering on summer grass? A dream, perhaps?

"Let's get on, mate." This was John, of course, leading the way in a frenzy of impatience. He was, like most birds, truly conservative, disliking change, regarding anything out of the ordinary, any deviation from the norm, as a disaster waiting to happen. He had fought Ben's decision to return the pie plates until he ran out of breath; no reason, was there, why the birds couldn't return the bloody things the way they'd taken them? No reason, was there, for Ben to get himself involved?

But Ben, usually so tractable, had shown a solid stubbornness the ravens had never seen before. She'd been feeding him, hadn't she? It was her pie plates, six of them, he'd deprived her of, wasn't it? Bloody rude, then, really bloody rude, to not apologize, to skulk in his little house as if he was scared to show his face.

So here they were, walking the winding road between Killiford and Sparrowdene in the summer sun, the pie plates carefully washed and neatly packed into a green plastic carrier bag that said Harrod's on one side. And Ben, for the first time in his adulthood, was feeling stirrings of an odd nature, remembering little bits of a life he had ignored during all the long, bad years he had been forced to live it.

The Home, Willowbank it had been called, was something he never thought about; now he thought about it, dimly and glancingly, and little things, faces and foods and smells, came back to him. Fish and chips for supper more often than not, tasting of salt and vinegar and leaving his fingers thick with grease. A young woman, calm most of the time, who would occasionally and for no discernible reason fall to her knees and raise her hands to the heavens and shout, "Will! Will! What have you done with Will?" The matron, with her inexpressive face and thin permed hair that showed patches of scalp beneath, pink and vulnerable as the flesh of a newborn puppy. Deeper than that Ben did not go; he had no language for his feelings, no reference point for the day that his father, who had placed him in the home when the old man grew too sick to care for an idiot son, did not come and never, after that day, came again.

His toe met a small rock and, like a child with a football, he kicked it delightedly, watching it land some ten feet ahead of him on the grass. Another nice noise. Thump, thump. He laughed aloud and the ravens hovered, startled.

"How long until we get there, Johnny? Soon?"

"A while." Some of the truculence had died from John's voice; Ben's delight in his expedition was mellowing his bad temper. Yet it was impossible not to worry. Ben was so young, so old, so helpless . . . Into John's voice crept the loving hectoring note of a parent. "You packed some food, didn't you, mate? Crackers, and cheese? Right. Let's have a rest and some grub. We can sit in this nice field. Okay?"

Ben opened his mouth to protest, looked at the flat yellow eye regarding him, and shrugged. Possibly he understood John's need to regain some of his lost position, his need to assert himself and he obeyed in some small matter; possibly he was simply hungry. Certainly he knew no urgency, there was nothing of Max's knowledge in him and nothing, either, of the desperation that too often comes with knowledge. He nodded, smiling vaguely, and plunked himself down. Thump, smack, a scattering of pebbles beneath his weight. He opened the bag and took out his lunch, looking up to find three ravens instead of four. He asked, happily, "Oh. Where's Luke gone, then?"

"Hunting." This came from Matthew, close by Ben's feet, his wings tucked in close. "Lunch for us, too." He added, thoughtfully and with simple pleasure, "Maybe a rabbit this time, wouldn't that be lovely?"

"Ah," Ben said, and began to eat. To the birds, he was a pleasure to watch, though adults had always turned their faces away when Ben ate. Deemed from childhood as too stupid to be taught manners, he ate like a child, tearing off chunks of cheese, chewing with great unrestrained noises, smiling beatifically. The ravens alternated between eyeing him in paternal pride and scanning the heavens for

Luke, who had soared high and disappeared over the woodlands, his neck arched to spy out the land.

He reappeared suddenly, laden, a dot in the sky; one claw clutched something dark and the other a splash of color, a deep and heartbreaking blue. It was not until he was directly overhead that he realized he could not possibly land with his claws engaged. Something fell on either side of Ben; another squirrel, bloody and limp, and an enormous jay, its brilliant feathers unruffled and unmarked. Thump.

He landed clumsily—ravens, while possessing size and efficiency, are not overly graceful—and sat panting for a moment. The other ravens crowded around, exclaiming and poking. When he regained his breath, he answered the spray of astonished questions with a grin.

"No, I didn't get one with each claw. What do you take me for, an eagle or something? I'd got the squirrel and was coming back over the top of the woods when I looked down and saw this beauty staring up at me from the top of a tree." He nudged the jay with one claw. "He gave an almighty shriek, went stiff, and toppled out of the tree, dead as a nit. Ticker went on him, I think. Anyway, here's plenty for all." Some obscure feeling, perhaps a reaction to the oddity of the entire day, made him turn to Ben. "Want some, Ben? Like I said, plenty for all."

"No, thank you." Ben, who had been staring at the jay, wrenched his gaze back to Luke. "But, um, do you think I could have a feather? Such a lovely color. Would you miss a feather, just one? You don't eat the feathers, do you?"

"Course we don't." Luke was gracious. "Take all the feathers you want, mate, I don't mind. That's right, a nice long primary—you're right, it's a gorgeous color. Proper little quills jays have, don't they?"

The meal eaten, the slender feather tucked safely away in Ben's pack to find a new life in paint at some future time, the five travelers resumed their journey. And eventually the road became narrower, the paved tar giving way to crushed pebbles, and there was a tall stone gate with a little bell set high on the door. Ben, with no sense of doing anything momentous, reached for the bell and pulled the string on the clapper, sending a long, deep peal through the orchard on the other side.

Silence, then voices. Footsteps. The door was pulled open by a small girl, her whole body borne backward at an impossible angle by the weight of an even smaller child. At her feet, welcoming and cool, was a gray cat.

The morning sun has ever been a provider of comfort; one of its nicest attributes is that there is always enough to go around. The same morning sun that had highlighted the bat's blood on Gad's feet, that had touched Max as he sat down to a morning meal near a British Rail station just west of London, spread itself effortlessly and settled its mantle across Sparrow House.

Julia, lying on her back—oh, those earlier days when she could flop on her stomach and bury her face in the pillow, with no Bump in the way—opened her eyes to it. She lay awhile with tears on her lashes, following the movement of ray and mote across the painted ceiling, registering the warmth without noticing, her mind reaching back into the lost hours, trying with the futile desperation of waking to recapture the night.

She had been dreaming, dreaming of Max; this was something that had never happened before, and the sense of loss lay on her, a murderous weight. She closed her eyes, fierce in her need to once again picture him as he had appeared in the darkness, miraculous bones, eyes out of time, walking with his long easy strides. She had seen the streets of London, her old flat in Bloomsbury with the bare bulb in the sitting room (the little cord that held the cloth lampshade in place had broken shortly before the Big One hit and things had moved too quickly, after that, for her to waste time replacing it), children, standing in ritual patterns. And then Max, shockingly clear, lost Max, stalking the empty city in the dark . . .

Julia was not surprised at the clarity of the dream; since early childhood her dreams had come clear, in color, always remembered on waking. Yet they had been dreams, no more than that, shadows and reflections in fancy dress. This last had a different feel to it; even in her sleep she had seen that. She had felt more as though she were sitting in a cinema, watching only, not a participant.

She had not appeared in this dream at all, another change from the usual; Julia was one of those who always starred in her own dreams, good or bad. Yet she had felt herself over it, watching and presiding, and the dream had gone on, children singing and Max walking, always walking, until the moment when she had unknowingly called out his name to the painted ceiling in her need and wretchedness and he had looked up, his hooded eyes suddenly wide and alert.

It was no good; the dream had faded, its contours blurred with roused consciousness. She sat up slowly, knowing that violent jerky movements, the expression of sorrow and frustration that her body craved, would end in no better satisfaction than an intolerable dizziness and perhaps a cramp in her belly. The Bump stirred softly as if in sympathy, and Julia suddenly became aware that she had been weeping, was still weeping, tears moving in runnels down her cheeks.

"What's wrong, child? Are you ill, shall I call Gad?"

That was Simon, outside her window two floors below; he had slept in the wet grass, politely refusing her invitation to come indoors, explaining that sheep belonged in the meadow and were happiest there. She reached a hand up and rubbed the tears away.

"I'm all right. I was dreaming, that's all, a sad dream, about someone I loved, at least I think I loved." She slipped her feet into her espadrilles and stood unsteadily, her distracted mind sending out random thoughts. "Do you ever dream, Simon? Or do only humans do that?"

"Oh, we dream. All cultures dream, every one of us, all creatures, great and small."

She had made her way into the hall, but at this she stopped, startled. " 'All creatures great and small'?"

There was a shy wickedness to his thought, like a child who has played a successful practical joke on an adult. "Ha, I thought that would make you jump. It was the name on the spine of the book you were reading when I arrived; I saw it lying on the terrace when I came up."

Julia suddenly felt better. "Naughty. Well, I'm going to make some breakfast, tea and toast. Do you know, Simon, when I chose this house to live in, I didn't realize it had its own electricity from the mill. I can still plug things in, if I want to. I'll be out in a moment."

"Yes, do come out." Something in his mood had altered. Julia, still new at the business of hearing and interpreting, felt the difference but could not put a name to it. It had sharpened somehow. "You will have visitors today."

Visitors. The thought stirred something, a sudden wild hope, fading almost immediately. No, it had been a dream, only a dream. Max was lost to her, lost, never to be retrieved, part of the fodder of flesh that had rotted with such uncanny speed to meld with the earth that had, for so long, given it space. He might come at night, available to her in dreams that left her cloyed with sweetness and sorrow, but the flesh was lost, gone, disappeared. The visitors Simon referred to must be Dilly and Maddy.

And yet Gad had told her that Max was still alive, had stated it, moreover, with absolute knowledge. But it would hardly do to hope; she had loved so few things in her life, the need to love twisted for so many years into poetry instead of contact, that hope had been translated into nothing better than an object for suspicion long since.

Three volumes on the shelf, the publisher's imprint a gaily colored blotch on the bottom of the spine, the titles in the royal purple used by those dead surveyors of language to designate their poetry line. She passed the stately bookshelves in the great library with her tea and toast held firm, catching with a feeling akin to guilt the three titles. *Breathing Rainbows. A Colored Edge. The Liar's Game.*

Well, she had come to know all three of those realities, and far better than anyone would ever want to. She shrugged and continued out of doors, nothing to do, nothing to hold her attention, the gentle opaque cloud of calm granted by late pregnancy always with her.

Visitors. Well, let them come, human or bestial. The sun was warm and peaceful, she had nothing else to do, and there was plenty of tea for all.

In the great garden orchard, three people sprawled on flannel blankets rendered soft by innumerable washings. The ravens, close by, had relaxed their vigilance; however poorly Ben might have dealt with his fellows in their time, his understanding and acceptance of the children was immediate and complete. In Dilly, in Maddy, Ben had found equals.

And the cat was no threat to them; she had made that clear at once, welcoming them to Dills Cottage with a stately courtesy and quick, cheerful reference to Old Trout. Though John remained wary—he had been raised into a cold distrust of cats and would not easily abandon those teachings—the other three had begun to cope with Gad, cautiously at first, with polite and general talk of the countryside that soon degenerated into cheerful libel of some mutual acquaintances in the fields, the trees, the streams. They discussed the stupidity of blue jay and robin, the stubbornness of squirrel and hare, and sagacity of hawk and horse; Mark, returning again and again to Dilly's note, applied the mind that was so similar to Ben's to the written word and taught himself, in an astonishingly short time, to read.

Luke, in particular, soon discovered that, in Gad, he had found a hunter after his own heart; Gad had heard the story of their lunch today, and had been frankly admiring. It was she who suggested that the jay had been so impressed by Luke that it had simply keeled over with fright, and she stifled the moment of mischief, the desire to tease the birds about the cannibalism of birds who ate other birds.

Ben, too, had provided a surprise. He had handed the pie tins to Dilly with a shy apology, muttered and gruff at first, as was to be expected from a man who had spoken to none of his own kind for some years. But Dilly's pleasure in her tins, her delight in Ben himself, had worked some internal magic in the painter; within a few minutes he was finding words, his speech becoming easier. Gad, her paws tucked couchant on the green lawn, chatted with the ravens and looked benign; with plump fingers Maddy picked chocolate chips out of fresh cookies and gurgled to herself.

The surprise had come with the picture. None of the ravens had been aware at the time that Ben, succumbing to some long-forgotten etiquette about visits to other people's homes, had brought a small drawing he had done as a gift for the children. The picture was a delight, done in soft shades of chalk; the meadow around Ben's easel was a green eternity, pocked with pimpernel, campion, bluebell, little individual spheres of color that danced on the eyes. In the foreground of the picture, the four ravens were sly shapes in purple and black, glossy and pure. Ben handed it to Dilly with a shy ceremony, hoping she would like it.

Even Gad stretched her neck for a better look. Dilly, holding the heavy paper down at the edges by planting her knees on it, stared at it for a long moment, her face creasing into a deep smile. Then she laughed, joy ringing through the orchard.

"Look, Maddy," she said, and the baby turned her face from the enchantment of the cookies to stare, wide-eyed and solemn, her poppy cheeks smeared with chocolate. "Birds, flowers, grass. Oh, lovely!"

They stared at the picture. Only Gad, looking at Ben, felt something move in her stomach, a realization of power in this enormous innocent. She rose and stretched, letting her long leg bones settle silently back into place, and climbed daintily to Ben's lap.

After that, even John relaxed. The innocence of these creatures' intentions was so patent that to persist in his wariness would have been inexcusable bad manners, and ravens place a high premium on manners. The day marched on, the sun moved to zenith. At teatime, Dilly rose to her feet, a small but gracious hostess, and announced that she would put some food on for supper.

Ben, with Maddy set high on his shoulders, followed her indoors. The animals remained on the lawn, even Gad, who knew there would be something put in her dish if she came; Dilly had gone to the stream that morning and come back with her father's old wicker creel full of fry. No, the fish could wait, must wait. There were things to discuss.

The fish was fried in lemon and egg, and Ben, eating with the same greedy abandon as Maddy, had three times cleared his plate before he was sated. Looking up at Dilly, who was taking a loaf of bread from the oven, he took a long deep breath of the food-scented air.

"You're the best cook I ever saw," he said simply, and made a friend for life.

When they returned to the garden, the sun was slightly lower in the sky. Luke and Gad had disappeared; at Ben's raised eyebrow, John merely shrugged and said, "Gone hunting, back in a bit." He was lazy and unworried, relaxed to a degree unusual in him, but before Ben or Dilly could frame a question, Luke fluttered over the wall and dropped a rabbit into a clump of forsythia. He was laboring for breath.

"Open the gate," he panted. "We had an idea, Gad and me. Open the gate, would you?"

"Yes, open the gate." Gad had appeared on the top of the wall; she made no attempt to jump down, glancing behind her and downward. A soft sound drifted over the wall to those inside, a gentle whicker, high-pitched and patient. "We've decided we must go and visit Julia, so we've brought home a way for you people to get there."

5

Stasis and Movement

MIDWAY THROUGH THE second day of Max's journey, it began to rain.

A summer storm in the English countryside is both scenic and frightening; the heat bounces off the ground in sheets almost visible, a placid sky becomes, with the shortest of warnings, a wild backdrop of impossibility. The very air loses its clarity and takes on the qualities of sentience, beating viciously at the land and the life that moves across it like a furious spoiled child with enormous fists, deprived of a toy or a cuddle.

Max, caught between townships when the voice of the season took on its idiot whining note, quickened his pace. Though death was denied him, discomfort was commonplace; he had no desire to be soaked to the skin, perhaps to come to the end of his wanderings with a cold in the head. There had been a signpost, weathered wood and pointing like fingers, a half-mile back: one finger had said Camford, one Little Carbury. Which one had he taken? He could not recall, and it didn't matter, really;

a town would have buildings, and buildings would cover him until the storm was spent.

He broke into a trot, seeing the horses in the distant fields casting uneasy eyes to the sky, smelling the onslaught to come with their huge flaring nostrils. The birds, those signposts of weather fair or foul, had disappeared in the mysterious way they do at such times. The air was thickening by the moment, darkening with internal pressure; to the south, lightning rippled in a mindless plume of power.

The rain had begun to fall, its first soft ominous drops spattering his bare head, when the village loomed up before him. Little Carbury, was it? Fine; it would serve. A small cluster of thatched roofs showed, a modern barn of a building that was probably a supermarket, the crenelated stone of an early Norman church, an elderly Cortina on the High Street. On the horizon, shocking and somehow indecent in this rural setting, he saw the twin spires of a factory smokestack, pointless now, denuded of purpose.

The church, a beautiful little building made of stones quarried somewhere in the open fens eight hundred years before, was the first shelter he reached. As he gained the steps, thunder rumbled; the old building shook with it, gently but perceptibly. And suddenly the storm broke in an access of rage and all the world was water and violence, everything heaving, all obscured.

Max stood in the shelter of the porch and breathed deeply, unwilling to go inside; silly of him, he supposed, yet he simply did not wish to risk another spite session with the Son on, so to speak, his own ground. Only his fancy, probably, but the memory of the angry little cloud with its cracked, harshly inflected voice seemed particularly strong as he leaned against the church door, and Max had learned long since to regard these inner flashes of light and knowledge as solid, real, no more to be ignored than his arms or legs.

He moved away from the doors, therefore, and craned

his neck around the ancient pillars, getting drenched in the process. Beside the church was a graveyard, small and serene, and beyond that the first shops of the High Street. They would likely be locked but, what the hell, he could break a window. Who, after all, was left to complain, what angry shopkeeper would come shouting after him, calling to the town bobby to take him in charge, demanding that the hooligan pay, in time or money, for his vandalism? Put it on my bill, he thought grimly, and then laughed out loud; the sound was snatched by the rising wind and sent echoing away through the ranks of well-tended gravestones.

He hitched his pack more securely to his shoulders, thrust his chin as far down into his neck as it would go, and ran out into the rain.

And here was the High Street, curving graciously up a steep hill and away into the afternoon. Shop windows, some leaded and edged with oak, others the featureless and faceless plate glass that proliferated in this century, reflected one another in the glinting rain; the supermarket windows showed a bald and barefoot mannequin in a pink twin set, the windows of the harberdashery opposite showed a series of posters announcing a bargain, sixteen-ounce tins of new peas, only ninety pence for four, buy today.

He ducked beneath the first awning he came to, a brave little affair of red and white stripes, and pushed at the door. Surprisingly, it opened, or perhaps it was not such a surprise, after all. It is true that habits die hard, and the habit of this age had been to lock doors to keep out the evil that men do. But what use, what use in the world, to lock your doors against a plague that fed on fear, against a death that no weapon could stop, no prayer could defeat, no locks could keep out?

He pushed the door closed behind him, feeling it fight him as the rising wind demanded entry at his back. Jumping a little at the valiant little tinkle of the overhead bell, he turned to survey his surroundings and found himself in a tea shop.

For a few moments, his senses oddly concentrated by the electricity in the air outside, Max let a feeling of tactile memory take him. How many of these places lay dead and empty across England, how many? He knew this place, he had eaten its fresh-baked scones and drunk its hot sweet tea in towns and cities the length and breadth of England's green and pleasant land. No doubt it had been owned by an older woman, a widow or a spinster; no doubt she had prided herself on the wholesome goodness of her home-baked pies and pastries, the elegance of her little fancy sandwiches. The white wrought iron tables carried salt and pepper and small cut-glass vases of silk flowers, choked with the detritus of neglect now; there were small jars of pebbled and cloudy glass, too, covered and with the tips of tarnished silver spoons poking through: catsup, mustard, marmalade. Here the vicar would have sat, and there the local bridge club after an afternoon at the shops . . .

Oddly disturbed, strangely sorry, he trailed through the stuffy room like a ghost. His fingers found the edges of a lawn tablecloth, a copper teapot, a menu that said, in curling gothic script, The Gray Cat.

The Gray Cat. The gray cat . . .

"To everything a purpose," he said softly, and his breath plumed on the stale air. The gray cat. Movement. Turn, turn, turn. He had been right to desert the beckoning finger of the old church, right to come back out into the rain, after all. Setting his pack down behind the ornate brass cash register—and where had she found such a thing, that woman who had baked the pies and served the tea with such painful gentility?—he went into the little kitchen at the back of the shop to brew himself some tea and wait for the visions he knew would come, out of the west.

* * *

James Wren, that rising young expert on maritime law, had found the pony cart in the old stables at Dills Cottage. The cottage, built originally in the seventeenth century and added to in height over the following hundred years, had been standing empty since the First World War; owned by a wealthy but crazily inbred family called Viner, it had been the least of their several residential possessions, and none of the family had cared to live in it. They kept it in a modicum of repair and otherwise let it be, leaving the tiny attic full of Toby jugs and mezzotints, and the Victorian pony cart to molder in the old stables, converted now to a serviceable garage.

During the decade when the cottage came into the possession of James Wren, Victorian paraphernalia had been once again in vogue. He had left the thing where he found it, only hosing it down and oiling its wheels and, when these things were done, moving it to one side to make room for his estate car. Perhaps he had secretly enjoyed the unrelenting kitsch of the thing, or perhaps having it removed would have cost more than it was worth; certainly he never expected it to be used again.

Now his two daughters, twelve and two, stood with a painter and a cat and four birds and a horse, looking in wonder at the faded painted flowers on the sides, the buckled wood of the perch, the great iron wheels. Small it was, yet quite large enough for one adult and two children; even the heavy iron hitches, where a horse's leads might go, were whole and intact.

Of the little group, only the gentle old gelding named Whiskey regarded the thing with a truly expert eye. He was a large horse, fourteen years old and quite fond of people; he had been owned by the same man since his birth in the grassy paddock of Farmer Coughlan. Always well treated, never used for hard labor, his memories of the human race were kindly and pleasant; an apple slipped to him by the farmer's son, a blanket on a cold night, a pasture full of food growing in the summer and a stable full of hay when snow came.

He had known Gad a long time, as time was measured in his life; horses are gregarious by nature and Whiskey, fond of talking and bewildered by the lack of this ability in the horses that shared his space, had made friends with the gray cat years since. He had been stuffing himself with grass when she jumped over the fence a few hours ago, to introduce him to her friend Luke—odd sort of friend for a cat to have, Whiskey had privately thought, but had said nothing—and make her delightful suggestion.

So here they stood, solemnly regarding the pony cart, amazement on their faces. Whiskey, noting the well-greased wheels and solid construction, gave a snort of approval and turned to find Gad watching him, a question in her eyes.

"It'll do," he said briskly. "That thing there, that's where you loop the reins and fasten the harness—look, there's an old harness up there on the wall, it's the leather contraption hanging on that hook—and that's where the driver sits. Nicely built, a proper pony cart. Don't see many of those anymore." He sensed satisfaction in Gad, and essayed a mild joke. "Course, I'm not hardly a pony, but not to worry; I'll get you there, all shipshape and Bristol fashion. All you've got to do is provide a little elbow grease and hook us up."

"Well, but who's going to drive the thing?" This plaintive question came from Dilly, and held a note of trepidation. Whiskey turned his head and regarded her; a child who did not know how to cope with a horse was outside his ken, and he did not know how enormous his fifteen-hand height looked to her, a child of the automotive age. Dilly, in fact, had been intimidated by his sheer size from the moment Gad led him through the garden gate.

"What, can't you drive a cart?"

Solemnly, she shook her head.

"Have you ever even *been* on a horse before?"

Another shake followed the first.

"I'll be damned, excuse my language, whoops, sorry,

children present. What do they teach kids these days?" The horse rolled an eye at Ben, who was still rapt in his contemplation of the pony cart. "What about you, mate?"

Ben forced his gaze from the charming toy, and smiled at Whiskey. "Oh yes. Yes, I can drive this."

"You *can*?" This was John, perched on an overhead beam. He regarded Ben with frank disbelief. This was a new thought, that Ben might possess so useful and impressive a skill; coming hard on the painter's sudden understanding of the written word, the way his shyness and inarticulation had dissolved before Dilly and Maddy's openness, it was a bit eerie. Ben turned his endearing smile on the ravens.

"My father had one, when I was small; I think, I seem to remember, that I was taught once. And, anyway . . ." He gestured at Whiskey, who stood beside him, and Whiskey nuzzled the top of Ben's head with his velvet muzzle. Horses, above any other animal, are gentle with the simple of this world; the annals of man are pocked with puzzled tales of village idiots who handled the most intractable of horses like masters born. This, in fact, is merely a kind of nervous sensibility on the part of the species, and it is one of their chief charms. Ben touched the long face with love. "Anyway, it wouldn't be proper driving, really. Whiskey's a smart horse, isn't he; someone just needs to hitch everything up and hold the reins and tell him which roads to take." He looked momentarily doubtful. "At least—that's how it is, isn't it, Whiskey?"

"Dead right." The gelding, vastly relieved—at least one of these people had some sense—pawed gently at the floor. "Now, let's get the harness down and get it oiled. You'll need some saddle soap and some good grease; what's in that little lot of tins, up there on the shelf?"

They made a party of it, Ben and Dilly, whistling and laughing and trying not to spill the glutinous stuff on the garage floor. The birds, safe overhead on their beams, offered advice and encouragement; Gad, amused as always by the noise and vigor humans seemed to bring to the simplest endeavor, washed the dried fish sauce from Maddy's cheeks. When the labor was done, Dilly scrambled to her feet and regarded the shining harness with pride.

"Lovely," she said fervently, "lovely, look at the color that's come up."

"Color," Ben agreed—was he already seeing the harness, dingy beneath and gleaming on the surface, as an abstract reality on a backdrop of white canvas?—and solemnly shook Dilly's hand. His voice was very pleased. "Did that little job half properly, didn't we?"

"Too right," Dilly agreed. Her fear of the horse had become a thing of the past, swallowed by the larger pleasure of working on the harness. Ben, sharing his delight, smiled at the horse; Whiskey turned his great head Dilly's way. "Why don't you and Ben mount it, and I'll try it on for size. Let's see if it fits."

"It will," Dilly said with confidence, and suddenly her face went blank, the white skin nearly lost in the sudden widening of brown eyes too big for her face. Her mouth slackened; she had begun to tremble.

"Dilly?" Ben's voice and heart held urgency, a feeling to which he was unaccustomed; his tenor cracked into a reedy falsetto, rusty and afraid. Like Ben, the others stared at Dilly, a small arrested statue of bewilderment; only Gad, lying on the floor beside Maddy, was knowing and relaxed.

And Dilly did not at first reply. She was lost, lost in wonder at the voices in her head—the click beetles, the sense of knowledge between ravens in a bright sky—and suddenly the resignation of not understanding was gone in the wake of perfect, easy comprehension. "I heard you," Dilly whispered, and suddenly her knees gave out and she sat down hard on the garage floor, thump, thump. Unrealizing, unaware, she lifted her hands toward the roof in a gesture Gad had seen, over and over again, across three millennia—the hands of the priestess, beseeching the heavens. Joyous, elemental, unique in itself.

"I heard you, I understood you, you spoke to me in my head and I heard you, I truly did." She turned to stare at Gad, and the high unemotional voice came clear as a memory, the voice of the gray cat, Gad, her Gad, complete at last.

"To everything a purpose, and all things in their season," the voice of the guardian said. "Wheel turning; movement, all along the line. Don't look so amazed, Dilly my Dilly. It was time, that's all. You had more than anyone else to unlearn, and you've unlearned it quite nicely. I always knew you would, too."

"Gad," Dilly said, not speaking, laughing and weeping. "Gad, Gad."

"Are you going to help Ben with that harness, or not? Because if we're going to go to Sparrow House, we'd best do it soon. It's getting late and, unless my nose is mistaken, there's rain coming."

Julia, utterly and unabashedly lazy, had decided to forsake the marble terrace with its ornamental statuary for the broad green lawn of Sparrow House's southern face.

In doing so, she had set up a chain of mixed feelings in Simon. Trepidation at her physical nearness, and at the fact that she so clearly expected conversation; of the few of his ancient circle, Gad, and Old Trout, only the sheep had never attained the gift of comfortably sharing his opinions. Offsetting that feeling was a sneaking pride that she should want to spend her time with him, that she should trust him with her thoughts, her proximity, the thing she carried.

"Mind your head," she called down, and the golden quilt, used by Maddy and left on the terrace, billowed like a parachute to land on the grass beside him. For a moment he knew alarm, his long face pinching and wrinkling with it; surely she did not mean to follow the quilt, leaping over the side as well? But no, the notion had been absurd. Carrying her plate of sardine sandwiches in one hand and a cup of tea in the other, she descended the eight marble steps and came to sit naked on the quilt at his side. In point of fact, a suspicion had been growing in her, a hazy idea that had to do with time and life, and she had a question for him.

"Simon," she asked, as soon as she was settled, "how old are you?"

"Oh," he said, startled. He had not anticipated this question; though traditionally opting for a policy of ignoring the infuriating and stressful thoughts of man over his time in the world, the occasional unavoidable bits he had picked up had all had to do with things that concerned themselves and themselves only. Proper curiosity had seemed beyond them; he had long ago decided that they were dangerously selfish, caring about the world only insofar as it related to themselves. Julia's simple question, therefore, threw him for a loop, and for a moment he said nothing, wondering how to reply.

She mistook his silence for annoyance, and made haste to retract it. "Oh, I'm sorry, I didn't mean to pry. Of course you needn't answer, if you'd rather not."

And that, too, was outside his set opinion of humankind; in his experience, when one of that lot wanted something, they'd smash anything and everything in their way to get it, flesh and feelings alike. Sensitivity, he had long ago decided, was not a virtue they possessed. But of course Julia was different, she had to be different, considering what she held . . .

"Not at all, not at all, of course I'll answer you . . . hmm, well, it's just a bit tricky, that's all. Answering, I mean. You see, my kind measures time differently than you do." He knew a deepening of her curiosity, and hastened to explain. "You do yours in, what, years? Yes? Well, we don't, at least not exactly. Seasons, more or less. Although not exactly, not exactly." He had never really stopped to consider it before, but he did now. "A long time, anyway, I do know that much. A very long time."

"Oh. Seasons." She sipped her tea, her stomach jutting out before her like a rose, pink and white, showing that vital network of blue lines just beneath the skin. He looked at her in admiring silence. "Well, seasons," she went on. "There are four in one of our years, you know: spring, summer, fall, and winter. So tell me how many seasons and I'll translate it into years." She laughed, reaching out to rub his head where the roots of the ivory horns met; liking the sensation, for her fingers had found an insistent insect bite and were doing wonderful things to soothe it, he pushed at her hand and snorted, deeply and pleasurably, in his throat. "So?"

"Well, I don't know," he answered. "Hard to say." Her face fell; she had not considered that math, as it is understood by people, might be unknown or seen differently by the rest of the universe. The scratching hand stilled in her disappointment, and he spoke hastily. "I'll tell you what, though. Name a number of years, and tell me what was happening then, and I'll tell you if I was around to see it. Right?"

"Right." Julia, who knew her history in the thorough manner of one who truly enjoyed the march of faces and lives through time's panoply, gave the matter a little thought. She decided to give him an outrageously distant time in the past to start at, and move forward from there. "Nearly five hundred years."

"My!"

"Queen Elizabeth was Queen of England then, red hair, fighting the Spanish Armada. The Inquisition was happening in Spain, Jews and Moors being killed because they weren't Christians—"

"And Shakespeare," Simon said eagerly, astounding her. "I remember him, quite well in fact. Stratford was a pretty town, and his people quite prominent; who would have thought that a common little bloke like that could have had such words to say? My, he had a lovely touch, didn't he? There were fewer people then—there had been a plague; I had already come to England by then, long since.'' His eyes had darkened, remembering; he did not see Julia's jaw drop, or feel her sudden stillness.

She took hold of herself, and went on. "More than that? Goodness. All right; nearly nine hundred years. Richard was king then—''

''Was he the stocky fellah with the mop of ginger hair? Bad temper, loved to kill people, any people, didn't matter who?'' Stupefied, suddenly dizzy, she could only nod at him. His voice held satisfaction. ''I remember *him*, all right. Heart of a lion, they said, but that's all wrong; lions only kill from need, never from pleasure or boredom or because they want another lion's territory. Heart of a man, and make no mistake about it.''

His thoughts had taken on an almost bardic tone of reminiscence. ''I grazed the hills of what they called Cyprus then; he came through with an army, nasty noisy lot they were too. Going to Jerusalem, I seem to recall. Old Isaac Comnenus, wicked old sod, was in charge of Cyprus then, and he drove everyone half-crazed with his tricks; this Richard lost his temper with the old misery and shoved him in a cage.'' He chuckled, the black nose creasing with amusement. ''Oh, he turned them upside down, Richard did. Odd bloke. Not nice, really, but likeable, somehow.''

An incredible suspicion was growing in Julia, sending shock waves through her system; The Bump, responding, kicked and settled. ''Two thousand years ago. A man called Herod.''

And Simon's voice in her head was sorry, very sorry. ''What a mess he made of things. Those babies, you know, and all out of fear. He didn't even get the one he wanted out of it, though there's plenty to say it would have been better for all if he had. He wouldn't, he couldn't have done, but of course he had no way of knowing that, did he? Turn of the wheel, you can't alter it. Gravity works.''

But the incomprehensible words were lost to Julia, suddenly cold, staring into space. Two thousand years, at the very least. How old, how old? "Simon," she whispered. "Simon. Were you—are you the only one? Or are there, well, more of you?"

He had bent for a mouthful of grass; the face that regarded her moved in an endless rotation of cud, impossible and silly. Two thousand years, four thousand, ten thousand? "What, as old as me? Course there are. Not many, though; only a few. There's one or two even older."

A high clear voice in her head, a presence, protection. Golden eyes, gray fur. "Gad?"

"Oh, Gad, well. She's always been around. You couldn't have proper changes without old Gadabout, could you now?" The answer, oblique and indirect, was an answer nonetheless. Julia felt a clutch around her heart and suddenly her memory came clear, the high voice prodding at her, pushing her down the forbidden roads that led back in time: Yes, I know of him, I remember him. He was forbidden to die.

The storm had subsided at last, not to a clear sky, but rather to a thin, steady rain. The tendrils of wet and fog seemed to creep under the red and white canopy and permeate the tea shop, chilly and depressing.

In the wooden cupboards lining the kitchen walls, Max had found a number of candles; these he had set up all across the shop, lighting the windows and the counters. Each table now had a white candle to bear the salt and pepper shakers company, and the pale apprehensive mallards asymmetrically placed across the flocked wallpaper now lifted wings dappled with tongues of firelight.

Max, supine on the soft bedroll he had stretched across the floor, lay wakeful and alert. He had waited all day and all evening for some word from Gad, but nothing had come; he had reached his mind out, calling her, but had received no response. Otherwise occupied, no doubt, and he only hoped it was with Julia. Once he had felt something, a feathery touch on his heart, but he had closed himself to its appeal, for he had known where it came from. He had no mind to squabble with the Son just now. After a while, his eyes closed and he grew drowsy; no harm in sleeping, every body needed sleep, even his. Gad could speak as clearly in dreams as she could waking . . .

Knock, knock. A tapping. Fingers against the glass? And was that the bell tinkling? No, impossible. He was dreaming, dreaming of one of the two thousand years, the days past counting gone by . . .

"Hello?"

Suddenly pulled completely into wakefulness, Max sat up. He was not dreaming; he was awake, and someone had come into The Gray Cat, some shape conjured up from the small hours and the rain.

The voice came again, a man's voice, cultured and calm, with a hint of singsong in its cadences. "Good evening, is someone here?"

"Yes." Max got to his feet to face this improbable newcomer; unconscious of the splendor of his naked body, he placed his hands on his hips and craned his head into the shadows beyond the candles. "Who is it?"

"My name is Raj." The man stepped forward. "Good evening, yes, and hello. You need not be alarmed by me, no, not at all. I am unarmed, traveler, and mean no harm to you." He opened his hands, long olive fingers splayed out in emptiness. "See, no weapons and nothing harmful meant. I was walking through this town when the rains came. There was lightning and lightning is very bad, very dangerous. So I looked for shelter."

He gestured at the candles, a clipped wave of one arm, beautiful in its grace and economy. He smiled at Max, and even in the negligible light Max was warmed by the sweetness of the smile and its lack of guile. "I saw the lights. It is a great pleasure to me, to find another person.

A very great pleasure. May I share your light? I will go away again, if you wish it."

"Why should you? Stay, by all means. They're not my lights; they're just lights." Indian, was he, or Pakistani, or Nepalese? Yes, certainly Indian. His skin was dark and smooth, his black hair grown long in the lack of cutting; his eyes, those indicators of the soul within, were obscured by enormous horn-rimmed glasses. Max spoke again, wondering why he was unsurprised by this man's appearance. There was something, something that he knew, a reference that lay, taunting and shadowed, at the edge of conscious knowledge. "My name is Max, just Max. I've got a Bunsen burner in the kitchen. Would you like some tea, a sandwich, coffee?"

"Thank you; tea would be very pleasant." Raj bowed, a short courtly bob from the waist, and Max realized how tall the man was—six foot five or six at the very least and incredibly thin; if he weighed an ounce over twelve stone it would be a miracle.

Raj followed him into the kitchen, and stood beside him as he measured tea leaves into the little metal strainer. "I am most grateful to you, for it is days now since I saw anyone, and then it was children and they would not stay to talk with me. Are you from this place? Is this your shop?"

"Not mine, no. I'm just traveling through here, on my way to somewhere else. Like you, I was caught by the storm, so I came in here to wait it out. There's plenty of food; tins of milk and potted meat and things, you know. And tea, of course, all the sorts of things you might expect to find in a tea shop. Sugar?"

"I thank you, but no. Tea only." Raj took the cup gratefully. As their fingers brushed, a flash of gold glinted in the light: a ring, beautifully worked, very old. Max felt something move down his spine, a recognition; was this why he had come here, then? Led here, and if so by whom? The Gray Cat . . .

"You are looking at my ring." They had sat down at

one of the tables; in the light of its single candle, Max saw an apricot bloom on the dark man's skin. "Perhaps you are thinking me very effete for such a self-adornment? It is very beautiful, of course, but more than that; it has a history, and a future. I do not wear it out of vanity, I assure you, but out of need."

A history and a future . . . Max kept his voice carefully neutral. "Really? Sounds interesting."

"Oh, it is." His equilibrium recovered, Raj explained. "I am from Kashmir, and of course my people place a high premium on gold; it is magical, you see, it has healing qualities and protective ones too." The bare hand moved to touch the ring with its interlocking symbols, in a gesture so natural that Max recognized a ritual born of long custom; Raj had touched this ring in just this way many times before. "This ring is a gift, a linking; it is as old as my people and was made, the story says, for gods. To gods it belongs, to gods it must go." The sweetly modulated voice was matter-of-fact, explanatory. "I guard it only."

"Gods." The single word might have been either agreement or exclamation; Max was tingling, the warmth running through him like electricity. He reached out a hand to touch the ring, and was somehow unsurprised when Raj drew his hand away and spoke apologetically. "I am sorry; it is merely that I did not wish for any harm to come to you. Only a god or a guardian of a god may touch it; those others who try receive a nasty burn."

Movement, movement, to everything a season. "And that's why you're wandering around England, to find the god to give it to. It's loosening on your finger, is it, my friend? Times changing, world turning, a new season?"

Raj regarded him steadily, the candlelight winking on the thick lenses. Slowly, easily, he reached the hand that bore the ring out to Max.

Max's hand closed over it, feeling its life and its power. A smile broke over his face.

"I shall come with you, of course," Raj said simply. "It is my honor, to give the ring. Gold."

"And frankincense and myrrh." Max was laughing and alight, the wheel was turning, yes, here was Gad's message in all its glory. "We travel together; I know who you are now. Do you have a sleeping bag?"

6

All Along the Line

DOWN THE LANES went the pony cart, clip clop, its brave high wheels churning up clouds of dust, moving past hedgerows and walls of stone on its way to Sparrow House.

The wooden signposts were still there, of course; five months of emptiness and lack of care had not been nearly long enough to make a difference to the painted guides showing weathered white in the twilight. They were the winks and nods of the old England, beckoning the traveler to a preordained destination or merely to a place whose name sounded inviting: Killiford, Sparrowdene, Little Bunting.

The cart, pulled by the old horse Whiskey with the knowledge of rain to come strong in his nostrils, flashed by sign and field and empty barn, and was watched all along its route. The rows of wheat several feet tall, insects and mice sent it distracted glances before returning to the urgent business at hand, that of burrowing deep into the ground to avoid being washed away when the cloud cover broke. In the tall hedgerows small fat wrens who had not yet fully recovered their consciousness that was their natural birthright felt a stirring of curiosity and fear at the great black ravens. The flash, based on instinct, was a brief one; a moment only, and they pushed their heads deep into their feathers, sucking the heavy air into their miraculous system of lungs, prepared to wait out the storm in drowsiness and warmth.

The recipients of Whiskey's good nature tasted the water-laden air as well. Dilly's nostrils pinched and flared, pinched and flared, and she all unaware; Ben, who like all of nature's simples rarely caught cold or anything else, put out his tongue to taste the moisture with simple pleasure. He often stood in his meadow, brush in hand, covering his canvas with wide sheets of brilliant light as the weather changed around him.

Maddy, held firm and upright in Dilly's lap, was unfamiliar with this new sensation; slightly premature and tending toward bronchial infection as early babies do, she had been kept firmly indoors by an anxious mother for the whole of her infancy and long after she had grown plump and healthy and the danger was past. Now, her spirit sensing Ben's delight and Dilly's calm acceptance of the electrical tingling that grew around her with every passing moment, she felt no alarm.

Of the group, only the ravens were less than happy. Birds, sensible creatures that they are, do not care at all for flying in heavy weather; water thickens the feathers and makes the wings nearly too heavy to lift, and in the raw storms of summer the brutal eye of lightning can come from any corner of the heavens, catching you, ripping breath and bone away. Creatures of the air, they held the pony cart as something beneath contempt; still, as John had pointed out to the others, it might be necessary to have a little sitdown, if the weather got too nasty.

They discussed it now, flying low and in a sketchy formation, keeping pace with Whiskey. Mark, unperturbed and a short way behind the others, concentrated on keeping the beat of his wings measured and even; the single-minded Luke, knowing how food reacts to the variety of sky now closing in on them, occasionally broke high above the others, his eyes scanning the open fields for the small furred shapes dashing for cover. Matthew and John, leader and aide-de-camp, stayed directly above the cart, talking and casting anxious glances overhead. Thunder rumbled in the distance, a magisterial and arcane warning, and Matthew ruffled his feathers unhappily.

"Whole sky's going off like a bloody gun in a minute."

"You got that right," John said in fervent agreement; he disliked summer storms as much as Matthew did. "Crash! Bang! What a time to be flying!" The sky had taken on a brutal yellow tint. "Cor, I hate this weather."

"Think this house we're going to will have eaves?"

"Oh, bound to, bound to. A big old house, Gad said; all the old houses have places for such as us to hide."

Matthew, suddenly hit with a few enormous drops of rain, lurched and swore. He seemed determined to look on the negative side. "Yeah, right. Lots of places to hide, and very likely with a nice big barn owl already in possession."

"Ugh!" John shuddered as this new demon raised its head, for ravens and owls are old enemies. He spoke bitterly. "That's right, we haven't got enough on our plate, make it worse. Thanks lots for nothing, chum."

"Sorry, sorry." More rain; the drops were falling closer together now. "I don't know about you, Johnny, but I'm getting out of this. Me for the cart." And he suited action to word, tucking his wings and landing hard on the back edge of the pony cart. Since the road was gravel and rough and the cart was lurching over a particularly deep rut as his body made contact, his action was harder to perform than to describe. He gave a startled screech, turning heads from the driver's bench; for a moment swaying wildly, his claws scrabbling for a grip on the rail. Then it was done and he relaxed, his body adjusting itself to the rocking motion of the wheels on the road.

Luke, who had disappeared, suddenly rose from the wheat and fluttered back to John's side. A very bloody mouse dangled from one claw; as if in protest at the unfairness of being chosen for lunch when it already had the threat of rain to contend with, the mouse had led Luke a merry chase, running like a mad thing, zigzagging crazily through the thick stalks. Luke's feathers were dusted with chaff and pollen, and his eyes were bright.

"Look, a mouse. Think I'll go sit with Matt; the rain's getting worse." And with this brief speech he, too, made for the comparative safety of the vehicle below.

And really, John thought, that's sense. "Mark! Landing time, look lively!" The smallest bird jerked his head up, though the easy rhythm of his wings never altered; a single comprehensive glance and he changed his course. Another tucking of wings, another thump, another startled screech as he underestimated the speed of the cart, and then there were three ravens, an unlikely trinity riding pillion.

John, scorning the back of the cart, landed neatly and gently on Ben's shoulder. "How much farther, Ben?"

Dilly, already used to this new way of hearing so miraculously granted, answered. "Only about ten minutes. See that wall up ahead, with the stile? That's the outer wall, it leads to the house. If we weren't in a dip in the road, you could see—oh. There."

The cart, laboring up the side of the small hill, had suddenly emerged with Sparrow House in view. And a very effective view it was; the men who had built it had placed it with an eye for the effect it would have on the passerby. Huge and pale, its sandstone glinted behind its curtain of rain; there was a broad lawn, emerald under the ominous sky, and several stables. And the ravens knew at once that there would be cover, plenty of cover, for the roof of the welcoming house itself curved beautifully at the corners and the stable buildings might have been designed to cover roosting birds in shelter from the rain.

"Nice," said John, startled into encomium.

"Shelter for all," Dilly said, and Whiskey pulled the cart across the wide expanse of grass and up the sweeping drive to stop, at last, before the eight marble steps. It was only when Julia came out to hurry them indoors, exclaiming at the dangerous color of the sky and sending Ben off to put the pony cart in the stable where Simon slept the storm away, that they realized Gad was no longer with them.

Gad had slipped away, unseen by any of the others.

Dilly and Maddy, with an indifference born of long custom, had tactfully ignored her disappearance; if Luke could hunt in this weather, why, then, so could Gad. Ben's attention was divided between the joy of the rain and the horse whose reins he held, and Whiskey, that old traveler, gave his whole mind to the road.

Between the high walls of wildflower and blackthorn Gad went, a gray ghost of silent movement stalking through the fields. Something had come into her as she lay curled on the seat beside Dilly, a notion, a feeling, an expansion of her blood. She could not put a name to this feeling, but in fact it had been a picture, merely stranger than the rest, and its strangeness had been enough to spur her to motion.

Still a few miles from Sparrow House, her sudden burst of energy caught up with her and she stopped, panting, to rest. One of the more irritating drawbacks of great age, of life lived so long, was the tricks one's memory played; a significant face first seen a thousand years ago might suddenly reappear, teasing the heart to place it, no easy task, for there had been so many faces and so much time. Movement, movement, and now the time had come to try and make some sense of it all.

The image had come fleeting and blurred: a girl in a

boat, a small boat to be sure but out to sea, far from the land, far, far. A slim hand trimming a sail, a small vibrant body that was browned and salted by its travels, taut with expectation under a dirty white dress. What the picture had meant Gad did not as yet know; that it was part of what was coming she did not doubt.

What disturbed her was the familiarity of it. For, beyond doubt, she knew the girl; every line of the small body was familiar, and the brief glance of the face, eager and hungry as a flame in the hills at night, had brought to Gad a confusion of passion that had badly shaken her. Important, to take herself far from the others, to trace and find, chasing the picture and this new inner storm to its source.

So she wandered, paying no heed to the nervous rustling in the grass or the rain that felt cold against her skin, her paws carrying more than just the burden of her own bodily weight. Memory, intolerable and sweet, haunted and stalked her as well as she had ever stalked the mouse and the finch. She emptied herself, opening to the voice of the ages she had lived, and gradually it began to come clear, a story she knew, a story man had set down for his children to read, not knowing that the story would, in the end, outlast him.

A girl, a girl alone on an island. White sand, bare feet, a garden smelling of the sweet things that grow cupped in the hand of the southern sun. A different time, different gods. A walk in the sand under a drifting curtain of morning mist, the heat of the day still to come. The thin body stopping, startled; the brown foot reaching out to push gently at the man who lay there exhausted, spat from the sea which had taken his ship and then mercifully rejected him, freeing him to sail another day.

And how long had she kept him there with her, tending to his wants, warming him when the sun burned its way into the edge of the sea at night, before the hard call reached him once again and sent him back to wrestle with the world of men? Years, perhaps: Gad was unsure, and it hardly mattered anyway. The story had been told, handed down, transmogrified by the poets of the men who worshiped those long-dead gods, so meddlesome and so petty, that little group who ruled where Sappho sang and the black olives grew.

Another picture flashed through the rain now falling steadily, perhaps spurred by Gad's slow understanding of the first; familiar, less incomprehensible this time, and yet not without its mysteries. Max, beautiful in his nudity, with his fathomless black eyes fixed on a man; he stood indoors, a shop of some kind, facing over burning candles a tall man with dusky skin and the sweetest of all possible smiles.

And now the picture grew more clear by the minute. Movement, Gad thought, movement, and she knew a deep excitement; it had been too long a time since this brand of anticipation had taken her in hand. Something was trying to get through, a voice, and she sat down to wash, the self-discipline of long survival reasserting itself. She was a guardian and a vessel too, a sailing ship across many centuries, and her place was to give and to receive. Movement. If a voice desired to speak, she would listen.

"He's found one of them." Old Trout's voice, falling clearly and without warning into her head, might have been part of the growing storm around her. It held an echo of her own racing joy.

"Or one of them has found him."

"Now then, now then, no splitting hairs. Doesn't matter who's found whom, does it? Point is, they're together, and high time too."

"High time." Gad, falling back on the comfort of ritual in the face of this strangeness, began painstakingly to wash her face; the silvered paws were licked and sent rubbing across brow and chin. "One down, two to go."

"One to go."

The old voice was flat, and so sure of itself that Gad was surprised into immobility. "Two, surely? The pantheon calls for three, always three; three priestesses, three nymphs, three wise men. Why two this time? Is it really to be so different now?''

Max watching, a hand on his ruffled white hair, and the thin man smiling, stretching out a hand, and the hand bore a ring, a token, golden symbols that were snakelike but not snakes twined a long dance and she knew that, too . . . ''Three, isn't it?''

''Max has found one.'' The voice held patience, tainted with a hint of sarcasm. ''One is on her way. And you already have one. That makes three, unless I've forgotten how to count in my old age.''

''I've already—oh!'' And she saw a big gangling body and a smile like the dawn, pale hair streaked with paint. ''You mean—do you mean—is Ben—''

''Got it now, do you?'' And he sniffed. ''Certainly took you long enough.''

''You can't know everything all at once all the time,'' Gad defended herself. ''Things have been fairly quiet these two thousand years, and now it's all happening at once and I'm smack dab in the middle of it. Don't be such an old caution; it's enough to addle anyone's wits.''

''True.'' She could feel the alteration of mood in him, a sudden fixing of concentration. ''They've reached Sparrow House; now you've got what you came away for, maybe you ought to get back.''

''I intend to.'' Gad, her dignity unimpaired, lifted her tail and turned to go. ''Tell me—though you've gone so uppity on me, I'm almost afraid to ask—what is her name, that girl on the boat? I knew it once, but I've forgotten; after all, she's even older than the others.''

''Calypso,'' Old Trout said, surprised. ''It wasn't her name, but that's what they called her, and now it's the only name she knows, maybe, at least it's the only name she'll ever answer to.''

Far from the land, far, far.

Calypso stood on the deck of the trimaran painted silver, listening to the sough and sigh of the sea wind. It belled the green great sails above her head, giving them the look of the Greek women, shopping for grapes and bread in the agora, vastly pregnant, with modesty and white linen veiling their faces. She thought briefly about those women, so long dead now, and a small shudder took hold of her. Patience is my lot, she thought, but no man's acceptance is ever total, no, and no woman's either.

She was alone now, though she had not been when she began this journey. From the shores of her island, past the Golden Horn and down the straits, the dolphins had borne her company; they told her small shy jokes and sang her rude songs about sharks and lobsters to keep her spirits up, which she sorely needed, and gave her advice about which way to sail, which she did not. They had accompanied her for as long as the warmth of the current would allow. Now, with the coast of Normandy vanished over the horizon to the south of her and the coast of England yet to come, she was alone; the chilly waters of the Channel were poorly suited to dolphins.

Far from the land, it was true, but she had been farther than this, all along the way. And sometimes nearer; though she had never set the silver boat in to land, she had sailed out of curiosity close to the shoreline, when she could do so without danger to her craft. The land was not empty of people, as she had feared might be the case; there had been scattered life, small groups of children and adolescents. No one had shown any surprise at the sight of her moving on the water. Once she had passed a colony of old men in the garb of lamas, servants perhaps of Buddha or Shiva; they had merely waved at her, a conventional and cordial gesture, and she had waved back at them before the wind took her ship once more in hand and sent it rocking back on its course.

Soon now, soon. Calypso, so many years spent in contemplation of the past, had since the Big One discovered a change in herself, a yearning toward the future. And that was strange, a strange thing, for she had for so long been the repository of the past that the future had come to seem like an uncouth joke. And this journey by sea had done something else to her, or perhaps merely triggered a change that had been lying dormant and watchful, waiting for an excuse to happen. She had listened for so many centuries to her own songs and the voice of time passing that she had come to see herself as a shade out of history. Now she was beginning to see herself as alive, a thing unique and whole within herself.

Calypso raised her long eyes to the sky, gauging the quality of the light and the density of cloud and breeze. Fair weather, the wind perfect, night falling; she felt a slight contraction of her stomach and tried to remember when she had last eaten. Yesterday at sunrise; well, that was too long ago, small wonder she was hungry. She looked at the rudder, tied securely in its proper position, and walked to the trimaran's starboard rail in search of her dinner.

On some level, she supposed, she ought to feel guilty about using her gifts to deceive the fish. She did not, however, and never had; life goes on, and one must eat even if one has been taken far from one's own lush garden. If a song would procure supper, why, then, sing she would. It was no different from those wanderers who sang for their suppers under windows, or by the turning spit in some taverna. The ship, three thousand years old and, against all tradition and superstition, nameless, was built very low to the water. It was a simple matter for her to lean over its edge, her face a scant inch from the brine-scented foam.

She began to sing.

The words were unimportant, and in any case were couched in the high Greek of the halls of Mycenae. It was one of many she knew, a simple plea for a child to sleep through the night, written before the birth of Homer by some exhausted nursemaid in the palace of Minos or Crete. Its effect was immediate and charming; bubbles, an answering call to her siren's voice, broke the water's surface and materialized into a large cod.

For a moment they regarded each other, woman and fish; black eyes met and spoke, the woman slightly apologetic, the fish, with its perfect understanding of the facts of life, merely resigned and accepting. A sort of dialogue went back and forth between them, currents of that speech which is not speech as we understand it.

FISH: Ah. This is the end, then.

WOMAN: Yes. I grieve for you, even though I'm hungry.

FISH: No, nonsense, not at all. I understand your need perfectly. You'll make it quick?

WOMAN: Of course; no pain, I swear it. After all, why would I force you to linger?

FISH (sighing): Well, then.

And it swam into Calypso's hand to lie there, breathing its last. Perhaps for reasons of tact, it closed its eyes; humans were notoriously superstitious about last rites, and it saw no need to upset her unduly by fixing her with an accusing stare. Calypso carried it back to the prow where she kept the portable altar that served so well as a cooking stove; the cod twitched once or twice, and was still.

Olive oil, from one of the ten precious jars; she had not wanted to overburden herself, but she must bring an offering of some kind—it was unthinkable that she should come empty-handed, and olive oil was useful as well as valuable. She lit the altar, watching its scented smoke for the density that would tell her the heat was sufficient. When the moment came, she draped the cod, dead now, across the little grille and began to cook her dinner.

Ritual is an anchor in the face of change, and some things never change. Four thousand years and an eternity of dinners had passed since the morning he sailed away, and at every fish dinner she had eaten since then she had thought of him. It seemed appropriate, for he had been a man of the sea, that wandering man, cast onto the shores of her bright island and into her waiting arms, lost on his way home from seven years of battle at the walls of the city.

So the fish spat and sizzled in its invisible coat of olive oil, and Calypso remembered.

And there was so much to remember. Oh, the tales he had told her—the son of the goddess with his bad temper and his weak heel, what had truly become of him? And the woman who had been the pawn in this liar's game, that beautiful queen abducted, stolen, spirited away to the wide red plains of Anatolia, what of her? Had she gone home to her husband, perhaps still loving her young fancy boy in secret, perhaps embittered? Or had she been glad to be rescued, that sad-faced woman for whose beauty ten thousand men had immolated themselves in anger and blood?

The stories of the gods, told in the awestruck tones of men, had not moved Calypso; was she not even older than they, and would she not remain when the wheel next turned and they were sent spinning from their lofty perch atop it? No, it had been the tales of men and women, the taste of the dusty Turkish soil, the vividly imprinted walls of the city, the cunning contrivance of the enormous horse, that had taken her imagination in thrall and held it over all this time. There was, in fact, only one small detail in all of his wonderful stories that she had forgotten, and attempts at recall had woven themselves firmly into her nightly memory play.

The fish was done now. She ate with her fingers, shaking the hot oil from them, muttering in Greek under her breath. Would she have to speak English, where she was going? Very likely, very likely, and that was a pity, for she found it an ungainly language, overfull and without subtlety. She knew it, of course; no language was unknown to her, and none of their words held mystery. Still, she was a Greek, had always been a Greek, and in her insular eyes Greek was the fairest of all tongues.

There were birds overhead, gulls and albatross and harbor pelican, attracted by the smell of fish. She shot them a dirty look and they retreated, intimidated, to a greater height. Her message had been clear enough: You are thieves and scavengers, and I will not cooperate with you, or share my food with you. Go and catch your own fish. And over the three sails they hovered, watching and envious, frightened to come closer because they could smell her dislike.

Pheromonal stimulus, science would have called it, but science is notoriously pompous and very slightly crazy. History is what it was, no more than that.

And so Calypso, glaring at the birds, eating her fish, trying as she had done since the morning he left her to remember the name of the man who had warmed her bed and sweetened her life and told her his pretty stories, came imperceptibly ever nearer to the southern coast of England.

"This," Raj said with the judicial impartiality that is such a hallmark of the educated Asian mind, "is very beautiful. Very beautiful indeed. I must thank you for showing it to me."

They were standing on a small tor, their faces turned to the south. Before them spread the downs, a panorama with an air of gently tricking the eye; at their feet and in the immediate vicinity of sight things seemed enormous, trees and sheep and flowers beginning to taper in size and shape as the angle of the slopes changed and faded out to meet the sky. The earth was drenched in flowers, vast banks of buttercup and primrose and daffodil; on the far horizon, their individuality ran and blended into patterns of color.

"You're welcome." Max, in fact, had not led Raj here to show him a pretty view, nor was he paying any attention to the view himself. He was, instead, trying to make some sense of a sudden conflict in his signals, pulls that came from different directions, west and south, each direction tugging at him, and the simple solution, heading southwest, almost certainly not the correct one. Which direction? There were roads that led each way, shining ribbons of pebble and tar, and from each of these roads Max felt an intolerable pull.

"You are troubled about something?"

Startled out of his reverie, Max turned. Raj was watching him, the eyes behind the pebbled lenses remarkably shrewd and sympathetic. An unexpected bloke he was turning out to be. Was it possible? Well, maybe . . .

"A bit, yes. I'm certain about direction."

"Ah," Raj nodded with perfect comprehension. "You feel a need to go this way and also that way, and you cannot feel which way is right. Possibly I can help?"

"Possibly." West, south, and from each an urgent feminine pull. Well, what harm could it do? "I'm not sure how, though. What are you doing?"

Raj had sat down in the mud, his eyes closed and his legs lotus-crossed. "You must be quiet a moment, please."

Max shrugged. South, no, west, the children had said so and he'd felt it himself, Gad, Julia, south, why south? Raj, motionless on the ground beside him, breathed like a man deep in sleep, even and regular.

The silence stretched out so long that Max, pushing off the frustration of uncertainty, had almost forgotten Raj's presence. He started galvanically as the placid voice spoke beside him.

"Thank you, thank you, you are very cooperative. I have your answer for you now."

Max blinked. "Answer?"

"Oh, yes." Raj was as serene as ever. "We must go

west, but not yet; south first, then west. There is someone we must go and collect."

"Collect?" Really, thought Max, I sound exactly like a parrot, or a myna bird; why can't I do anything but repeat what this odd person says? And why can't I think?

"Perhaps collect is not the proper word; meet, find, greet?" There was something very humbling in Raj's self-deprecation; he had plucked an unspoken conflict of directions from thin air, meditated for a while, found the answer; now he was apologetic because his command of English idiom was imperfect. He went on, modest and patient.

"There is someone who is coming to join us. She is on a boat, out to sea, but she will make landfall somewhere to the south of here. We must go and meet her there, and bring her with us where we go. Very important, *most* important in fact. You see?"

"Her?" Bloody hell, he was doing it again. "Sorry, Raj, I don't usually make sentences of one word; I'm just a bit distracted, that's all."

"Yes, I see that very well." Was that a glint of humor behind the spectacles? "You have not even asked me how I came to know what I know."

"No, I haven't, have I? I'm not at all sure it's really any of my business. I'm curious, certainly; if you feel like telling me, of course I'd like to know."

"Well, I would like to tell you. But I do not think I can, because I have no words in your language, no words that would describe, although in my language the words for such a thing are common." Raj looked at him sadly. "A matter of different cultures, different ideas. I am sorry."

It was no use; try as he might, Max was simply unable to resist a bit of surprising on his own account. He looked full into Raj's eyes. "And what, my friend, makes you think that English is either my mother tongue or culture?"

The graceful head with its long bones cocked alertly. "Not? Not English?"

"Not in the least."

"What, then?"

"Oh, different things at different times." Really, exhaustion and confusion were making him petty, and pettiness had gotten him into this mess in the first place. "I'm teasing you, Raj; it's one of my worst habits, and I apologize for my bad manners. But what I said is true enough. I'm English right now, but that's only because it's suitable. Originally, I was a hybrid; my father was a Hebrew, my mother a Greek."

"Oh, my." And Raj looked at him with simple respect. "Yes, yes. I see it now, Hebrew and Greek, very old. I pay my great respects to you, wanderer, but it does not change my problem. I have some Hebrew and a little bit of Greek, but again—not enough."

"So tell me in your language. Don't look so surprised, I know four dialects of Kashmiri and seven of Hindi." He watched the surprise grow, rather than lessen, and touched Raj's arm gently. "Dravidian, too. Come along."

Raj told him. It was a long tale, a tale of men who wove silk, of bronze idols with a multiplicity of arms, of a guardianship of knowledge passed from father to son over fifty generations. Knowledge that was bred in the bone and nurtured in the blood, women who were queens of herbal lore and accumulated wisdom mingling with men who traveled on wings of the mind to find some jewel of understanding in the weak and fragile clay that had shaped them. It was an old, old story, a story Max knew very well and respected, and when Raj was done he nodded, his winged smiling a blinding light across his face, the thin lips that had captivated Julia like a bird flying.

"Yes," he said peacefully. "I know all that; of course, you would see clearly, wouldn't you? It's one of the reasons we called to each other, or were called together; I'm not sure just what happened, and frankly I don't care. The important thing is that you've got my answer for me, and that's enough for me. A woman on a boat; fine."

"But we go south?" Raj, for the first time, sounded anxious. "You believe me, then, and we go south?"

"We go south." And, indeed, now that he looked for it, he could see the gleam of the southern road and hear the whisper of approval from the unknown source where all such instinct is held. "South first, then west. You didn't happen to learn just who this sailing lady is?"

"No. Only that she is coming, and will be welcomed."

"Damn right she will. Let's go meet her."

7

Storms

WEATHER, SO STRANGE and mutable, so remarkably different in different places; perhaps the most astonishing quality it possesses is a discerning eye, a capacity for mercy.

In London there was only a brief fury, a few flashes of lightning, a few rolls of thunder. The storm, after this brief show, became a steady downfall, sending dusty water running down the gutters, startling the rats who foraged by the rising Thames. It splashed down white Georgian houses in Mayfair and Kensington and streaked the windows of the hulking shells of the British Museum and the Post Office Tower; during the night a small wind rattled gleefully through the deserted dressing rooms at Covent Garden, stirring a pair of satin ballet shoes that hung on the wall to brief uncanny life, making them tap against each other in a momentary dance before they fell still and silent once again, and the wind moved on.

In London, too, there were small crowds of children, mostly around Holborn and Bloomsbury; they went laughing through the rain, their eyes wide and unalarmed, some of them enjoying the sight from beneath the shelter of the Holborn Viaduct or the feel of it running in rivulets around their shoulders as they stood out in the street. It meant no harm to them, the rain, and let them be.

To the southwest, all across the dusky reaches of Salisbury Plain and centered at Stonehenge, the sky was angry; storms were always focused near the old stone pile where so many had once come to gape. The rooks that lived on the trilithons protested to whoever might be listening; they were nesting, damn it, they had eggs to think of and could live quite nicely without this weather, thank you, was it really necessary? But the sky ignored them, lashing and mad. Lightning turned the blue stone to crimson and gold, rain filled the postholes and streaked the empty parking lot, and all the while the stones sat silent and knowing, bearing the brunt of the weather as they had always done.

In Little Carbury, the rain had a definite purpose in mind; it sought out a thin dark man who wore a golden ring of curious design and drove him in search of light and company. This purpose achieved, it waited until the two who must meet had come together and recognized each other; then, as if tired out by its anger and the energy required by its pyrotechnic display, it backed off to a drizzling curtain that was as dreary as it was persistent. Almost as an afterthought, it looked down on Little Carbury and, disliking the smug symmetry of the factory towers, let one more streak of heat fly; one of the two smokestacks screamed as it was hit, toppling with an enormous crash to lie shattered, a useless and amorphous heap of scorched bricks. The wind whispered something about balance, balance, and went off to search the land, wanting to be busy awhile.

On the gray water that divided England from France, where a small silver boat sat low, no rain fell. It remained a distant beacon, its only manifestation a bloody sky off to the north; Calypso sailed for the coast in a clear salty wind that blew lightly through her hair as she sang, and her trimaran hove through a swelling current, carrying her always landward.

And in the west of England, in Sparrowdene and Killiford and all those other places so charmingly named, it found the unseen eye of energy and put on a show for whoever might still be alive to see. Here, with so much intelligence waiting to watch it, it was neither mindless nor angry; instead it was stately, a majestic performance, every detail considered for beauty and maximum effect. Old Trout, massively anchored near the bottom of his stream, looked up and admired the bubbles that broke downward toward him as the rain found the surface of the current. Whiskey, deep in conversation with Simon—and such a pleasure, how different was this old sheep from the others he had known, silly creatures with their heads stuffed full of grass—heard the crash of thunder and peacefully munched straw as Simon told him marvelous tales of olive groves and dancing women and a shepherd's fire at night on a Cypriot hillside. Above them, sheltered by the timbers of the stable roof, four ravens slept the hour away, waiting for the sun.

Across the wide lawns, the rain-streaked windows of Sparrow House blazed with light, and smoke drifted from one stone chimney to mingle with the rising wind. Four people and a cat curled in comfort around a drawing room fire; on the marquetry table was a huge pot of tea, a tray of drinks, some freshly baked biscuits. On the floor a small plate showed a glutinous streak of oil; the sardines had been eaten, but Gad was far too well-mannered to lick the plate clean in company.

Julia, who had wrapped herself in a lush bathrobe against the chill of the evening, stirred lazily and put a half-empty cup of tea on the floor beside her chair. "I love this weather."

"I do, too. Unless I'm outside, of course; my race is not one of the water-oriented species, as a general rule."

Dilly, who had just come down the broad staircase after tucking her slumbering sister up for the night, entered the room in time to hear Gad's comment. "But you can swim, Gad; I've seen you in the stream, hunting fish."

"Oh, I can *swim*; all cats can do that, for better or worse. I'll get wet for food or survival, Dilly, but that doesn't mean I have to like it."

"No, I suppose it doesn't." Dilly helped herself to a biscuit—she had gone rather wild with baked goods, her delight in Sparrow House's emergency generator and the immediate availability of a modern electric oven going to her head—and looked at Ben from the corners of her eyes. "Well, I like the rain, but I like it best from indoors; being all warm and wrapped, you know, and everything else in the whole world looking in at me. What about you, Ben?"

"Um." Ben had been staring blank-faced at the great logs where they smoldered in the fireplace, slowly reducing to ash. He shook his head, as if to clear water from his ears, and smiled at Dilly. "Rain. It doesn't bother me."

"A nice, succinct point of view." Julia laughed, hearing Gad's appreciative comment in her heart, and The Bump moved. It was not a kick this time but something different, more obscure; Julia was suddenly taken with a picture of the child, sentient and potent, nodding in agreement, the tremendous translucent head of a fetus almost complete in formation moving in the placental waters that held it, sending currents through it, the great linking cord with its engorged veins shuddering slightly . . .

Dizzy, nauseous, good grief, what in hell was this? The picture had been so clear, the room was fading in and out, she had ceased to be a temporal entity and time itself was shifting, moving, the painted ceiling above her head showed angels dancing, nameless winged things . . .

"Julia!" Gad was beside her, sharp and commanding as a midwife. "Put your head down between your knees."

"I can't reach my knees." Steadier now, better, the

picture was fading. The room gave a sickening lurch and settled itself, a room once more. Her voice was absurdly weak. "I can hardly even *see* my bloody knees."

"What happened?" There was no relaxation in Gad's voice, it was still sharp, and Julia became distantly aware that Ben and Dilly were staring at her, one in wonder and the other in alarm. The quality of Gad's tension frightened her; was the gray cat thinking of a sudden stab of pain, the body rejecting the unborn, the litter of kittens lost? She got command of her voice somehow.

"Nothing—I don't know. I saw something, that's all. A picture of The Bump, nodding or something." Dizziness returned momentarily and was gone. She knew her words were inadequate, it bothered her, but somehow words would not be found for this. "It—it was awfully clear, somehow."

"Movement," said Gad, a faint thought but still a thought. She was staring intently at Julia's swollen belly with something like awe in her eyes. "No pain?"

"Pain? Oh, no. It didn't hurt." Julia began to struggle for words, nearly drowned in her sudden sense of urgency, a feeling that Gad must be told and told properly. "It wasn't anything to do with my body, Gad; I mean, it happened in my body, yes, but that's not where I felt it."

Dilly had come to stand beside her, her mouth pursed in thought. Something had flickered in her, too; a memory, a warm dim cavern of a place, where hunger never came and one could lie still in a vast encompassing silence broken only by a distant booming that was more a physical vibration than an actual sound. Somewhere she had been, but where? Frowning, she stood and puzzled over it; warmth and security, food on demand, no words spoken. She could not know, had no way of knowing, of the great distance this image had reached; in his swollen stream Old Trout shared her memory, and in the stables outside in the wet darkness Simon broke off what he was saying to stand in silence a moment, puzzled and moved.

And then Ben, too, climbed to his feet. He pushed Julia's bathrobe aside with the easy love of a doctor, laying a beautiful paint-stained hand on the ripe belly beneath. At his touch Julia became very still, her eyes closing, lost in a blissful sense of peace.

"Hello," Ben said, and the others knew he was not talking to Julia, but rather to what waited within. "Hello, hello. It's night, you know." And he laughed, the soft hand never moving, the outsize knuckles with their pale hairs glinting in the firelight. He sounded strong and sure, unlike himself and yet utterly himself, Ben, speaking as always with knowledge and innocence. "Night, night. Go back to sleep."

Other eyes saw the child nod in weighty approval of its mother's laughter. The Son was outside time, himself a temporal anomaly; still, he could be affected by its passage and its tricks, and he had excellent reasons for watching the dim shape with all the vision he could muster.

When the laughter had stopped and the vision faded, he came back to himself; it had almost mesmerized him, that shimmering fetus whose eyes were closed tight against an early birth. The knowledge of its power frightened him. For two thousand years he had wielded the reins of man, and he had paid dearly for that privilege, too. Was power to be wrested from him so painlessly, so easily? Never again the crowds kneeling in scarred oaken pews, never again the paintings offered up to him in atonement for an infinity of nameless sins, never again those voices lifted, *benedictus domini*, praying for his blessing. No, it was not to be thought of. There was a way to avert this catastrophe, there must be. It was simply not to be borne.

And yet, and yet . . .

"Come out, lord."

And here he was, the gadfly; may his soul be taken from him, was there nothing the old nomad didn't see?

Furious and resentful, still shaken from the beauty and serenity of his supplanter, he tried to tune out the mocking voice that sucked his will from him. Wretched child of vanity and spite, he thought, you wandering bastard, be quiet now, be still, let me be.

"Bastard? A modern idiom for such an antiquated tongue, surely? Inaccurate, too; I was born in full wedlock, which is something you can hardly lay claim to. I'd abandon that phrase if I were you; people who live in glass houses, and all that."

I will not hear you, I will not, I will *not* . . .

He failed, as always. Max, awake under a sky washed clear by the day's rain, had seen what he had seen; it was hardly fair that, even as he weakened, Max grew stronger. For a moment the Son was shaken by a surge of self-pity; he had died for them and forgiven them, and all for what? So that they might all die when he needed them most, still wailing for his help on their deathbeds, never once pausing to consider that, just for once, he might need their help instead? Greedy, thoughtless, infuriating. Dead.

"Come out."

It was useless; that voice, mocking and familiar, hated from the bottom of the Son's being, took hold of him like a vise and pulled him into the light. He felt the stars cold around him, and the chill of the earth at night rose to brush him where he hovered, hating and impotent, above Max's head.

"Exquisite, wasn't it? I take it you saw?"

More mockery; Max knew very well that the Son had seen. Max had felt the helpless fear and, reveling, had grown that much stronger because of it. The Son looked down at the fertile earth which slipped daily from his grasp, and spoke against his will.

"I saw. Yes, it was beautiful. And make no mistake, taunting child of doubt, I will kill it if I can."

On the soft damp ground, Raj opened his eyes. He lay quiescent, listening, his regular breathing never altering;

the man beside him and the shadow from above continued their parry and riposte, unaware that, for the first time in their long history of such dealings, they performed for the eyes of an audience. What had he heard in the far chambers of his inner ear, one voice he knew, another he did not? The night was huge, an envelope of darkness and calm, and beside him the teasing went on, spiteful and malicious.

"The emphasis, of course, is on the auxiliary verb, *Can*. Let us add to the structure of the grammar here, a new designation; not an easy task, but an interesting challenge nevertheless. How shall we do it? We have verb passive, verb active, verbs both transitive and intransitive. Ah, I have it: verb impossible. Simple and neat. And true."

"You underestimate me, wanderer. As always."

"Underestimate you? Think you less important than you are, is that what you mean?" Max was grinning now, the sheer savagery of his joy apparent in the very timbre of his echoing thoughts; beside him Raj stirred, suddenly disturbed. "Believe me, lord, it would be impossible for anyone to think you had less power than you really do. Ah, once again, we have verb impossible in action; there now, I knew it would be useful."

But the shadow across the stars was gone, pushed by its own rage into the cloudy turmoil that waited behind every black hole, every sunspot, every flying meteor. Max lifted a hand to his brow to dash the sudden sweat away, and heard Raj's voice behind him.

"Who did you speak to? Who was the man whose mood was so distempered?"

Max stiffened, the hand arrested in its sweep across his brow. Raj had heard; he had lain awake, listening. In two thousand years they had met like this, he and the Son, a thousand times or more, sometimes within the hearing of others, sometimes not. No words were ever spoken; the exchanges of hatred and torment were conducted on a level of mystery, beyond any possible spoken words.

But Raj had heard every barb, every shaft, every arrow.

Slowly Max dropped his hand and turned to face the Indian. Raj was sitting up now, his skinny frame muffled to the waist in its down sleeping bag; between the blue of his bedroll and the pale moonlit earth, Max could see the edges of a large plastic lawn bag, protection against the chilly damp that would seep through to the skin. There was no fear in Raj, and his eyes, now stripped of their obscuring glasses, looked childlike and vulnerable and incredibly wise. He was passing no judgments, taking no sides; he merely sat and waited in courteous silence for Max to reply.

"You heard us, then."

"Yes. You dislike each other, you and this man."

It was a statement, shorn of the questioning lilt that is such an integral part of the Indian accent, and Max's lips tightened and thinned. "We do."

"But you require each other, as well."

And that, too, was a statement, a statement rather shattering in its implications. Max stared down at Raj, not really seeing him. A curious feeling was growing in him.

"Require each other. *Require* each other. Well, now. I never stopped to think about that, believe it or not."

Raj wriggled himself free of the sleeping bag. He slept in his clothes, not from modesty, as he had gravely explained to an amused Max, but for warmth; for children of a warmer climate, the English nights were a penance and a malediction. His bright yellow shirt, reflecting the color of the ring he wore, was rumpled.

"Never? You have known him a long time, this man?"

Max laughed, a short sharp bark. "Too long. Far, far too long. Maybe I'll be rid of him someday."

"But who is he, please? A friend, an enemy?"

Max bit back the reply which sprang immediately to his tongue. The question, asked with all of Raj's frightening perspicacity, demanded some consideration; in the short time they had traveled together, Max had already learned that his companion possessed a quality of insight as rare as it was uncomfortable. And the question was pertinent. The Son, now. A friend, an enemy?

One thing was certain; the Indian had hit the nail on the head: need each other they did, he and the Son, though he had only just now understood that. The sharpening of the blood, the quickening of the heart that came before the Son's appearance, they were shadow and light to each other, though which was shadow and which light was a question perhaps better left unasked. And the Son, what of him? Had he thought of Max as Max had thought of him all this time: enemy only, a source of irritation? Or was he, in truth, what Raj suggested: a basic need?

The soft touch on his shoulder made him jump. Raj was inclining his head in a gesture part apology, part dismissal.

"I am sorry," he said quietly. "I had no wish to pry. It is only that, if the answer is not one you know, you should learn it. There was power in you, dark mostly, and power can turn on you in the end. That is all."

"It can turn on you in the beginning, too. That's why I'm still alive." What would he say, this product of fifty generations of Indian wise men, if Max were to say to him casually, The man you heard me speaking to is Jesus Christ, the last outpost of Jehovah's trinity, and he is frightened half out of his wits because the wheel is about to turn and he will no longer sit in its most eminent space? Would Raj exclaim, waving the long hands, sending the bright ring dancing? Or would he accept, bowing his head with his peculiar brand of stately grace?

The question, for the moment, was destined to remain unanswered. Raj, his nostrils pinched in concentration and a hand held up for silence, had turned his face to the south; he had the look of a hound who scents the wind. When he turned back to Max, he was smiling widely.

"She has left the sea behind her," he said, and laughed.

"She has come into a town of hills where the river divides the land, where many ships have always landed. Her ship is behind her, lying in close water, and she is walking on the railroad tracks, northward, northward, this way." He saw the momentary confusion in Max's face, and shook him gently by the arm. "She, the woman we are to collect, meet, greet, find. Forget your enemy for now, and your need with it. She is on land, and coming."

She had made landfall at Plymouth, repeating without knowledge the feelings and actions of many who had come there by water before her.

The harbor was full; the death that had come to the world had not been escapable by ship or plane or any other means of transportation known and the majority of the population had not bothered to try. A few of the ships were enormous, huge gray navy transports that loomed across the night sky, covering the small gayer yachts and schooners like beasts out of legend. Calypso, admiring the size of these ungainly monsters even as she despised them for their overindulgence and lack of grace, put the silver trimaran to anchor at the harbor wall with perfect ease.

She clambered gracefully across the barnacle-crusted pilings and stood a few moments, until tactile memory of the sea's motion heaving under her faded and died. She looked at the city, a graduated huddle of roofs and roads, and decided that it must have been crowded and ugly in its time. Then she shifted all her attention to the northern sky, seeking and finding the brilliant dot that was Polaris, sighting herself along the road, trying to determine, a stranger in this new and bewildering place, which way to go.

To a Greek who had spent uncounted years in the heat of the island sun, the night should have been insupportable. Calypso hardly noticed the chill, despite her thin dress; like a flame, she burned from within, and it is doubtful she would have noticed anything less extreme than fire or snow. Her small clay jar of olive oil held firmly on her shoulder, carried in the same fashion used by women throughout recorded time, she set her feet upon the tarmac and walked into Plymouth proper, leaving the silver ship rocking gently behind her, lapped by the hands of the current.

The city, of course, was dark; there was no one now to run the power plants, no one to extract the electricity and send it along the wires to all these gloomy houses. But it was not empty. As she came into the heart of the city she saw children, small groups of them; they ranged from infancy to adolescence, the smaller ones being carried in the arms of the elders or pushed along in prams. They did not approach her, nor did she make any attempt to attract them. If they knew her they would come, and if they did not they would let her be. It made no difference; she would be met, it had been promised, and one did not question a promise.

She walked, quick and eager, down the broadest street she could find, reading the signs in the windows. Pill's Fine Meat and Poultry, Boots Dispensing Chemist, Saxone Shoes; useless, all of it, the meat and poultry would long since have rotted, and she needed no medicines or shoes. And then, unexpectedly, she found herself staring at a sign, a name painted in gilt letters on a restaurant window, a name she knew.

Stavros and Son. A Greek restaurant, then; she reached out a thin finger and traced the letters of the name, the small Greek characters beneath it. Had he come here, this Stavros, after the Nazis had abandoned the shores of his homeland, come here to seek his fortune? Perhaps he had come from Salonika, or Larisa, or Piraeus; perhaps he had come down from the sweet green mountains of Delphi, or perhaps he had been a man of Crete.

He could cook, of course. He had possessed a love of food, an inner empathy with the lamb on the spit, the rice mixed with garlic, the sun-dried tomatoes in the jar.

And his wife, what of her? Had he brought some strapping girl with him from his native land, or had he come alone, to marry some placid Englishwoman with her lighter skin and cooler blood? Had they together produced a curious mixture of two cultures, an olive-skinned boy with his mother's blue eyes and the crisp black hair of his father's people? Had he missed the ancient stone monuments, this Stavros, sighed for the rocky walks, the feel of the morning rain against his skin in the morning, the towering hills that echoed his cry back at him as he stood calling the sheep to fold?

Calypso pushed open the door and went inside.

It was uncanny. The place looked as though, at any moment, the lights would blaze on, the waiters in their black jackets would rush to seat her, the air would be redolent of mysterious and succulent aromas. Trembling a bit, she set her clay jar on the floor beside her, touching with a sense of wonder and loss the bright velvet chairs, the flocked wallpaper, the plaster statuary copied from the temple guardians of home.

She did not linger there; the feel of a Greece that she might never again see had saturated Stavros and Son, moving and uncomfortable, a clutch at the heartstrings, the first thing in too long a time to actually hurt. She took with her a menu, a picture of the Acropolis on the front, words that were achingly familiar on the inside: moussaka, souvlaki, dolmas. Her mouth watered, reacting, as her eyes found these dishes listed; memory was painful, and she was sick of fish. She went back out into the street, the menu tucked into her wide leather belt and the clay jar back in its place, shutting the door softly behind her, to find herself facing a crowd of children, a circle of youth and life, watching her in unsmiling speculation.

So; here it was, then, directions at last. She gave them back stare for stare, letting them absorb her, see her as she was, no danger to them. Calypso held no falsely sentimental views of children. There were good things about them—their eagerness to know and unwillingness to be lied to—and bad things too; she remembered the village children tossing casual cruelties against each other like bread crumbs, their iron determination to come first at all costs, the bitter manifestations of an egocentricity that she, for one, had never found charming. Still, they could and must be spoken with. She beckoned to a girl, some twelve or thirteen years old, a pale-haired waif with the budding breasts of approaching womanhood.

"Speak with me, please. I must go north from here, to bring a gift to someone. To go north from here, which way is the best way?" Her voice; rarely used except for song, came out cracked and rusty; her accent was atrocious. Ah, well, it could not be helped, and the girl seemed to understand her, for she immediately pointed.

"There's train tracks," the girl said. It must have rained here a short while ago; the child's hair was stringy, plastered to her face, and her clothing showed patches of damp where the driving water had caught her. Her voice was reedy and high, and totally devoid of curiosity. "The old Brit Rail Intercity used to run there, to London and Wales and places. Follow the tracks until you find the north spur. Then take that."

"My thanks to you, kyria." Calypso gave the girl the ancient courtesy title, usually reserved for older women, and saw a shy smile split the round face. For a moment she was sorry that she had nothing with which to reward them. Before she was able to allow the regret to sink deeper, the girl, as if sensing Calypso's gratitude, had stepped forward and taken her hand. The touch, which should have been shocking after so long an absence from human contact, was reassuring instead; the girl's hand was warm and dry, and her breath brushed Calypso's bare arm. The children crowded forward, smiling now, dirty hair and tattered clothing eddying and breaking and, at the last, forming a protective phalanx around Calypso.

"We'll show you," the girl said simply, and tugged at Calypso's hand. "Come along, come along. This way, up these stairs and through that little park there and around the corner to the left. You can't miss it, it's there."

"My thanks to you," Calypso said, and allowed herself to be pulled forward. The children were patting her now, touches like birds' wings, though they said nothing at all. The girl who was leading her tossed long blond hair out of her face and smiled directly into Calypso's eyes.

"A gift," she said clearly. "A gift. You said so. We'll show you the way. Come along."

And the tracks were there, the long railroad ties stretching like ribbons out of sight in all directions. The children, who had obviously come to play here many times before, gleefully gestured her along; the station itself, modern and gleaming, held long benches and counters of polished wood and machines, tipped over and broken now, that had once dispensed chocolate bars for fifty pence each to bored or hungry commuters. In one corner, a ratty-looking brown dog lay sleeping; he opened one eye to regard her briefly, and closed it again in apparent disgust. There was no other sign of life in the vast building, and the children and the dog seemed tiny, dwarfed by the high roof and the smooth walls, specks beneath a microscope in the belly of a preposterous whale.

Calypso had never seen anything like Plymouth Station and would have lingered there, fascinated, to explore. The children, however, would not allow this; they seemed to have been infected, one and all, with a sense of urgency, of time passing, and they pushed at her, still wrapped in their cocoon of silence. The small hands all carried the same message: movement, movement. You must not stay, you have no time to wait, you must be moving, moving, moving . . .

Calypso put her feet tentatively down on the tracks, having been warned by the blond girl to avoid the rail at the far left, it used to be dangerous and even though there was no electricity left to come through it, it was still possible that some power might be sleeping under its worn hood, anything was possible and after all you never knew, did you? And Calypso, thanking her once again, lifted her face to the heavens and saw Polaris, a frosty steady pulse, beaming out at her.

They stood on the station platform and waved goodbye as she hoisted her jar higher on her shoulder and began to walk.

8

A Little Night Music

FOR THE FIRST time since attaining a room not shared with another person, Julia left the door to that room open as she slept.

She lay drowsing, thinking of the vision she had seen and the reactions to that vision of those who had so miraculously come around her. Something, a lingering fear or a premonition of some indefinable danger, prevented her from easily relinquishing her grasp on the waking world.

So she stretched out on her back beneath the feather quilt, her eyes closed and her mind preternaturally clear. She seemed able to see the others as they slept in their borrowed rooms down the long hallway: Dilly and Maddy, small angels of light, Ben with a soft flush across his brow and a smile that never altered, undisturbed by dreams. Gad, that creature of the night, would not be sleeping; she would be curled before the dying embers downstairs, her gray paws tucked beneath her chin, alert and aware to any change, any threat . . .

And here, at last, was sleep, sleep and its companion,

dream. It took shape slowly, evolving into oddity, and something in Julia warned her not to intrude through the fabric of events or to make her presence felt; only observe, and later to remember as best she might.

A man in nondescript clothing, she could not see what he wore. A bathrobe, a nightgown, something? Whatever; at this level of dream, importance sorted itself out, making it easy for her, subliminally defining priorities. He was familiar, though not actually known; he moved across moon-washed cement under a night sky, a man with rich olive skin and long black hair and a face that spoke of camel trains and poppy plants, of precisely rhythmic caravans across the face of the hills of Lebanon. It was a strange face, not cruel, but chilly with a look of sad abstraction that seemed more an imprint than an indication of any particular mood.

And now, though she could not place the traveler, she recognized his setting. She had often walked where this stranger now walked; it had been one of the great delights of living in London, carrying with it happy memories of Saturday crowds, children with their ice cream cones, the assorted sounds and smells. Regents Park Zoo, of all places, and why in the world was she dreaming of a stranger walking through a zoo at night? His bare feet slapped against the concrete paths, but made no sound; his long hair lifted and fell behind him in the soft breeze as he walked the barren ruins of the famous menagerie like a shadow.

The cages he passed all shared one thing, doors that had been opened long since. Some were empty, some still housed the animals who had always lived there. With the lazy prescience that is the gift of dream, Julia knew that the creatures who remained had done so from choice; perhaps they had been bred here, these lingerers, born in captivity, and the wide world outside was alien and unwelcoming. Yet the choice had been theirs; man was dead, the gates were open and freedom lay down any road you wandered, so long as you were willing to make it your own.

He stopped first at the cage which had once held the panda, that large lovely black and white beast with its strange opposable thumbs and its soft clown's smile. The cage was empty now; its erstwhile occupant, perhaps understanding that the daily gift of food was gone and that she must now take to the streets in search of meat to replace the diet she had grown accustomed to in the valleys of Xizang, had left behind her a large toy ball in one corner and decaying strips of bamboo tied to the bars.

The walker gazed a moment at the striped shadows, seeming to consider. Then he turned to face in another direction, making his way toward a long low building, its roof showing red in the gauzy moonlight at the end of a short well-tended path. Letters of black marble announced that this was the Reptile House and welcome to it, the smaller sign on the door asking only that visitors please refrain from teasing the animals or tapping on the glass.

Deep in sleep now, Julia stirred at the sight of what lay within; he had pushed the door open and was standing among a multitude of snakes and lizards. The serpents, some big, some small, were all beautiful with their patterned skins and flat diamond eyes; they lay piled against each other, making the most of the warmth. A long pale cobra moved across his instep and, as something fell with a plop onto his shoulder, he glanced up to look at the Javanese python, twenty feet long, who had lowered its tail from the fluorescent light fixture to make its presence known.

"What do you want?"

The voice had come from a monitor lizard, stretched out on the grubby floor. The great reptile's yellow and gray skin was elegantly wrinkled as he lay watching. The black-haired man, his eyes seeming somehow to keep them all within sight, spoke politely.

"Good evening to you, my friends. I have come to ask a favor, which I hope you will perform."

"A favor to your own benefit, of course?"

This seemed to bother the traveler, for he frowned and looked momentarily worried. "Why do you say that?"

Above his head, the python replied. It had a small thin voice, not unlike Gad's, ludicrous in a creature of such proportions. "Surely that is obvious. We have known your kind long years, and never once have you required anything that would benefit anything but yourselves. If you come to us, it is because you want our skin for adornment, or the use of our killing grip and our poisons to destroy an enemy. Come along, come along, out with it. No blathering, now. Which do you want?"

"The second. I have an enemy I wish dead."

"And why should we oblige you in this matter?"

"Because I am who I am, the crown, the king."

The monitor lizard snorted. "Typical human, greedy and pompous to the last. Crown and king, indeed! Why should we give a flying damn who you are? What's it to do with us?"

"My father created you, it is written in the Book," the traveler whispered, and recoiled from the vibrant hissing and the concentrated amusement around him.

"Not us, mate," said a small adder. "You had nothing to do with us or your father either, whatever else he might have created. I've picked you now, I know who you are. Coming to us for a favor, that's rich, that's killing, that is. Wasn't it your father that destroyed our reputation, painted us in this precious book of his as the lowest of the low, and all in a fit of pique?" The adder's voice grew ugly. "We don't like your father, and we don't like you, and we won't help you. Be off, now. Go on, get out of it!"

Far away in her soft bed, Julia's unconscious brain heard the single word *enemy*; it sent a signal to her hands, lying open and relaxed, and the hands wove together to form a protective shield across her stomach.

The man, his contemplative face never changing, left the reptile house and walked on. His footsteps took him up a slight incline to an outdoor exhibit, this one a microcosm of the African savanna; a lily pond lay stagnant under a crust of green scum, and artificial boulders, poured from the same cement as the path, had been tastefully arranged in towering piles. He walked to the open cage door and rattled it, summoning the occupant.

The lion, several hundred pounds of sleek-maned power, rose from his place at the pond's edge and strolled to meet him. The amber eyes, large as they were, were nearly lost in the surrounding tawny fur; they gazed at him unwinkingly, and from the broad chest issued a rumbling question.

"Well?"

The man stared back at him. "Where are your females?"

"They are not 'my' females, naked monkey; they are their own females first, and then each other's. After that, they belong to their cubs and to the killing ground. That is why we are called a pride. At the moment—to answer your somewhat impertinent question—they are out on the hunt, searching for Alsatian or Great Dane in the streets of Camden Town. What's it to you?"

"I have come to ask a favor, which I hope you—or the females, which you insist are not yours—will perform."

"To ask a favor." The lion showed yellowed fangs three inches long in an unpleasant parody of a human grin. "I'll bet you did. It involves spilling blood, no doubt? You have an enemy you want hunted down and killed?"

"You could eat her, you know; I just want her dead, and what happens after that makes no difference to me." The quiet voice was persuasive, gentle, and far away in Sparrow House Julia gave a tiny whimper. Through her sleeping terror, she heard the lion's amused reply.

"You want, you want. Humans always want and be damned to the consequences, why do you think they're all dead? They died of wanting, every man jack of them." Every hair of the sable mane was bristling, and the lion's amusement had transmuted to something that reeked of malice. "Bloody nerve you've got, coming to us to do your dirty work. We don't kill for gain or pleasure; what do you think we are? And just for your information, chum, my people only eat yours if it's that or starvation. Mangy stringy things, full of worms and disease; you rot our teeth to nothing and our fur falls out from the swallowing of you. You've got an enemy, you kill it. It's your problem, not ours. Where do you get off, asking us for favors, bothering us with your problem? Kill it yourself."

"I cannot." The voice had gone thin. Was it anger at the lion's attitude or dismay at the truth of its own words? "I am forbidden to do that; I can order death, but I can't give it by my own hand." The voice became a small flicker, whispering strange words. "It was one of the conditions."

"Well, isn't that a shame?" The great cat turned away, every line of his body compact of disgust. "The answer is no, flat out. No. Go find someone else to get their hands dirty for you. And if I were you, I'd scarper; my nose tells me the ladies are on their way back. They're a pretty mean bunch, by and large, and what's more they don't like your sort. What, are you deaf? Didn't you just hear me tell you to go? Go on, twit. Get out of it."

The man went quickly, finding the gates that led to the street, leaning against the high stone walls with their overhanging shrubbery, staring out into the darkness at nothing. And as Julia saw his face and heard his voice speaking incomprehensible words to someone or something hidden from her, she became aware of a new element in the dream: Gad's voice, tense and utterly convincing.

"Give it up; you can't do anything about it, and you'll only make it worse for yourself. I know it's hard for you, but try, just try. Can't you just accept it with a little dignity, it's time and you can't do anything about time, not even you."

The traveler's voice, more hollow now than when he had been speaking with the beasts, filled the air around Julia's head. "No, guardian. This I cannot accept."

Julia had a sense of Gad shrugging. "To your cost."

Suddenly the man's voice was full of pain, the wild accusatory misery of a child betrayed. "You, you of all of them, to say this to me! You were there at my birth, you guided my first steps, you cared for me. Under a new star in the winter sky, you were my eyes and my heart. Can you refuse me now? Can you cast me off so easily?"

And Gad sighed, a deep mournful sound with patience at its root. "Foolish, foolish. All this time in the high seat, and you still haven't learned that guilt makes a poor gift? Yes, I was there at your birth; I remember your mother, a lovely woman, a gem of her species. Yes, I guided your first steps, but I guided the steps of all your predecessors too, and I watched them reign for a turn of the wheel before they faded away, even as I'm watching you."

The man made no answer, and Gad's voice softened. "Poor silly sod. You never learn, you people, never. Two thousand years; that's your turn. It's just about over, the guardians have gathered for the birth. I'm here, Trout's here, Simon's here. One of the Three is here, another is with Max, and even now the third is on her way. Time moves on, my child, the world won't turn any other way. Accept it with grace."

"Not yet." The traveler's voice was fading, joining with the first streaks of dawn, and Julia swam a step closer to the waking world. "Not yet."

She opened her eyes to a room full of gray and rose; morning waited just over the horizon, clear and bright. The rain had blown itself out and the grate in the drawing room would be full of cold ashes. Gad lay beside her on the wide bed, her eyes filmed with tears, and Julia, her body coming alive in its morning ritual, knew with the certainty of the blessed that what she had seen was of vital importance to her, because it had been no dream.

"Who was that?"

Gad looked at her, considering, and Julia could actually see her thinking it over, reaching the decision to tell. She could feel Gad's relief that the burden would finally, now, be shared.

"Oh," said the gray cat simply, "that was God. He's upset, poor silly man, upset because he's dying and he doesn't like the idea at all."

"God?" Julia blinked in disbelief, even as she knew, felt in her bones, that Gad had spoken the incredible words as nothing but the simple truth. "Did you say *God*?"

"God, or the man your kind has called God for the past two thousand years. Get up now, Julia, and I'll tell you a story. There're things I must be doing and things you need to know, and it's high time we were up and about."

"She wants you to do what?"

John perched on the edge of the terrace and stared in complete disbelief at Mark and Luke. Behind them sat Gad, her eyes on the smaller ravens; there was confrontation here—she could smell it in the air and see it in every line of John's stiffened feathers. If there was to be a battle of wills, she must be present to throw in whatever weight she could.

Mark, the perennially unflappable, simply lifted his shoulders and cast a yearning glance to the skies. Luke, sharper and more tuned to John's moods, was truculent.

"Fly to Plymouth and guide three humans back here. Bloody hell, Johnny, you make it sound like we're supposed to fly to the moon and bring back a herd of elephants. What's the problem here?"

"The problem is that neither of you has ever been any farther away than the county borders, that's what the problem is. And *you* make it sound as if Plymouth was a half mile past the stream. It's a whole day's flight from here, and the weather's been treacherous. Suppose it starts that damned storming again? Suppose one of you is hit by lightning, or attacked by a hawk, and I'm not there!"

Luke, the tiny air holes above his beak glinting in the morning light, mustered up every ounce of patience he could. "John, you're being a prat. No other way to put it, sorry, there it is: a prat, I said. I'm the best flier and the best hunter in this part of the world, and you know it. And what would you propose to do if I was hit by lightning while you were there, anyway? Scream at the flame to leave me alone?" He saw the absurdity of the question strike John, saw the downward pull of the flexible neck as his leader tried to stifle a laugh, and pressed his advantage. "Gad'll watch us all the way down and back again, tell us what kind of weather to expect on the way, keep you informed. Won't you, Gad?"

"Of course I will." She had already read the violence of John's disapproval for what it was, part sulk at his two subordinates enjoying an adventure denied to him and part honest worry for their safety, for Mark the simpleton in particular. It was praiseworthy, but annoying. Moreover, it was wasting time, and they had none of that precious commodity to spare. There was a cold breath of threat waiting in the wings, and the child had begun to stir.

A month, Julia had said, but Julia was wrong. Several thousand years of experience at the fine art of bearing young had honed Gad's eye to a sharpness unobtainable by mankind. No matter that Julia knew with accuracy the moment the child had been conceived; this one had its own ideas as to when it would be born, and a month had nothing to do with it. It would be sooner than that, much sooner; a week, two at the most. The stars in their courses were moving, gathering above them for the change; the people who should be there by right were on their way. No time, no time . . .

She forced herself to look John in the eye and speak calmly, though she would have greatly preferred to use her full majesty and scare him into cooperation.

"Now look, John. I've tried to explain what's going on here, I have explained it in fact, and I don't have the time, we don't have the time, to argue. To the south of here are two men; one of them is a wise man with a gift for Julia's baby, and the other is the baby's father. There's also a woman, a woman as old as me—and believe me, mate, that's really saying something—who has come from the other end of the earth in a little boat to be here. I can only guide them by little—ah—signals, and that simply isn't good enough; there's someone out there doesn't want them to get here, and signals can easily be confused or misconstrued. And they've got to get here, all three of them; I can't even guess what might happen if there's any delay. Now, I've told you what I can. I've told you how important Ben is, I've told you that the baby Julia's carrying is no ordinary human child—you'll see that for yourself when it's born. And I've told you the truth; it's as I said, there's another player in this game, someone who will kill the child if he can. He's frightened and furious, and hard to stop. Now, you're wasting time. You and Matthew must stay here to guard Ben, and the others must fly south to make bloody well certain that those who seek each other find, and after finding, come back here as soon as they can. I'll keep in touch with Luke and Mark along the way, and give you news as it comes." The pupils in their amber pools had contracted to pinpoints in her intense concentration. "And that's flat, John. All right?"

She had captured John's eye, and with it his obedience; the yellow bird eyes were glazed over. She put the weight of her whole time in the world, every ounce of whatever it was that made her something to be obeyed, into her voice. "I repeat, John. That's the way it has to be. Understood?"

John looked at her, not blinking. "Not an ordinary child."

"No."

"Then what is it?"

"A god," she said calmly. "A new one. For us, for them. Now will you do what you're bloody well told?"

"Right." The other ravens were dumbfounded. Had she hypnotized John, laid a spell on him, put his beady mind in a box for her pleasure? He rapped at Luke with his head, and spoke irritably. "Well, what are you waiting for, are you deaf? Get a move on, no slacking about. I'll come to the edge of the wood, to see you off. Fly careful, now."

"Can you teach me how to do that?" The tiny whisper in her ear came from Matthew, who had watched this power play with admiration. "Never seen the old sod so meek."

"Behave yourself." She was watching the ravens, Luke and Mark soaring high, John escorting them to the edge of the wood before turning back again. "They're on their way."

"Gad?" She turned to find Matthew regarding her with some shyness. "Was—I hate asking, but—was all of that true, I mean really true? About Julia's baby being the new one, not only for people but for all of us this time?"

She suddenly loved them, all of them, clever Matthew and childlike Mark and feral Luke and cantankerous John, and the love spilled out of her in a warming torrent that covered Matthew like a sprinkle of autumn leaves falling. She reached out to pat him with one paw, the claws well sheathed.

"Yes, Matt. All true, every word. The thing is, I've only just told Julia this morning, and she's a bit stunned."

"What?" They moved from terrace to lawn, the raven with his wings slightly spread, hopping from step to step to meet the grass at last. "You mean she didn't even know?"

"Bizarre, isn't it? No, Max never told her; he probably thought she wouldn't believe a word of it. Myself, I think he underestimated her." Her voice turned wry and acerbic. "Your sex has always underestimated mine, whatever time, whatever species. Always. That may change, with this new one coming; things may get different in a big hurry."

Matthew laughed, a harsh happy croak from deep in his throat. "Underestimate females? Not me, Gadabout my only love. They frighten me to death, if you want to know."

"Do they?" And now Gad, for the first time since the early morning and her painful disclosures to Julia, was free to smile. "Good. That's as it should be, and we'd rather be feared than not." The smile dying, she spoke more to herself than to her companion. "And I shall have a few choice words for Max, when he gets here. Imagine him not telling her she was going to wind up pregnant with the savior of the world, whether she wanted it or not!"

Matthew, who had heard only the first half of Gad's statement, seized on her remark about fear and replied to it with a consciously wicked glee. "Johnny must be half female, then. Talk about wanting to scare, that's our Johnny! Fear's just a way of being controlled, isn't it—hullo, Sim, how's the food today?"

The sheep lifted his stained muzzle from the grass to acknowledge them; beside him, Whiskey bade them greeting through a mouthful of breakfast. Simon fixed his eyes on Gad, and his voice was terse.

"What's wrong with Julia, old cat? I've tried to talk with her about ten times since sunup, no luck, none. She's like a woman in shock. What's the story?"

"The story, my friend, is the same as it always was. What's wrong with Julia is that she now knows it, all of it. She'll be all right, Simon; she just needs a bit of time to take it all in, nothing more. Well, it's a bit of a stunner, after all. Falls in love—if that's what it was, and I wouldn't give anything for the truth of that feeling—and winds up accidentally responsible for the death of most of her species and pregnant with a god, to boot."

"Good grief." Simon was gazing at her with great respect. "What did you do, sit down on that great ruddy lap of hers and say, pardon me, Julia, but it's just occurred to me that you may not realize that the child you're carrying is the next protector of the universe, and the protector running the show at the moment is a bit browned off at the idea of making a change, oh and by the way if you hadn't slept with a handsome stranger your people would still be alive?"

"Something like that, yes." She saw the slow shake of his great woolly head, and spoke defensively. "I had no choice, Simon. My hand was forced during the night."

"How?" He was angry, or as close to angry as a sheep can get; Gad recognized its source, love for Julia, and kept her voice soft.

"Two things happened, that's how. First, the child shifted last night; you must have felt it, even through the thunder. It's engaging itself, getting itself into the proper position."

"Is it, now? Well." The sheep's caustic sarcasm had died; he had begun to look thoughtful. On either side of them, the raven and the horse cast puzzled glances at each other, as if to say: This is all beyond my ken—do you understand it? No, somehow I didn't think so.

Simon went on, quietly now. "And second?"

"Second, the child is gaining vision. Julia saw the Son last night, or thought she did; of course it was the child's eyes she was seeing him through, but I really didn't think it was a good time to explain that. She's got enough on her plate at the moment."

"The Son." Simon had gone very still now, his horns warlike and ready in the brilliant sun. The horse and the raven pulled closer together, infected without knowing why by the danger in the air. "What happened?"

"He took a little walk through the zoo. He tried to talk a few snakes and an African lion into wandering out this way for the purposes of spreading poison or fang. They told him where to put it, and he took it out on me."

"He wants her dead?"

"Can you doubt it?" Gad was suddenly tired; her entire body remembered the tension of that confrontation, the cold deliberate placement of all her mind, her heart, her soul between the slumbering Julia and the raging deity. "Can you doubt it?"

"No." Simon took a step toward the house and stopped, forlorn, worried, irresolute. "Can—can he do anything?"

"He can try."

Clip slap, clop thump, Calypso's bare feet rose and fell, rose and fell, on the wooden railroad ties.

The stars had come all the way out for her and the planets shone brightly, Orion and Scorpio jostling for position in the hectically crowded heavens with Venus and Jupiter. She walked across the Tamar and up, always up, following the North Star's beckoning light, her eyes taking in the new land around her, searching for the northern spur.

She sang as she walked, a song of the sea and a woman who took on the form of a dolphin to make love to the deep waters. The rich contralto shaped the ancient words in her own language and sent them out over the fields, and under her the track lengthened and narrowed, twisting like a smile across the face of this unknown land, this England.

The night was very calm, its stillness accentuating the vastness of the light-studded canopy above her. If there were rustlings in the wheat fields, if the owl cried to the moon, Calypso did not notice. She was intent on her song, on the perfection of her feet as they slapped the wood, and the soft sloshing of olive oil in the old jar at her ear. At first light the great North Star would begin to fade; she gave all her concentration toward keeping it in her eye.

Toward dawn she realized she was hungry. The moon had come up and retreated again, though a faint phosphorescent circle still clung dimly to the coming morning; the first light of day fell on a field to her left, its divided patches with their wooden markers and wire barriers oddly truncated by the turns of the railroad tracks. She looked thoughtfully at the overflowing little allotments, her mouth watering. There were potatoes, tomatoes, an abundance of cabbage.

She made a meal of vegetables still dewy and cold from the transition of the hours. Her breakfast consumed, she put her ear to the ground, listening for a stream.

"To the north, kyria. Fifty feet to the north."

Calypso froze where she squatted. The voice—in her mind, in the ground, out of the soft clouds banking behind her?—had been wise, pleasant, sympathetic, and the words had been in no language, in every language. She stood and walked due north, hearing the bubble and chatter of flowing water, listening for the voice that had pointed her. But for the moment all was quiet, except for the stream itself.

The water was very cold, and tasted like love. She drank like an animal, dipping her face between the reeds, and it sank in long grateful spirals down her parched throat. When she had splashed her face with it, she lay down to rest awhile at the water's edge, her waiting ear tuned to the air around her, hoping for further communication.

She was not kept waiting for long. This time the voice came from the water itself; it was very clear and spoke to her sensibly, telling her things that she wanted to know.

"You are making good time, kyria. The children were

wise, to set you on the railway line; it will take you to where the others will find you."

"Others? Ah, yes. That was promised." She asked the voice no questions; if it wished to inform her, she would be informed. A life of marvels may not wear away the capacity for surprise, but it does make coping with those surprises a bit easier when they come.

The voice had gained some definition: old and rather grumpy, definitely male. "Of course it was promised. You are necessary, and expected as well. The child's father will meet you, and another of your own kind. Have you brought an offering, as the custom requires?"

"A jar of my finest olive oil, to nourish and soothe hurts." Curiosity stirred; surely the voice was familiar? Calypso rolled over on her side, propping her face up on one hand to stare into the stream. "I have no wish to be rude, kyrie, but it would be better if I knew whom I spoke with. Who are you, and where?"

"Where I am makes no difference, kyria. My voice, which is the only important part of me as far as you're concerned, is in the water. It's in the water because the water is where I live."

Remembrance, sharp and bright. The man with the brown face weathered by his years of wrestling with the sea. He stood on the deck of a ship made gradually sea-worthy again during the years its master had spent in Calypso's arms; he stood with his hand on the tiller, putting his small brave craft to the harbor's mouth and out past the rocks that waited with their dangerous patience. Calypso herself, standing barefoot and tearless in the sunlight, waving farewell, knowing that he would never return to her. And in the tidal pool at her feet, an enormous fish watching her with its flat eyes never moving, sympathy in every scale.

Now tears filled her eyes and words tumbled out, irrelevant, or perhaps not. "A song," she wept, "about love, and the bottom of the sea. Dolphins. The waters of Babylon."

"Oh, I've traveled a lot since then." The grumpiness had given place to weariness, or was it merely exhaustion? "Across the wide seas, over and over, four thousand bloody years of it. I fetched up near Bethlehem last time around—the other guardians helped me out a bit there—and then back out again, across the wide seas, over and over, another two thousand years, would you believe it? England this time, another birth to attend. What a life's work for a fish."

He sighed, a long sweet descant of breath. "Anyway, you're here now. Keep a lookout for those you need. You'll see them in your mind's eye soon enough, I imagine; Max wouldn't contact you, he's concentrating on Gad and Julia and a bit of spiteful work on the side, but Raj can see you just fine. A good eye, his people have." Calypso heard sly laughter, and found it incomprehensible. "A good eye, a third eye."

Lighter now, softer, the words carried away on the ripples dancing toward the sea that had ever carried him. "Goodbye now, goodbye, stick to the northern roads. Eyes on Polaris, forget the rest. Eyes on the skies, too; birds. I'll be talking with you soon."

"Please—"

But it was too late; the voice was gone, its presence in the water fading to echo and, finally, silence. A pity, but he would return to talk with her, he had said it, and then perhaps he could answer her question, the one she really wanted answered: the name she had forgotten. He had been there, the owner of this voice. Another wanderer. All of her life it had fallen to her lot to deal with wandering men.

"Once," she sang softly, testing the air, "once I loved a man, a man to whom all roads were one; he left me and I made this song, for him, for me, for a fish in the sea. Can someone give his name back to me?"

But nothing came back at her but her own echo, and the first brazen trill of the lark, taking its head from beneath its wing to greet the dawn. She took up the clay jar, its roughly hewn black silhouettes frozen in the sculptor's dance, and made her way back across the fields to where the tracks waited and beckoned with their siren's song.

9

More in the Air Than Just Dust

"I," SAID MARK simply, "need a rest. Okay?"

"Okay." Luke looked sideways at his small companion, and felt the surge of protective instinct that the runt of the litter will always raise in a discerning heart. "Poor Marky, it's the hell of a hike, innit? Are you hungry?"

"Getting there." But Mark did not look hungry, or tired for that matter, and neither body nor thought expressed anything other than a huge contentment at the feel of the wind in his feathers, the ballast under his wings, the vast green panorama of England spread out below him like a child's picture puzzle, bright and beautiful.

"Look, Marky, trees, off to the south about a half mile. Let's have a nice sit-down, shall we?"

"Ta, lovely, let's." And Mark veered sharply, blinking as the sudden shift of his body against the wind blew some fragments of pollen into his eyes. Luke, one eye on Mark and one automatically scanning the earth beneath him for signs of supper, cut south to follow.

Luke saw Mark settled in the highest reaches of the tree and turned back over the woods. Plenty of food here, grouse and pheasant and badgers—the little stand of trees was just swarming with life. To the east of the trees ran a little stream, no doubt dense with fish for the taking; wouldn't Gad have herself a proper old dinner down there!

Luke circled once, low around the trees; he noted the spoor of some other hunting bird, a wild peregrine he thought with a stiffening to attention, for the peregrine is a bird even a raven has second thoughts about sparring with. Still, the skies above him were empty and, for the moment, the wood was his to hunt as he chose.

He decided on a fat pheasant, a prey so easy to take that he was almost ashamed of himself. One swoop and a loud threatening croak to separate it from its companions and flush it from cover between the larch trees. A second swoop—the sound effects omitted this time—as the foolish thing broke cover screeching and the one he had marked as his own fled the raven's shadow toward the open fields. One last swoop, and in less than no time it dangled, limp and bloodied, from between his talons.

He was bringing it back to the tree to share with Mark, had almost reached the tree, in fact, when Gad's voice sounded in his head. He had not been expecting it; he gave a harsh croak and a convulsive jerk of his body and the pheasant, suddenly freed from his grasp, thumped to the earth with a sickening splat, fifty feet below.

"Pox," he muttered, and Gad apparently picked up on this vagrant thought, for she replied with a hint of apology.

"Sorry, Luke. Did I startle you?"

"A bit. I've just dropped my pheasant. Hang on a tick, will you?"

He landed beside the limp gaudy huddle of feathers with a clumsy series of bumps, managed to get hold of it a second time, and dragged it upward until he was airborne. He was highly conscious of Mark's eye fixed on him during this series of maneuvers, whether critically or with approval it was impossible to tell; one can look very foolish while struggling in the air, and Luke knew it.

"Pox, knickers, *blast*," he muttered under his breath, as he gained the top reaches of the larch and thrust the pheasant up against the bole of the tree, wedging it in tight to hold it there. Though Mark's eyes held no undue amusement, a bad mood was threatening; ravens have a high regard for their dignity, after all, and are often victims to self-deprecation.

"Now," he said to Gad, "what's on your mind?"

"Nothing much, my friend. I promised John I'd keep my eye on you two, and I am. How's tricks?"

"Tricks is tricks. I'm fine, Marky's fine, I've caught a whopping fat pheasant for din-dins and all's right with the world if you like this sort of thing. We're sitting in a larch tree, I'm not sure where; the last sign we passed said Middle Crendale or some such thing, according to Mark. That was on the motorway, an hour ago. We're heading south. How's Julia, Gad? Is she still in a daze, still upset?"

"Yes and no." The good cheer in Gad's voice disappeared abruptly, replaced by gloom. "No, she's not in a daze, but yes, she's still upset, and I don't really think she's all right, either. She's been sitting locked in her bedroom since yesterday morning, writing poetry, good grief. She won't let me in, she won't let Ben or Dilly in, she won't talk to Simon, and what's worse than all that, I don't think she's eaten. It scares me, Luke; things are too close."

"Writing poetry? What in hell for?"

"Oh, that's right, I keep forgetting. You don't know humans the way I know humans. She's writing poetry because something hurts, that's why. I think she feels betrayed, and she won't let a single thought through, not one, so I can't tell her Max is on the way."

"Good job you can't, if you ask me." This, to Luke's

surprise if not to Gad's, was Mark; he had entered their stream of mental cross-talk like an expert wiretapper on a company pole. "If she feels like this Max bloke has got her into a mess and you were to pop in all happy-like with the news that the wonder boy will be along any day now, she'd likely meet him at the front gate with a shotgun."

"Mark!"

"No, really, Luke. Writing poetry, is she? Well, I may not know what poetry is, but I know why she writes it; she writes it like Ben paints his pretty pictures, because maybe what they see with their eyes don't match what goes on in their heads or their hearts or their stomachs, and the picture is the halfway point between all them feelings, a way to tell themselves what they think ought to be the truth of things. That's what Ben does and I'll bet poetry is no different from pictures, when all's said and done."

There was a long moment of quiet as Luke and Gad took in this little speech and assimilated it. Mark, Gad reflected, was surprising. In a way, he was like Ben; you thought he was a harmless idiot who wasn't safe out, and then you'd all be poring over something, looking for a complicated answer to a simple enough question, and he'd pop right in with some beautifully delicate perception of his own that made everything clear in a way you hadn't considered before and honestly couldn't argue with.

"You'd win your bet," she said. "And you're probably right, too; the last thing she needs to hear right now is that Max is alive and well and coming to Sparrowdene for a piece of the action."

"Vulgar," said Luke with an inner grin. "I'd say he'd already got the best of that action he could hope for."

Gad properly ignored this bawdiness. "I did tell her he was alive, the first day I saw her and I knew—well, never mind. I don't think she'd believed a word of it."

Luke, realizing simultaneously that he was very hungry and that eating would not interfere with this kind of communication, ripped a large part of the pheasant free of its bones and tossed the meat down his throat. "Well, we'll warn him when we see him not to expect a kiss and a cuddle by the back door. Speaking of which, beloved kitty cat . . ."

"I know, I know, that was the other reason I wanted to talk with you. I can see you, you know, and very clearly too; is that a woodpecker's hole behind Mark's head?"

"A woodpecker's hole?" Mark, busy eating, ignored this. Luke craned his neck over his friend's bent head and noted the gray deadwood around the hole with pleased surprise. "A woodpecker's hole it is, empty, I think; there's no resin left in the upper part of the trunk for protection against climbing bird lovers, so I'd wager the occupants have gone elsewhere to live. Where's this Max bloke, Gad?"

"South, still south, and the woman is south too. Her name is Calypso, by the by, and it was no joke, what I told John. She really is almost as old as me, so be polite to her. She comes from a much hotter place than this, an island far away in the south of the world, and if you want to make a good impression and probably a friend for life, address her as kyria. It's her proper title anyway, so it can't hurt."

"Will do. Do we just continue south, then, and hope we spot them, or what?"

"Go south until you reach a town called Wildebourne. You'll know it from the air, no need to worry about signposts this time; it's got a massive old cathedral, with three spires instead of the usual two, and the leftmost spire is far and away the tallest of the lot. When you see those spires, turn to the southwest and keep your eyes peeled for the old British Rail lines laid down there. If you see two men sleeping in the open, you've found Max and his friend, and if you see a woman walking north along the tracks, you've found Calypso. She should have your speech down to a fine art by this time, so just tell her who you are and why you're there. I have a feeling she's expecting you; Old Trout may be a cantankerous old bugger, but he's certainly thorough."

"Kyria." Mark, swallowing the last of his food, rolled the word around his mind like a wine taster. He surrounded it with lushness, brightness, some sorrow. "What pretty sounds the humans made, didn't they? Prettier even than birdsong, sometimes. Is that in any special language? I never heard the word before."

"Greek." Gad was beginning to fade now. "Something's happening—I think Julia is calling me, and I must go. It's full moon tonight, in case you didn't know, so keep flying. There'll be plenty of light to see by, for you and for the humans too. Happy hunting."

"Kyria," Mark said dreamily, but Gad had gone and there was only empty space where her spirit had sat. "Pretty."

"Pretty or not, we've got to go find her." Luke stretched his wings, letting the sky take him, understanding from the temperature and pressure that it would be a clear night with mild winds. "Up and bloody away, excelsior!"

Julia, with the summer sun washing her feet and the smiling ladies painted by Angelica Kaufman guarding her bent head, sat at the little desk in her room for a day and a night, resolutely barring her thoughts from the world beyond her door and wondering what to do.

Gad, she suspected, was feeling badly about the whole thing. Still, she could hardly lay the blame on Gad; Julia had always disdained the concept of killing the messenger who carries the bad news. It was not Gad who had allowed a lifetime of hard-won defenses to crumble at the first sight of a lint-haired man with eyes that were tunnels into time. Nor was it Gad who had taken him into her flat, into her bed, into her womb, to set the destruction of her fellows in motion.

And Gad, barred from Julia for that day and that night, had made two incorrect assumptions. Julia had, in fact, eaten; she had been pregnant long enough to discover that the condition tends the sufferer toward a sudden longing for food at odd hours, and the kitchen at Sparrow House was far enough from her bed to make the long climbs up and down the stairs a misery for a woman carrying forty extra pounds. She always kept a supply of tins in her room, sardines, tuna, potted meat, and pâté, and while Gad sat downstairs and worried about her hunger and its effect on the child, Julia had actually been eating steadily, guzzling really, taking solace in her little cache, numbing herself as best she could against the staggering fact that her pregnancy had resulted in the greatest cull of humanity in history.

Gad's second mistake had concerned her occupation during that time. The foggy, fleeting image of Julia, a pen between her fingers and her hugeness hunched over the desk, had been accurate enough. But Julia was not writing poetry. The shock of Gad's story, the realization of her own part in what had happened, the sudden clutching knowledge that what she carried, the seed that Max had sown, was not human, all of these things had combined to produce a reaction not dissimilar to that gained by drinking a bottle of brandy. Julia, in short, was feeling both giddy and detached, and for the first time since her adolescent years she was putting pen to paper, not for poetry, but to write a journal.

So the pen moved, the feelings marched and hid, and the words came down. They were stark and ugly and yet somehow comforting in their very lucidity.

(I remember when the Big One first hit, it was so fast and so unexpected, the first days there were just a few cases of people going into emergency wards in the big cities. Headaches, aching limbs, a sudden radical increase in heart rate. Flu, the doctors said, an outbreak of Hong Kong B or something. Wrong. Then the news from America and Asia and Africa, people came to sit in the emergency ward and died in their chairs while they waited for the doctor to be done with those who had staggered in before them; tea cooling on the tables beside them, spilling across the magazines about sex and money as they flung about in a last convulsion.)

How had it happened, how? How had a woman who had never loved anyone fallen into such a dirty little pit, so cheap, so badly dug. And Max had known, Max, oh dear lord, Max, lying beside him and tracing the hard wash of muscles across his torso, listening to the light regular breathing, which, now that she thought about it, had remained light and regular even during their coming together. He had known and he hadn't told her. Together, they had murdered the human race.

She leaned back in her chair. staring up at the fat women in their Regency gowns, and a tiny bubbling laugh escaped her. Talk about irony. You make a conscious decision and stick to it, never get involved because love opens you to being used . . .

The laughter was bitten back as it moved toward the edge of hysteria. One slip, and bob's your uncle. A pawn in some monstrous game, she thought, and tears moved slowly and painfully down her face to discolor the writing paper. Julia had never wept easily, but she wept now, and the pen ran inexorably across the smeared blue lines.

(Newspaper reports, shrill frightened voices on the BBC, speculation. An emergency meeting of the Royal Society of Surgeons here, an emergency meeting at Downing Street there. Hysterical accusations from Washington about Russia, indecent quantities of stupid Moslems howling for Western blood, it was all an imperialist American-Russian-Israeli plot. All their usual rubbish. And then the reports from Moscow and Atlanta, three million people dead in six days, all adults. Never children. Always adults.)

Julia paused, holding the pen like a talisman against the past, and remembered the worst days, the things she had pushed from her mind by sheer force of will.

She had come home to Sparrowdene to die—surely she must die just as everyone else had died. Driven by some obscure homing instinct, she was willing, as the death toll mounted to over a billion, to risk her parents' certain fury at her unsanctioned pregnancy. Too late, of course, too late. The sinking of her heart as she laid her hand grip down on the steps and pushed at the front door of the little house was with her now, vivid and dreadful, a nightmare that might visit a child who had eaten too much, impossible and unreal.

(The door was hanging open, unlatched, and I pushed at it and called; there was no answer but then something inside squeaked and a rat shot past me and I knew that the house was empty, that all the life had gone out of it. Mum, Daddy, Lizzy, Richard, Michael, Trisha and her American lawyer in Chicago, Stephen and that foul-tempered bitch he married in Madrid, they were all dead. All gone, gone, and the rats were in the pantry and there were chewed boxes of things strewn all over the floor, cereal half-eaten, a tube of oatmeal with fang slashes in the sides, oh god, why do I keep seeing these filthy pictures in my head? Why won't they let me be? Why can't memory be blind?)

She hadn't died. Incredibly, unbelievably, she had tripped over putrefying bodies in the streets of Sparrowdene—and how fast those bodies rotted to nothingness, something to do with the acceleration of the mutated adrenaline—and she had never felt physically healthier; indeed, she felt herself as a climbing plant, thriving in the midst of terror and decay, and The Bump as a vampire, sucking the life from the living to make itself strong.

One day she had walked up to Congreve's, that last bastion of her lost world, and jumped at the sight of a woman looking out at her from the lead-framed windows, a beautiful woman with the bloom of high health on her cheeks, and red hair that shone. She had stood frozen, torn between a sudden wild hope for company and a fear that what had happened was turning her brain. Several heart-stopping minutes passed before she realized that the face staring so peacefully out at her was her own reflection.

(Static on the radio and the rats in the gutters, and then the rats disappeared and the grass began to look greener, even the rain fell softer and everything was so bloody quiet. I couldn't understand why I hadn't died, the rest of the world died, didn't it? I didn't know then that the children would survive. Unkempt children moving through the alleys in little groups during those last bad days and then disappearing altogether. I thought they had died too, but I was wrong, they simply vanished, or hid. Something, anyway. Why didn't I die, Bump? Well, we know now, don't we, my darling, we didn't die because we were the death that came to everyone else, and only death is immune to itself. Max, are you dead? I hope so.)

What to do, what to do.

She could kill herself. That was always a possibility, the final choice left to her, the one move the pawn could make without approval from the heavy hands who worked the board. She could do that, yes. She could die, and The Bump would die with her. Justice?

That would be unwise.

The pen slid from between fingers gone suddenly cold and nerveless. The voice was not Gad's, nor Simon's, nor anyone else's she could put a name to. It was huge and soft and familiar; it came from the walls, the floor, her head. She got to her feet, holding the edge of the desk for support, and heard herself whisper.

"Max?"

Very unwise. Also useless, and wasteful, and far too late. I would have expected better from you; you understand the movements of the wheel, after all. Such a reaction is unworthy of you.

The detachment that had held her awake and writing for the past thirty-six hours slipped, cracked a bit, shifted. Something slid through her mind's eye, a great translucent head shaking in weighty sorrow at the foolishness it beheld, a pair of black eyes that watched her over a great distance. Above her the painted ladies bowed and curtseyed in their endless galliard, and the lush carpet was soft as vair beneath her feet. The placental fluid rippled and shimmered, the great cord trembled in its cavern of silence . . .

Please, she thought strongly. No. Stop.

A pawn, you think. That is not the case. Everything you have done you elected, on some level, to do. That is the turning of the wheel, the vagary of choice. There is nothing that has happened, or is yet to happen, that we can ever call random. How do you think the wanderer knew that you were to be the mother? He saw it in your face, he heard it in your speech, that night in Paris. No lies here. Not now. This is unworthy.

Something was pounding, was it the door or her heart or the roof of the world caving in on top of her? She was unaware of having cried out, her hands flying first to her face and then to her belly, and only vaguely aware of the dancing ladies seeming to bend closer over her, smiling and unconcerned. She was unaware that Gad and Simon and even young Maddy playing on the lawn had been rocked by the shock waves of the child's first real display of power. She was unaware of anything but the visions that shot across the walls in front of her, the dancing ladies and the great rosy head with its closed eyes, the waves of intolerable light, bitter vetch running like flame through her veins.

She was unaware, too, of Ben lifting her thrashing body as lightly and easily as he might have lifted Dilly, and laying her across the bed. She did not hear Gad's voice filtering through her to reach the child inside. Even if she had, she could have made no sense of Gad's words: Not yet, we are unready and incomplete, bide awhile, sleep.

The light died, the tumbling pictures stilled and went, and Julia crumpled into stillness. She lay in a long faint of utter exhaustion, one hand cupped beneath the pillow, her face empty of expression. All around her the others stood guard, keeping watch during the long hours that came and went, though Julia never felt them. In its sheltered haven, the child subsided into stasis once more.

Waking or sleeping, Max rarely wasted time on memory. His waking hours were filled with the perpetual motion that was his pride and his curse, and his sleep was neat and economical, never more than he needed. Occasionally he would dream, fleeting shapes and words that he would invariably remember in the morning, keeping what he thought was useful from those dreams and coldly discarding the rest.

Tonight something had planted itself in his brain that was not a dream. He came awake immediately, as he always did; the disorientation usual to waking in a strange place was absent in him, for to a wanderer every place is a strange place and all corners are known.

The night was mild and easy around him; even the residual moisture left by the storms had baked out of the ground. What in hell was that, he thought, and knew a flicker of fear. Julia, something to do with Julia, something had rocked her where she waited, she had said his name and then something had happened, her face had exploded into a whirlwind of light and panic.

The child.

He stood, emotional antennae probing the air. Had the Son succeeded, then? No, it couldn't be. Odd little echoes came and went in his mind; Julia's red hair fanned across a white linen pillow slip, strangers standing around her in a protective circle, two black birds soaring gracefully through a cloud bank. And a sound, the sound of a fetus settling itself to greater comfort in its living lake.

He was wrestling with the moving sensations, trying to extract some nugget of sense and purpose from their core, when he realized that the steady breathing that kept him company these nights was absent. He turned his head to look at the empty bedroll a few feet away. Raj was gone.

Max knew another flash of panic, quelled instantly. What was wrong with him, anyway, after all these years of imperturbability? Why overestimate the Son's powers now, of all times? Something woke Raj, he told himself firmly, something woke him and he went to see what it was. The Son can't hurt him, and would gain no advantage even if he tried. Everything is as it should be, exactly on schedule, and you will walk to the tor some fifty yards to your left and climb it and look for him . . .

"Max?"

So, something had happened after all. This, for the first time, was Gad's voice, a clarion call against the night. He promptly forgot Raj, and turned his attention to this more urgent summons.

"Gray cat?"

"Yes, it's me. Are you faring well?"

"Very well; I'm on my way, and a charming Indian holy man named Raj is coming with me. He's carrying gold."

"Fine. Look, things are moving faster than I could possibly have anticipated. Where are you?"

"Near Exeter, northeast of Plymouth. Why?"

He felt, rather than heard, Gad's sigh of relief. "Near Plymouth, good, good. Listen to me now. There is a woman, coming up the railroad tracks from Plymouth. She's on her way to meet you, and—"

"I know; Raj has been tracking her every move."

"I said, listen. I've sent two guides, ravens, to lead you back here. Send them to find Calypso first, tell them to lead her back to you. Then follow the ravens back here, all three of you, and please don't dawdle. The child's on its way, and soon."

"But that's impossible!" It had been many years since Max had last been startled, but he was startled now. "Don't you think I know to the moment when the child was conceived? It has another month yet!"

So weighty was the slow shake of the guardian's head that Max, across the miles, shook his head along with her. "Trust me, wanderer. Sooner than that, much sooner; I know when it's due, but I also know when it's coming. You have ten days at the outside, no more than that, and that's a generous guess; it's very likely closer to a week."

"Gad, I—we can't get there in a week, or even in ten days. Be sensible; it's simply not possible, not on foot. We still have to find this woman—what did you call her, Calypso? And I don't even know where you are."

"We," she said crisply, "are at Sparrow House, a large Georgian manor outside the village of Sparrow-dene, county of Wiltshire. The house, which is set in arable pasture not far from Chippenham, is commodious, recently had all plumbing updated and boasts all modern conveniences. Stop quibbling; find a bookstore and get hold of a good Ordinance Survey map. You'll come up with Calypso shortly, especially if you send Luke and Mark—they're the ravens I told you about—to meet her. Find the tracks and wait at your end, and the birds will bring her. Simple."

"The hell it's simple." The announcement of the child's early birth had acted like a spur; Max was tense as a spring, and frustrated with it. "I'm not a bloody bird, and I can't fly. A week to walk through two counties!"

"Well," Gad said patiently, "don't walk, then."

Max was quiet a moment. "How, then?"

The gray cat's air of surface calm suddenly exploded into exasperation. "Will you stop being such a twit! Find a horse and talk him into cooperation; that's what the first of the wise ones did, and he's supposed to be a simpleton. If you don't like that idea, here's another; there are automobiles all over the place, the streets are littered with the filthy things, and there're petrol stations all over the place. Take a car, find a map, drive if you have to. That ought to take you less than a day, a good deal less. Just stop wasting my time with these defeatist interruptions, and get here!"

"A car," Max said aloud, but Gad was gone, the line broken. "A car."

Remembering Raj, he began to walk toward the tor, musing aloud as he went. "The batteries would be dead, but if I could find a place with an emergency generator, I could cope with that. Perhaps an auto service shop . . ."

He reached the tor, a nameless outpost in the moonlight, and climbed it easily. When he reached the top, he found Raj, his hands stretched toward the stars.

"I've just spoken with the guardian," Max said without preamble. "The child's coming early. We've got to find this woman, Calypso, and get up there fast. She's sent ravens—"

"Yes." And then Max felt his face brushed and something landed at his feet, a large black bird and then another, smaller this time. "This larger one is called Luke, and the other is known as Mark. They have come to guide us home."

Broken glass, bottles both ugly and nice, an old shoe.

Calypso, moving rapidly up the railroad line with her olive oil and the menu from Stavros and Son as her only baggage, had managed to quell her magpie instincts in the interest of expedience. It had not been easy; certainly the tracks held all sorts of interesting flotsam and jetsam, the effluvia of a different world, a different culture. She knew nothing of pop bottles or tennis shoes, found them a source of wonder and fascination, and the temptation to take some few pieces of this fascinating rubbish as souvenirs had to be pushed firmly away. Something was happening, something unexpected, and whatever it was it required her immediate presence.

She had reached the northern end of Newton Abbot without seeing any sign of life. Despite one ear kept always tuned to whatever mysteries might come her way, the Voice in the water had not spoken again, and the weather held clear for her. Calypso had a sense of things moving, things outside herself, short shining scenes that would flash through her mind and disappear before she could take hold of them. The feeling lent her an urgency that communicated itself to her feet; she had ceased stopping to rest, and needed no sleep.

Through the Newton Abbot rail station, where the edge of the platform showed a great black mark of charring where lightning from the storms had struck. Dodging her way nimbly between the silent trains, so long and sleek, that had come to rest there when their drivers had died. Over to the north end of the station, the northern spur . . .

"Nice evening, isn't it?"

Calypso jumped galvanically, nearly stumbled, righted herself. To her left was a dog, a large gray and white dog whose face was totally hidden by hair. Only the edge of a black nose and a dangling pink tongue showed clearly in the moonlight. She gazed at this apparition, entranced; she knew about dogs, it was true, but the dogs who lounged in the doorways of her native land had always tended to be skinny things, short-haired, with nasty temperaments. She had never seen anything like this one before, and found it charming. It had the look of a child's toy come alive.

"Nice, yes, very nice. Do you live here?"

"In a manner of speaking." the dog picked its way over the crossties and sat down at her side. "Strictly speaking, I used to live a few miles that way—where the moor is, you know—but I get around a fair bit. I'm a sheepdog, by the way, which explains my living on the moor; that's where they kept the sheep. Whimsy's the name. What's yours?"

"I? I am called Calypso. I am traveling north to meet up with some of my kind, and see a child born."

"Really?" The dog sounded rather doubtful. "Didn't know anyone old enough to have babies had survived the Big One. Sounds nice, though. Can I come along?"

Could this be the guide the Voice had mentioned? Perhaps, although Calypso doubted it; this meeting had a casual feel to it and, without knowing how or why, she knew that she would know the guide when it came. Still, company would be nice, and if she strayed from the proper path this native could perhaps set her right again.

She spoke graciously. "You may come to me, no, I mean with me. Certainly."

Whimsy fell into step beside her; his measured trot and padded feet were perfectly adapted to the rough tracks, and he had no trouble in matching her speed. Indeed, he seemed rather admiring. "Good pace for two legs."

Calypso dimly perceived a compliment. "My thanks to you. You, too, are very quick, for all you seem to have great bulk beneath this thick coat of yours. Did you live on the moor always, from when you were born?"

"Too right I did." They had cleared the abandoned Inter-City trains now and picked up speed as they moved along unobstructed tracks. "Born and bred on Dartmoor by a sheep farmer named George. Top of my class, I was."

"And did you enjoy that, to herd the sheep?"

His eyeless face turned toward her, astonished in the bright moonlight. "Well, of course I did. I mean, it's in my blood, isn't it? It's what I do, and my mother and father before me. Liking it's got nothing to do with it. We're not like your kind, you know; all that dithering about, poor sods, and not knowing what you were supposed to do. To everything a purpose." His voice changed suddenly. "Um, Calypso. Do you like birds?"

She glanced at him, never slackening her pace. "Birds? To eat, you are meaning, or only to admire?"

"Like them. You know, well, to admire, I suppose."

"Yes, very much." Gulls, pelicans, the broad wings sweeping the clouds away, her toes dug into the hot sand and the man with the salty face sailing away. Someday she might learn to cast the memory off; someday she might remember the man's name. But birds . . . "They are very beautiful. On my island they circle over my little house, and sometimes they steal things that grow, to eat.

I stay indoors and watch them. Often I have wished I might fly."

"Good," said Whimsy, and stopped so suddenly that Calypso nearly tripped over him. "Because there's a couple of sodding huge ravens coming straight at us, and I think maybe you ought to talk to them. Ravens have never much cared for dogs."

Black shapes against a blacker sky. The beating of blood in her temples. Here they were, sent to carry her to where she must be. The guardians.

And then the bird who flew in front stopped and hovered, his wings beating the air above her head, and his raspy voice spoke words she wanted to hear.

"Kyria Calypso? Will you—um, and your friend there—please follow us? The others are waiting."

10

Find Out, Find Out

WITH THE FIRST light of morning, a sleepless Max went into action.

He allowed Raj as little sleep as he decently could—waking the Indian at any time always caused a few stirrings of uncomfortably compassionate guilt, since Raj seemed not only to require a lot of sleep, but to actively enjoy it—and explained each of their new roles.

Max had already noticed that Raj's naiveté, such a prominent quality in the Indian's makeup, was at its peak during those first hazy moments between the abandonment of sleep and the acquisition of full consciousness. This morning, with his ears full of birdsong and a sense of purpose running liquid with the blood in his veins, Max felt more than ever that he was dealing with a child—not an average child, whose preoccupations were basically of the self, but one of those rarities, a small quiet boy who played chess and respected books and who could suddenly blind you with the sweetness of his smile and the generosity of his knowledge.

That impression was reinforced rather than lessened by

Raj's physical mannerisms. He passed from night to day, responded to the firm grip on his shoulder and the repetition of his name, without the smallest alteration of the gentle smile, and sat up with all the heartbreaking grace of one who is aware of his body as something intrinsically beautiful. Max, who on this new morning was noticing things he had for too long ignored, for the first time found Raj's pared-down physical perfection somehow depressing. He also noticed, for the first time, the small cloudy circles of growing cataracts in Raj's dark eyes and understood the reason for the thick, disfiguring glasses.

"Yes? What has happened, Max?"

"I never got to finish telling you what happened last night. We were interrupted by the ravens." Was the light somehow brighter this morning, cleaner, more illuminating? And that lovely smell, coming and going with the cool breeze that accompanied the sunrise, was that roses? "We dealt with the ravens and then you fell asleep. I have to go."

"What? What?" And now Raj, perturbation and alarm vibrating in every muscle, came completely to attention; whatever he might have been expecting, it was not this. He fumbled for his glasses and dropped them, enlightening armor that they represented, across the bridge of his long nose. "You are going, going where? And why? Why must you go anywhere?"

"Oh, I'm not going far, or for long. Just a few miles, a few hours. I'll be back. But you must stay here, wait for Calypso and the ravens. The baby's coming early, Gad said. She told me where they are, it's too far to walk, we'll never get there in time, not on foot. I'm walking into Exeter to find us a car to use. It may take a while; there ought to be plenty of cars, but none of them have been started for months and the batteries will all be useless. So . . ."

"So you must find an emergency generator and recharge these batteries. Of course." Max stared, fascinated; Raj, seemingly without recognition of the fact, had been slowly shifting his body as he nodded and spoke, stretching here, testing the pull of muscle and bone there, moving in place. Now he sat calmly, his extreme length tucked tightly into lotus, his breathing a slow pulse that met the morning and then retreated in perfect syncopation. "Very well, I shall stay here to wait for the others. I shall stay until all of us are together again, in this place, yes. If the others are here before you, I will keep them here until you return. If you return before they come, you and I will drive in the car along the railroad tracks until we have found them, and we will take them in with us and go away from here. Will you take some food before you go?"

Exeter, a place of churches and houses and shops; most importantly of all, there was the railway line. Sometime near noon, after three hours of steady walking, Max turned into Exeter's main shopping district and paused to consider his options.

Steal a car. Well, yes, but not just any car off the street; you never knew with an older model, it might have any number of problems, and the last thing he wanted was a machine with a faulty engine or a partially clogged fuel pump, something that would break down in the middle of nowhere and leave them stranded. Exeter was a good-sized place, and there was bound to be an auto dealership or two.

But was a dealership the likeliest place to possess an emergency generator? No, thought Max, it was not. A hospital for that, definitely, find a hospital and keep one's fingers crossed that it was not halfway across the city from the dealership. He could hardly carry a generator for, at the worst, several miles, and he had no wish to drag an acid-filled box in his arms for any distance at all.

There was also a book shop to be found, but that was the easiest of the tasks facing him; he had not gone one block before he found himself looking into a double-fronted window stocked with books. The door, this time, was locked; Max thought for a moment, shrugged, found an empty milk bottle in the gutter and smashed the glass. The maps were stacked in a tidy, colorful display behind the dusty counter, a complete line of both road maps and Ordinance Survey maps for the western counties.

Back out in the street, the maps and something else he had taken stuffed into a plastic carrier bag, he was suddenly overtaken with an odd sensation: eyes, yearning in their need, someone who wished to speak with him. He stopped, shaken and unnerved, and waited; the feeling had been familiar and yet unfamiliar—someone he knew, no one he knew. He set the bag down at his feet and stared down the empty street, his skin prickling. Nothing, no one, not a word; the feeling died. Max shrugged, dismissing it—if someone wanted him they would come again—and turned his attention toward the next necessity.

The dealerships, as he had expected, were next door to one another. Each had handled more than one breed of car. There were five in all: Jaguar-Volvo, Mercedes-Daimler, Porsche-Audi-BMW, Citröen-Peugeot, and, on by far the biggest lot, Range Rover of Exeter, Ltd. Max, for whom the automobile had always held a sneaking fascination, looked longingly at the sleek trucks. Lines of them, he thought, row upon row, parked in their silent serried ranks like the standing stones in Brittany, or the heads on Easter Island. They were the pith and muscle of man's greatest invention, able to handle any terrain, drive through any storm, push through any wall, emerge triumphant over the worst of roads.

Yet, in the end, he decided against them. Max knew a fair bit about the internal combustion engine and the machines those engines powered; taking that knowledge and his needs, weighing them against the pleasure he took in the great trucks, he regretfully turned his back on the low mileage they would get for each gallon of petrol used and, instead, opted for a Volvo. The Swedish cars were roomy, comfortable, dependable, easy to drive; they would get twice as many miles as the trucks would for the fuel provided, and the estate wagon had a large enough fuel tank, if filled to capacity, to carry all of them to their destination without any need to refill it.

The cars had been displayed by model: four-doors here, two-doors there, all-terrain vehicles grouped by model number. The estate wagons were kept at the back of the lot, fifteen of them, all sizes and colors. They made a metallic rainbow, their noses parked against the drab fence, their paint gleaming wickedly in the sunlight. On the windscreen of each car was a cardboard placard, and each placard bore a different number.

Max walked into the little office where the keys would be kept, hanging by display number on a pegboard. There he made an interesting discovery.

One of the keys was missing.

He stood for a moment, wondering, his eyes narrowed to slits. He knew precisely which key was not in its place; he had counted fifteen estate wagons back there. There were fourteen keys. The empty hook leaped to the eye, surrounded by bright red plastic numbered tags.

Footsteps, light and untroubled, sounded behind him. He wheeled to face the intruder.

For some moments, they regarded each other in silence. The boy was about fourteen, dark-haired, smiling a wide easy smile of welcome; he was, incredibly, dressed in a mechanic's overall that bore the name of the dealership in red letters. From beneath the overall poked ragged blue jeans and mismatched shoes; he wore no socks, and his hands were dirty.

The boy spoke first. "Morning, mate. Can I help you?"

Max, whose head was already reeling from his encounter with this strange apparition, suffered another shock at the traditional greeting. Really, this was turning out to be a most unsettling day. He pulled himself together.

"Good morning. I was hoping I might, ah, purchase an estate wagon."

"Purchase?" The cheerful face wrinkled. "Well, as to that, I don't rightly know. I mean, we *used* to sell them, that's true, but I don't think . . ."

"I need one." Max bit back on impatience; obviously, this insane game must be played using the old rules. "Did you—do you work here?"

"Well, I did. On weekends, you know. I was learning to be an auto mechanic." The boy sauntered over to the desk and rummaged in a drawer; he produced a small camping stove, a battered tin pot, a pair of china mugs with, again, the name of the dealership in red. "Time for a cuppa. Join me?"

"Thank you." Was this really happening? Yes, it was. There was something tantalizingly familiar about the boy, a resemblance Max couldn't place. "About this estate wagon."

"Yes, well, I couldn't properly sell you one. I could let you have one free, if you liked, but I couldn't sell you one. It wouldn't be right, since they don't properly belong to me. So I couldn't take your money. Anyway, money's not good for much these days, is it. Milk or black?" He carefully lit the little stove and measured bottled water into the teapot, humming gently under his breath as he struck a match.

"Ah, black, please. Sugar, if you've got any." Max suddenly recognized the familiarity in the boy's face; he was like Raj, not in feature or blood but in the gentleness of his honesty, the placidity of his speech. The boy's hands, oil-stained and deft, busied themselves with spoons, tea bags, a tin of condensed milk. He smiled up at Max. "Was there any one in particular you were wanting?"

"Any one will do, so long as it runs." The conversation was beginning to take shape now; Max accepted a steaming cup from the boy, nodded his thanks, sipped the scalding tea. "I'm in a hurry to get a bit north of here, and I require a good reliable car. I thought perhaps, a Volvo. The batteries . . ."

"Can't do better than a Volvo, then." The boy beamed at him, whether in approval of his choice or delight in once again getting to offer this vanished speech to living flesh Max could not have said. "Mind you, the Jags are nice, very nice. Posh cars, finely engineered, beautifully appointed, built for speed and power. Lot to go wrong there, though."

Play the game. "That's what I thought."

"Four carburetors." The dealer's name danced gently as the boy gave a weighty nod. "Four intake manifolds, four exhaust manifolds. Twelve cylinders."

"I know."

"Takes a lot of learning to care for a Jag. They're worth it, though, absolutely. If you've got the time for tinkering, that is." The boy swallowed tea, gave a gentle blowing noise of satisfaction, smiled at Max. "Those batteries, now. They're all good batteries, very strong. So why worry?"

"Well," Max said, and he was aware how feeble he sounded in the face of the boy's expertise, "I was afraid they wouldn't work. Sitting idle all these months."

"Idle?" The boy looked shocked. "Poor sort of mechanic who'd let his batteries die on him. I keep my cars in good working order, I'll have you know."

The boy seemed honestly offended. Max spoke warmly, and from the heart. He felt almost giddy with relief. "I'm sure you do. You're the best mechanic I ever met, knowledgeable and scrupulous, and I've known quite a few mechanics in my time. My name is Max, by the way. Yours?"

"Mick." The sweetness of the boy's smile, his obvious pleasure at the compliment, brought home to Max that he was dealing with little more than a child, however complete his understanding of his own obsession. Yes, the boy was like Raj, and in more ways than one.

Mick rose to his feet. "If you're done with your tea,

let's have a look at the wagons. You pick your color, I'll pick the key, we'll hose her down together. I keep all the tanks full, but I can give you a ten-gallon can of petrol for safety's sake, if you'd like. No way of knowing whether those motorway rest-stops will have kept their petrol pumps in good working order. Shall we?''

There were faces above her, soft breathing, a bright ring of worried eyes. The pillow slip was creased and uncomfortable to lie against, and a tingling in her right arm meant she had slept on it, cutting off the circulation. Stupid thing to do . . .

''Are you better?''

Julía, who had been staring through half-opened eyes for some minutes, blinked. The bed was hot and sticky with her perspiration, the room full of light; what was she doing, sleeping in the middle of the day? She rarely took naps. It must be some bizarre result of late pregnancy . . .

She remembered.

''No, it's all right.'' Though Julia had said nothing, had in fact scarcely moved, Gad had seen the sudden panic in her eyes, a stiffening of her face, and she spoke at once. ''You're fine, the baby's fine. You had a shock, that's all, but everything's better.''

''Better?'' A huge ringing voice, cathedral bells in her belly, a carillon shaping words against an empty world. The walls of the room dissolving around her. A sense of danger, a sense of threat . . . She stole a hand down to touch her abdomen, and spoke weakly. ''Better? Never.''

''Truly.'' Gad again, and why were the others so quiet? Dilly's fox face was solemn; Maddy nestled quietly in her sister's arms with her wide brown eyes fixed on Julia's face. Ben stood a little apart, his eyes closed, his face blank.

Julia sat up, her eye catching the beautiful sweep of lawn through the tall bedroom windows, Whiskey and Simon standing like ornamental rocks, their heads tilted toward her. She lifted one hand to rub her eyes; the hand seemed too weighty for her slender arm to carry.

"A shock," Gad said quietly. "You felt something wrong, something out of kilter, and the child reacted. Didn't it?"

"Reacted?" Julia, who had stood unsteadily, suddenly sat down again; she was very dizzy. Her laughter bounced off the walls, a harsh avian sound, and her voice was bitter. "I suppose that's one way of phrasing it. Delicate and tactful. Do you know, Gadabout, I'm not happy about this. Not at all. Why are you looking at me like that?"

But Gad, intent and sympathetic, said nothing. Julia's bitterness was intolerable, fierce, a flame that nearly choked her, offered to reduce her to ash. "Why me? What did I do to deserve all this, anyway? I spent a night with a handsome man, that's what, no more than any other woman ever did. And what have I got from it? What have we all got? I have the pleasure of knowing that I'm personally responsible for the deaths of a few billion people, and I'm pregnant with a child that isn't human. 'Reacted'!" The vicious anger soared, reached a flaring pitch, and faded to tears. "What am I carrying here, Gad? Why me, anyway? If that filthy lout had to choose someone, why me?"

"Don't you know?" Gad came to sit beside her; the others, living statuary in the opulent bedroom, held still. The cat's voice was gentle now. "It was the poem you wrote, for one thing. 'The Liar's Game.' Max heard it; it was a sign to him. He didn't choose you, Julia. You chose yourself. He simply recognized you. I don't say he handled it well; I don't say he did right, not warning you. He should have done, and when he gets here you have every right to wring his neck for it, not that wringing his neck will do any good. But he'd waited two thousand years for that sign. You can't really blame him for acting on it, you know."

"Two thousand—what are you talking about?" Julia lost once more in her wretchedness, had heard only the last sentence. Black eyes, tunnels into time. She had said that herself. A year ago this would have been ridiculous, absurd, not to be believed.

But anything was possible now. Some kind of internal gears had shuddered into movement, clicked one space, and all the universe was in that dark shadowland where all laws are revoked, all conceptions of normalcy suspended, all bets are off. Understanding, if not acceptance, was a heartbeat away now; it was time to know. She had been shying away from it since Gad had told her the truth, and she could hide from it no longer. And there was one thing Gad had not told her, the heart of the mystery, and she needed to know.

Julia looked around the room at the others, and turned back to stare directly into the cat's yellow eyes. She spoke simply. "Who is Max, Gad? Who is he really?"

"Max," Gad said sadly, "is just a man. No more than that, that's the truth, or at least it was true once. His name was Ahasuerus; he came from mixed Greek and Hebrew blood, and lived near a little hill in Palestine. The hill, by the way, was at that time a favorite spot for a rather barbaric pastime, something involving nails and pain and two lengths of wood hammered together. I see you understand me.

"One day he heard a procession going by and he went out to see. First mistake. It was a troop of Roman soldiers escorting some of their fresher victims to the top of the hill; one of the victims was a man called Jesus Christos, a preacher and philosopher with a rather unusual bloodline. Ahasuerus had, has, a streak of pettiness in him, and he took a sudden irrational dislike to this Christos bloke. Second mistake. He decided to do a spot of teasing, telling Christos to walk faster. Christos was carrying a rather heavy wooden cross at the time, so the gibe was both nasty and effective. That was his third mistake. I'm sure you've heard the official version of the story."

I go, but you remain.

The small Sunday school with its institutional green walls. The ineffectual little rector with his popping blue eyes, reading bits from the Children's Bible. The words, subtly altered from the original for children's ears and read in the rector's fussy pedantic little voice, seemed to sound once more. *And Ahasuerus spoke unto the Son of God, taunting him, that he should walk faster. And the Son of God spoke unto Ahasuerus: I go, but you remain . . .*

There had been a picture in the Children's Bible. Julia remembered her fascination with the gaudy colored plates, the ugly guilt-provoking scenes with which Christianity traditionally indoctrinated its young. A dark-haired man facing a white-haired man. One carried a cross. The other stood with his legs apart, a small cat between his ankles.

No.

"Oh, yes, that was me. I'd been there for the Son's birth, I was there for the death; that's my job, you know. In at the birth, in at the kill. In any case, Christos had a fairly nasty streak of his own, and he not unnaturally resented this bloody little sod teasing him at a time like that. So he laid a curse on him."

"A curse." She was losing her mind; none of this was happening, these words were not being spoken, this tale was not being told. Please, she silently begged whoever might be listening, let this be impossible, let me have a world full of people and noise and laughter, busy feet, history moving, no ghosts or no shadows. Make it be as it was. Please . . .

"Yes, a curse. I'll go faster, but you get to stay here until I come again." Gad shook her head. "Very simple, really. Only the disciples misinterpreted what was actually meant by that, and everything got cocked up."

"How?" Dilly had set Maddy on the floor at Julia's feet and was listening intently, her attention caught. Julia, grateful for Dilly and suddenly desperate for human contact, pulled the baby into her arms. Gad's voice, precise and patient, continued its impossible explanation.

"He meant, you see, to curse Ahasuerus with something as close to immortality as he could. A nasty thing to do; I'm immortal myself, and believe me, it's no day at the beach. What he meant was this: You were nasty to me at the wrong moment, you sod. You want me to walk faster, fine. I'll walk faster, but you get to stay here until my spirit, the spirit that guided me, is born into human flesh again. Until I come again, a new life, a new turn, the return of the Godhead." Gad glanced at Dilly, then at Julia. "You see?"

"No." She was clutching Maddy now, holding the child too tight for comfort, and the word was a lie. She did see, dimly and distantly. But . . .

Gad sighed deeply. "Think, Julia. For two thousand years, your people have been waiting for the Second Coming, expecting to see Christ as he was when he died. But that's not possible. It was never possible. When the flesh is gone it's gone, period, the end. Christ wasn't a man, not in the proper sense; even his church knew that much, and they managed to get everything else wrong along the way. He was an envelope for a spirit, that's all, for the light at the top of the wheel. His spirit, what you'd mistakenly call a soul, was only his on loan. He happened to come as a representative of the pantheon that crested the wheel before him: there was the father, he came as the Son. This last bunch, the Jehovans, are a greedy lot with a passion for continuance; they passed that on to you."

"Oh!" Ben, leaning against the far wall, broke his long silence. A pleased smile was stamped across his face. "What you mean is, the spirit's always the same, but the way people understand it is always different. And the people that heard him say that to what's-his-name at the foot of the hill took it to mean that he himself would be back, just as he was when he left. And that's wrong. Right?"

"Exactly." Gad's gratitude was enormous. "Now, that normally wouldn't have caused any trouble; you people insist on gods, and you never get it completely right. The problem is, what with millions of people chanting their own interpretation of his words right back at him for so many years, that the Son got to believing them. And they were wrong. He came to believe that the spirit was him, that he was the spirit, that one day when the time was right he would come back. But that doesn't happen; he's had his two thousand years, that's all he gets. One turn of the wheel, then change. When his turn was over it was over, that's all, bob's your uncle, and he had to hand the spirit to someone else. There was never going to be any second coming, not for him. As for the spirit, it's more like the tenth coming than the second.'' As if she had heard Julia's unspoken question, her voice grew gentler. ''And that's why everyone died. It wasn't random, Julia, anymore than Max's choice of you as the mother was random. Nothing's random, remember that and you'll live a saner life. The people who died were those who would never have accepted a new god, the people who could never, well, *unlearn* what they thought they already knew. They would have taken your child and killed it, rather than relinquish what they already believed. None of it was accidental, my love, none, none, none. You made it happen, and Max made it happen. Beginning, ending, we all contributed. Do you see?''

''Good grief.'' Maddy's skin was silken against her, her hair smelled fresh and clean; in Julia's own belly the new spirit lay at rest, waiting for its time. She looked down past the baby's head to her swollen stomach and began to laugh, ironically at first. Then the irony dissolved into honest amusement and tears of laughter began to stream down her face. Her whole body shook with it; she laughed until her muscles refused to support her and she had to set Maddy down on the floor. The others watched her as she rocked in ecstasy, gasping for breath.

'' 'The Liar's Game,' '' she wailed. '' 'The Liar's Game.' Don't any of you see how perfect that is? I wrote a poem about life and death that happened to also sum up the entire Christian mistake and Max heard it and that's not what the poem was about. He saw it as the ultimate omen, don't you see, he misinterpreted the poem in just the same way the disciples misinterpreted Christ's words, and he acted on it and everyone died. It's history repeating itself. Oh, lord, oh bloody hell,'' she gasped, clutching her sides and trying to catch her breath, ''don't let me die of laughing.''

Ben was grinning, not understanding Julia's amusement but infected by it nevertheless. Dilly, bewildered, looked from Julia, racked with silent painful laughter on the big bed, to where Gad sat silently watching her.

''Do you mean,'' she asked the cat haltingly, ''that it was all a mistake? Everyone died because of a mistake?''

Gad did not answer at once. She continued to watch Julia, who was slowly regaining control of herself. She watched her sit up and reach, with trembling hands, for a tissue to wipe the tears of mirth away.

''No mistake,'' Gad said quietly. ''No mistake at all. Nothing is ever random. Julia was the one. It's another conundrum, you see; words have many meanings, and Julia's understanding of her own words is only one of many ways to understand. If it was a mistake, do you think we would all be gathered around, waiting for this child to be born, waiting for the others?''

Julia's lips were shaking, but not with laughter this time. ''Others. What others?''

''We're incomplete,'' Gad said obliquely. ''Only one magus, that's Ben here; there are two more to come, and the father as well. I tried to tell you yesterday, Julia, but you wouldn't let me. The child's on its way. So is Max.''

Old Trout lay near the surface, the sun playing off his many-colored scales. He was listening to stories, told to a large woolly sheepdog by a vivid girl with a face like flame.

The words were pouring out of her, a rainbow of history slamming through a broken dam. For years past counting she had taken her life and put it into songs, songs that were given to the gulls and the fish and the lush flowers of her garden. The songs were taken by the wind and the waves, carried in the pollen that was caught in the upper air, distributed across the sky to settle in fertile ground. New flowers grew in distant places, emitting Calypso's scent, and the words settled into other people's hearts and minds, to be reborn as legends or theories on library shelves.

Now she was walking on alien soil, far from the sea, and the marvelous terrible words forced their way out to the avid ears of the living.

It was called Santorini, an island in the southern seas. I knew of it, of course; shaped like a shell, a jewel cast up by the water to rest with its face to the sun. There were people there, women in their white skirts with the red dust catching at the hems. The men went down to the shore and put their little ships into deeper water; they netted fish, the finest the sea could offer, and brought it home to sell or feed to their families. The children swam naked in the waves.

It was a heart of men, that place, but a heart of fire too. The island had a mountain, and atop the mountain was a cone, a cone with a hole in it, and steam blew out of it. Sometimes there was ash, sometimes hot rock, thick and liquid as mud. The ground would rumble and move; the people should have been frightened, but they grew accustomed, you see. When the buildings would shake, they would steady themselves against the walls and curse. You never see danger, until it's far too late.

Under the island, the sea floor was seething all the time. Huge rocks would break off, beautiful and terrible with their streaks of fire, and the surface of the harbor would bubble with heat. The people never knew that under the mountain was a little room made of liquid flame. And one day, the walls of the little room collapsed and fell in upon themselves, and all the fire and rock that had been waiting deep down exploded for the open air.

I heard it, though I was many miles from that place; the birds told me later that everyone alive then heard it. One bird told me that across the world, in the Sea of Blood, the explosion had sucked the sea from its bed and then pushed it back in again, and that slaves had run across the dry bottom to freedom; when their old masters came to bring them back, the sea pushed its way back and they all drowned. The sky rained black ash and scarlet rock for long years after.

What? Oh, yes, the island is still there, part of it, at least. It has a different name now, and a different shape, but it's still there. Thera, they call it.

Did you ever hear about the games? They were held on the mainland—women were not permitted to see these games, they would be thrown over the mountains to die if they were caught watching, but I laughed at them and they thought I was a goddess, so I saw the games in spite of them and lived to speak of it to you. Young men would come to Athens, to Salonika, and they would compete with each other on the hillsides and the open plains. Some threw the discus, others raced one against the other, and coins would be given to the best: gold, silver, bronze.

They frightened me, the games: they made me sad. What? Oh, because they were a kind of war, a kind of battle, and no one seemed to realize. After all, I had seen the children of Sparta, hardly more than babies, taken from their families and taught to kill before they could understand what killing was or what it meant. It was a cheap parade of glory, nothing more. Unimportant. The games were like that, and all the players liars, though they didn't know that. It made me weep, weep for their ignorance.

War, always war. Athens against Sparta, Mycenae against Crete. They never learned. Those were the first days of the sky gods, gods for men, and the sky gods always wanted blood; the women and children were forced to offer homage, though they were offered nothing in return. No balance, never any balance. Oh, yes, there were gods for women once, the worship of Earth the Mother, but that was hardly any better. No balance there, either, nothing for the men, you see. No one ever seemed to see the need for balance; I saw it, it seemed so obvious to me. Men and women different, separate, taking sides, each seeing the other as a lesser thing. I never felt that way. That's why I let him go.

Him? Well, that's what I call him; I've forgotten his name long since. He had been to war, another of their foolish wars, this time men fighting over a woman; they always managed to blame their greed on someone innocent. A walled city, he told me that. A thousand ships sailed for the wide plains; one of them, a father, sacrificed his own daughter for a fair wind. Years and years it went on. He told me of heroes, a man whose father was a man and whose mother was a goddess, a priestess of Apollo with true visions no man would believe, a great wooden horse with the army in its belly. Death in the morning, and the day won and lost.

He tried to go home, you know, often. He had a wife whom he swore would wait for him. It's a funny thing; I remember her name, though I've forgotten his. Penelope, she was called. He rarely spoke of her; I suppose that, after all those years away and so much of his heart turned to killing, she didn't seem very real to him anymore.

Yes, he wanted to go home, always, from the day I found him. But he'd angered the sea, and that is never a wise thing to do; we are the sea, we are of it and from it, and we must take its discipline even as we take its bounty. So few understand that. So there were storms, and his boat was wrecked, and he came ashore at my feet, and I took him into my care. Seven years, seven long years, nights in my arms and his skin going black under the heat of my island sun, salting him, healing him.

So many things, so many, so many. Oh, why are the black birds calling? Whimsy, why are you barking? Look, a car!

Old Trout lay in shallow water, warmth above him and cold below, and wept for his great age, the passage of time, the children of man.

11

Let the Magic Do Its Work

IT WAS A Wednesday, although nobody alive in the world remembered or cared except Julia.

Wednesday in England, midafternoon, and something was beginning to stir. In a small flat in Bloomsbury, a group of children found an expensively bound volume of poetry with funny words across the front, *The Liar's Game*, a game they were unfamiliar with and very curious to explore.

Most of the older ones had long since learned to read, and were appreciative of that magic art; feeling dimly that it would never do to let the gift of language die out, they gathered the younger ones around them and were busily instructing them. They read the words out slowly, carefully, exaggerating the vowels and pronouncing the consonants with small pops and stutters, stopping occasionally to fire abrupt questions at their pupils to make certain that they had been listening, that they understood.

The little ones, brows furrowed with concentration—and in a few cases an already dreamlike memory of sitting in school doing this very thing—learned the letters, and the words formed by those letters. After a while a girl of about seven began to hum, a low strange melody; immediately the others took the words they had learned and set them easily to the tune, and the walls of Julia's flat echoed and rang with the words of her destiny.

Wednesday, under a shimmering sky.

At the wheel of a blue Volvo estate wagon, Max gave a little cry and pushed his foot down hard on the brake pedal. There it was again, that sensation, those eyes with their need to talk with him and their owner's inability to do so—vision, in fact, through a brick wall. The frustration behind this inability came through to Max like a clarion call, and it turned him cold.

The others in the car with him had felt nothing, and they patted their safety belts and exclaimed. Max muttered something, shaking his head at Raj's gentle worry and Calypso's eager curiosity, and sat waiting in his shiny new car for his head to clear.

None of his human companions had noticed the sudden stiffening of the dog Whimsy or heard his low growl as he, too, felt a darkness around him. None of them heard the sudden loud croak Mark gave, soaring fifty feet above the hood of the car, as he was suddenly assailed with a vision of a despairing man, a strange anthropomorphic shape anchored in a strange sea; it opened its eyes, the flickering lids producing a booming in his head that was need and passion and a struggle to understand his own ending by someone who had never before needed to comprehend endings, and who was wrapped in a fog of miserable fear that drifted through the nerve centers of the afternoon.

Wednesday.

While the children in London set truth to music and the travelers regrouped to continued their journey, Julia walked slowly out to the stables with Dilly and Maddy at her side. It was not a proper day for going into Sparrowdene, but she was unsettled. She had dreamed the whole night through, dreams she could not quite recall but which had woken her several times, shattering her rest, sending her sweating and upright in her bed, trying desperately to grasp the pictures hovering just out of her reach in a darkened room that, in some way, now felt like a huge hollow vault.

She was so tired that even to walk was an act of courage. Her feet, which during the late stages of her pregnancy had tended to swell, felt like pontoons, and she had a small headache, persistent as rain. Still, she knew this mood; only the panacea of a stroll down Congreve's dim cool aisles and silent conversation with the shade of Eulalie Lufton-Hall would do.

She pushed open the stable doors, the two children and Whiskey pattering behind her. They had not attempted to argue, or to dissuade her from this foolishness, and Gad had surprisingly agreed that it might do her good, so long as she wasn't silly enough to walk the distance. The thought of walking from Sparrow House to Congreve's and back again was enough to make Julia shudder, and she told Gad so.

So Whiskey had cheerfully agreed to pull the pony cart into Sparrowdene, and bring her safely home again. At the last moment, Dilly had elected to accompany her.

The gaily painted cart moved down the gravel drive and swung out onto the Sparrowdene Road. Julia, holding the reins, had in five days adjusted to the new realities so well that she saw nothing strange in closing her eyes and giving Whiskey his head; the two children were silent beside her, and behind her closed lids ran a mélange of darkness, shot with color and light.

When the wave hit her, she kept her eyes closed. She knew it at once for what it was: the child speaking; the first time she had been shocked and frightened but now she was ready for it. Indeed, after the strangeness of the previous night, she had almost been expecting it. She tightened her grip on the leather reins and waited.

This time, the child was not talking to her. The lining of her lids, fragile as shells, stretched into vision; she knew the man at once, he had walked through Regents Park Zoo beseeching the beasts who still held sway there to destroy her, and had been rebuffed. She was not frightened; the fact that she could put a name to him, however fantastic that name might be, lent him solidity. The power had gone out of him, and the sense of threat with it, and he was pathetic.

She looked at the Son of God and felt nothing but sympathy, for he was weeping.

He was walking down the motorway; she couldn't see which motorway—the wide paved multiple lanes could have been any road leading anywhere in the world. Emptied of cars, the long curving tarmac looked strange, and the Son was a tiny painful nonentity against its vastness. As he walked, tears ran down his face and left dark patches against his robe; he wept as a child might, mouth cocked open and eyes screwed into puckered scars in a total abandonment to some limitless grief. The vision was without sound, and the silent tears were, to Julia, unbearable.

And then there was sound, the voice that came from nowhere and everywhere. Julia, the reins to the pony cart never moving in her hands, knew it at once.

Why weep? Is it for yourself, for you own ending, or is it for what had been and what can never be again? You need have no fear of telling me, carpenter's son. I would harm no one and nothing, for that is not my part; I am a protector, not a destroyer.

(A million voices raised in song, echoes of the Hanging Gardens: by the waters they sang, the waters of Babylon)

The Son stopped, listening, and Julia saw a streak of blood on the dusty ground; he had trodden on glass or a sharp pebble, cut his foot, never noticed. His beautiful olive-skinned face was turning to the sky, and his voice was the voice of the dying. Ave Caesar, Julia thought, but the rest of the inscription would not come.

(We lay down and wept)

"I don't want to die," he said simply, and Julia, in whom the words roused an intolerable empathy, yearned toward him. He was not terrible, her enemy. He had been great and now he was not; just a man, flesh and blood like all those lost brothers and sisters, afraid of death.

Like her, like her.

(For thee, Zion)

Is that all, is that why you have fought the truth so long? Did you believe that as I met the light you would go down into the darkness? You won't, you know, at least not immediately. You will live out the life of a man, a child of this earth. You will feel the sun on your face and the rain in your hair; you will go anywhere you wish, learn anything you can. My children will live longer than yours ever did, since all the things to decay them, fear and need and the burdens of those things, died at my beginning. Put your fears aside, my friend. You won't die.

(We remember, we remember)

"I won't die?" The Son stood still, his bleeding feet planted in the dust, and Julia felt the hope in him flicker and swell. "I won't die? How can I not die?"

(By the waters, the waters of . . .)

Is it so bad to be a man again, truly alive again, to live out the time stolen from you because those who knew you were ignorant and superstitious, feeding on mystery, and would not allow themselves to be guarded by one who walked among them? Sixty, seventy, perhaps a hundred years of life is due to you. Let us make peace. Let me love you and guard you. My father is coming to me, even as your father never did; you will meet with him and come to know each other better, and it's high time you did, both of you, for even in your hate you need each other. I am supplanting your place, this is true. But I am also giving you back your life, if you want it.

(For thee, Zion)

"You swear this to me?" The Son was trembling, his thin shoulders shaking like the leaves on an aspen tree.

Believe, Julia thought desperately, wanting to see peace come into the strong sorrowing face, wanting to see him safely wrapped in the enveloping arms of certainty and acceptance. The Bump wouldn't lie to you. Believe.

And the Son, straining, suddenly opened his eyes wide as if he had heard her, listening for the child's words.

There is nothing left to swear on, no relics, no lives, no deaths. Yet, if such things are important to you, then I will swear, and gladly. No more dying, not for you, not for anyone. Your life is in your own hands, and your magic is the magic you make. That is something that was forgotten, and must be learned again; to say Amen is only another way of saying So be it, may the magic do its work. So I will swear.

He was kneeling in the dust and the puddle of blood. It was an attitude of prayer, and yet there were differences; nothing in his posture spoke to Julia of fear or worship or even of need. It was joy, acceptance, and the taut mouth had relaxed into calm . . .

"Sparrowdene just ahead," Whiskey said cheerfully, "where to now?" and Julia opened her eyes. The man and the motorway and the titanic voice with its wonder and generosity were gone, and her companions, human and equine, turned toward her expectantly, waiting for her to speak. She felt her face curve into a smile, and for a moment she saw herself as she really was, a shining receptacle of joy at being alive, love for Dilly's thin face and Maddy's baby charm. Nothing in all the world had ever seemed so beautiful to Julia as she herself did at that moment. She had a place, a real place. She would never again be a stranger in her own world, there would be no more outcasts; all things had flesh, whether or not you could see it. All the world would be protected, and life would go on.

She was unaware of the tears in her eyes, and she laughed aloud. Two children and a horse, though they could not have known where her happiness came from, felt it as their own and laughed with her.

* * *

Wednesday, and the blue Volvo, which had picked up a fine layer of summer dust, hummed north along the motorway.

Mark and Luke, whose presence had been rendered superfluous by Max's acquisition of maps, had elected to escort them anyway. Each had his own reasons for refusing to fly home. Luke, calling to Gad to tell her that their task had been successfully accomplished, received a spoken permission to return to Sparrowdene if they so chose, and a strong underlying impression that she would much rather they didn't. Mark's reason was far less complex; to Luke's intense amusement, he had conceived a shy admiration for Calypso and wanted to keep her in view.

"In love with a human," Luke snorted. "Making a fool of yourself over a human." The day had cooled from scorching to bearable, the sun's lambent eye partly hidden by drifting white clouds. More rain in the air, Luke had decided, and conveyed this opinion to Max. Max had already been told the same thing by Whimsy. He had a deep respect for the instincts of the animal world, and had gravely thanked them both and begun to keep an eye peeled for road signs. Though he needed little sleep and would willingly have driven without pause through a stormy night, Calypso flatly refused to sleep either in a moving car or out under the rain, and Raj was frankly hedonistic when it came to his hours of rest. Beds were clearly indicated.

"I'm not in love," Mark said. "I just—don't you think there's something—"

"Spit it out, spit it out," Luke said irritably, and was astonished at how much he had sounded like John. Must be something to do with being in charge, Luke thought. Mark shot him a quick look and turned his attention away again.

"She's familiar, that's all," he said. "Something about

her makes me think I've seen her before. No need to get so shirty about it."

"All right, all right. Sorry." The car had slowed below a green metal sign: TAUNTON, it said, and gave a mileage figure. Luke watched Max turn the Volvo off the exit ramp, and swung his body to the east to match the car's direction. He was assailed by a sudden picture of Ben's meadow, the wooden easel left out in the rain, its contours swollen and sodden with water, the box of paints lying on the grass. "Familiar. Well, now, maybe. Not to me, though."

"In a dream," Mark said obliquely. "I was an owl, sitting on a big stone temple. Ruins—well, maybe ruins—open to the sky, and she came walking up the hillside. I'd rather not talk about it, if you don't mind. Where are they going now? I thought they were supposed to go north."

"The sign said Taunton. A stop for the night, I guess; they probably don't want to sleep outside in a thunderstorm." The car, with no policemen to stop it and no other vehicles in its way, had picked up speed; another vision flashed by Luke, very clear, this time of Max at the wheel, putting his foot down in a sudden access of sheer enjoyment. He could almost hear Calypso's startled exclamation, and see Raj's gentle smile. Luke fluttered and righted himself; really, he seemed to be seeing things very strongly today. Pictures, in fact, were simply jumping out at him. This was a new development, and not a totally welcome one. He had an uneasy feeling that John regarded strength of vision as his personal prerogative, and would take Luke's unexpected new ability as a personal insult . . .

In the end, Max stopped short of Taunton. He had not gone two miles down the road when Raj, sitting placidly beside him, touched his arm and pointed.

"Look," he said, "a farm. There may be sheep, and goats, and a garage for the car. Very convenient, very close to the road. Also, the birds may take shelter in the garage if they choose. Perhaps Calypso knows how to milk a goat?"

"Of course I can get milk from a goat. On my island I kept goats; they are friendly, and clever, and share their milk very willingly, if you ask them nicely." Calypso, who from the moment of closing the car door had decided that an unventilated automobile smelled like death, poked her head through the open window and craned her neck for a better view of Raj's discovery.

The house was a classic of its kind, early Victorian, practical and strong and very ugly; squat and lime-washed, a monument of solidity, it looked perfectly capable of withstanding a hurricane. There was something intensely comforting about that fact. The garage, a flat modern building in concrete, looked absurdly out of place beside it.

The living quarters were surrounded by several acres of pasture; beyond the distant fences they could just make out rows of what appeared to be cabbages. On the wrought-iron gates that separated the farm from the road was a wooden plaque on which was carved, in ornately curled letters, the legend MERRY FARM.

And there were, indeed, sheep and goats. The two flocks, thick in numbers, ambled up to surround the car; Calypso pushed the door open and squeaked as Whimsy, in immediate recognition of his duty, cleared her lap on the fly to hit the grass before Max had even brought the car to a complete stop. Possibly the sheep recognized an old master of the game, for they backed off bleating and huddled into a tight cautious mob. The goats ignored both sheep and dog, and stared knowingly at Calypso.

There were vehicles in the garage, a tractor and an old Austin; there was also a cord of firewood. Max, who had taken the Volvo to his heart, managed to squeeze it between the two resident machines, taking care not to scrape the blue paint; the two ravens, flying low, swept through the open doors and settled on the rafters. After a brief conference, Max opened the garage's rear windows so that the ravens might have egress if they felt the need. The low rumble of thunder, a familiar voice in the English summer, echoed through the building and was immediately followed by a violent streak of lightning as the sky flashed with heat.

Max, a log under one arm and a small bundle of kindling under the other, kicked the garage doors shut behind him and ran for the house.

Merry Farm, built in the early days of Queen Victoria, had been designed to house a large family in comfort. The family room was spacious and charming; Raj, with Whimsy asleep at his feet, sat on the large chintz sofa facing the stone fireplace and watched Max stack kindling. The Indian, although he would have considered it poor manners to complain, was shivering; the house, which should have been sweltering in the summer heat, had an air of disuse. It was both chilly and musty.

When the fire had caught and was spreading through the logs, Max stood and dusted his hands. "Where's Calypso?"

"She is getting the milk from the goats; also, she has looked in the little room behind the kitchen, the pantry at the back of the house, and she says there is food enough to make a proper meal." The front door crashed shut, and a moment later Calypso poked her head into the living room. Her face was alight with pleasure, and her arms were full.

"Milk," she sang, "goat's milk and wine and chickens, there are chickens too; we shall have roast fowl for our dinner and eggs for our morning meal."

Max, who had taken Calypso's measure from the first moment of laying eyes on her, looked at the laughing girl and the limp bundle of feathers dangling from her left hand with simple respect. "You killed a chicken? My goodness. I suppose you broke its neck?"

Reading criticism into this question, she broke off her singing and gazed at him reproachfully. "You have perhaps a better way to kill chickens? We must eat."

"That is true, although I must say that there is nothing so repulsive as the feet of a dead bird." Raj, who had gone to crouch by the fire, stood and bobbed his head in her direction. "And the chicken, shall I pluck it for you?"

"My thanks; that will save me much time and make the food come sooner to the table. There is flour in the little room, and oil; I shall make bread."

Max watched them go, Calypso crooning with pleasure, Raj courteous and deferential. He was suddenly shaken with a gust of silent laughter. Two thousand years, he thought ruefully, two thousand years, births and deaths and never a bed to call my own, and what does it come to? Making a fire in a country house. A nymph and a holy man. Plucking chickens and baking bread . . .

"There's someone at the door."

Max jumped; he had been so lost in his reverie that he had forgotten the presence of Whimsy on the hearth rug behind him. The dog, who possessed a quality of quiet rarely found in his species, had lifted his head. The round ears were cocked and alert. "Can't you hear it, matey? Knocking. At the front door."

But Max did not hear him. It had returned, the feeling of someone watching him, wanting him, needing desperately to somehow communicate with him, and it was stronger than ever this time. Something's happening, he thought, something, and everything he had ever done, ever been, poised and contracted around him in a breathless hush of expectancy.

Vision through a brick wall.

He stood quietly, holding his breath, and heard the soft fall of knuckles against wood. Odd words came into his mind, a soft sly echo, and for a moment he saw ragged people crouched by running water, their tears mingling with the rush and flow of the stream.

(For thee, Zion)

"Someone at the door," he agreed, and went to answer it.

* * *

Since his conversation with Gad, the Son had been trying to do what Max had been doing to him for two thousand years. He had failed every time. However easily the art of summoning someone by the use of finely honed spite may have come to his ancient adversary, he could not do it.

He could see Max perfectly; the fact that his eyes would obey him, while his will would not, only served to add to his frustration. Yet, after the Child had called to him, he was glad that he had failed at first, for his reasons for wanting to speak to Max had changed.

He had walked without stopping from Regents Park to the west country, his spirit a cloudy confusion. Two days and two nights he had strained to do what he had never before done; he had not taken human form since his physical death, and he had almost forgotten how. It was abhorrent, though necessary, and his hatred of this long-abandoned shell of skin and bone was intensified by the unacknowledged realization that his very ability to attain it was a sign of his returning mortality.

Well, so be it, amen; if godhood was to be stripped from him, then the conditions of godhood went by the board. Abnegation meant freedom, and he could kill Julia himself.

He had not, however, counted on the permanence of the change. Once attained, the physical world proved greedy. It took his spirit, more human than deity now, it surrounded him in a hungry claustrophobic shell, and would not let go. It was the final bitterness, the final proof of the cataclysm; the fate of an ousted god, tormented by the minutiae of the corporeal world, stuck in the body of man long after the body of man had died out.

You will feel the sun on your face . . .

With those words, that gift, the bitterness had lifted from him, an insubstantial mist of nonsense and wasted regret burned mercifully away. He did feel the sun on his face; he felt the sharp tingle of a cut foot, too, and the summer wind gentle on his back. How had he forgotten the pleasure of these things, how could he have forgotten? Had the Child been right? Had he floated in limbo too long?

And the rain in your hair . . .

Thunder shook the green-casted horizon, and the Son, stepping back from the open road into the shelter of the concrete overpass, looked into the heat-hazed distance. The embankment had been charmingly planted with grass, and above his head a large green sign said TAUNTON. The first large drops of rain blew into his eyes, another forgotten sensation given the flesh of miraculous new life. He laughed, the strange rusty croak of a man who has not laughed once during the passage of his own destiny, and balled his hands into fists to rub the water, rain or tears or both, from his eyes.

Sixty, seventy, perhaps a hundred years of life are due to you.

Blessings, blessing, the first gift of the Child, and it was all for him. *Benedictus domini*, or was it *domina?* No way to tell that, and it didn't matter; whatever the Child was, those who lived would sing praise to its name, and he would be there to hear. The wheel had turned, the hand was dealt, and all that remained of his anger was joy. He closed his eyes, delirious, and summoned up the picture of Max as best he could.

Even in your hate, you need each other . . .

Why had he never seen it? The simple truth of the statement was staggering; shadow and light, each incapable of reacting without the other, they were two weights balancing on some ludicrous scale with no name. Had Max not taunted him, given him that surge of anger and hate to imprint his last earthly moments, he could have faded into shadow long before. Nothing else would have been different; the masses who feared the abyss would still have lauded his name in terror and ecstasy, the cathedral bells would have tolled at Christmas and Easter, the disciples who controlled the world in his name would still have centuries of the blood of nonbelievers on their arrogant hands.

But would he have been aware of all these things? A shadow in the hinterland of time passing, would he have known, could he have cared?

Benedictus, amen, let the magic do its work.

The rain had begun to fall in earnest now, light sheets of it drenching him to the bone, and he reveled in it. Ahasuerus, Max, he thought, balance, where are you? and he closed his eyes and searched. He did not hear the sound of a car passing by on the blind side of the concrete embankment under which he stood.

A blue car. People, though he could not see their faces. It traveled on a wide road, twin to the road he himself stood on; it turned slowly under a green sign that said TAUNTON, twin to the very sign he stood under. A large house, sheep in the fields, violently backlit by a sky that had gone from celestial blue to mustard and purple and saffron. Smoke coming, fitfully at first and then with greater density, from one of the chimneys, carrying across the sky like a caress for the natural world.

The Son opened his eyes. He stepped out into the open road and stared at the sign: TAUNTON. There were marks in the slick wet coat of dust, tire marks. They wound away up the road to Taunton, the tread lines deepening where Max had negotiated the car at corners and turns.

My father is coming to me.

It had been many years since the Son had known humility. What would Max say to him? Would he slam the door in his face, refuse to take him to see the Child born, deny him, disbelieve him?

Only one way to find out. Only one way.

He reached Merry Farm much sooner than he had expected. It leaped out of the landscape at him, this house he had seen with his eyes closed from the motorway; complete in every detail, there were the sheep in the rain and the plume of smoke. He stood at the gate, his hand trembling as he laid it on the iron latch; alien territory and no sense of welcome. A distant laughter floated across the field to him, female laughter, high and happy, laced with incomprehensible singing that joined with the whining tenor of the wind, sweetening it.

With a sense of doing something momentous, the Son walked to the front door and brought his knuckles against it. There was a hush in the air, the very sky seeming to hold its breath, awaiting the outcome. He heard a murmur of voices, footsteps sounding inside the house, and the door opened. A man stood there, a man of compact body and eyes that were chips of onyx; the Son saw the long fingers whiten as recognition came, and they grew rigid against the doorjamb.

"Oh my god," said Max.

"Not anymore." The fear of rebuff had melted away with the grief and the bitterness; here he was, the adversary, the man the Son had consigned to wander the earth, and he was the one at a disadvantage. He stood like a stuffed dummy, his black eyes staring and his jaw slack.

The Son suddenly grinned, a smile of pure mischief, irresistible. "Not anymore. I have handed my place to the Child, and the Child has given me back my life. I'd like to be there for the birth, and I was told you were going there."

"What, what?" Max pulled himself together with a visible effort, but he did not move from the door. "You. It *is* you. What, no, it can't be, I don't believe it."

"Ask the guardian; she knows. Or ask the Child, that's even better. Do it; I'll wait." The Son saw the change in Max, the golden light that came up in his eyes as he recognized truth and heard the echoes of it ring through his head, and he laughed again. He could almost hear the Child's voice, the voice of rivers running and winds that blow, speaking its beautiful promise of the only eternal life that was worth anything at all.

Max stepped back from the door. He moved like a man in shock. Yet there was no invitation to be read from this, and the Son understood that he was now dependent on Max's belief and generosity, for he had come to Max as a supplicant, a fellow in need, asking his aid. He spoke plaintively.

"My friend, my enemy, my last and best reason for staying. You probably won't believe this, but it's good to see you. Please, may I come in out of the wet?"

12

Joseph's Coat

"TALK TO ME," Max said. "Talk to me, tell me, what?"

The fire in the family room was stoked and burning, the mustiness of disuse had been warmed from the walls of Merry Farm. Max, since hearing the strength and brightness of the Child's voice issuing its incredible confirmation of the Son's transmogrification, had been dazed in a way that is the only logical result of an eternity's worth of preconceived notions being blown to dust.

Under this cloud of unreality, Max continued to function. He moved back from the door and let the Son come in. He brought him in to meet a delighted Calypso and a strangely unsurprised Raj. He watched with an expressionless face as the Son fondled the dog Whimsy with a tentative hand. And, as the evening relaxed into night, he took his place at the mahogany dinner table opposite the face he had last seen spitting eternal hatred under the clouds of the Holy Land and which now flamed with goodwill.

"I wish you would stop saying 'what,' " the Son said

happily. "I'll talk to you if you wish, but there isn't much to tell. I haven't been doing very much all these years. You don't, you know, not in my position; there really isn't much to do. You're the one who ought to be talking; think what I've missed, after all."

Raj chuckled, a thick fat sound of pleasure. "He is correct, Max, yes. Where he has been there was no laughter, no pleasure, nothing to see unless he looked down." He turned the reflective glasses toward the Son. "Did you ever look down at us, watch us?"

"Of course. Well, in a manner of speaking, that is. Not down, because I wasn't up."

Calypso, idly picking over the remains of a chicken wing, paused in her exploration of gristle and skin to stare at the Son. "Where, then?"

"Oh, I don't know. Here, there, all over the place. Mostly in a gray haze, growing fat. Feeding on my own name, in fact." The beautiful olive-skinned face had clouded; somehow the memory of that stasis, a state that had represented all that was desirable until this afternoon, was disturbing. "I can't explain it, not properly. It was like—well, like—"

"Like being in a colorless room with darkened windows, and once in a brief while you could make out shapes through the glass?"

"Very much like that." The Son drank wine from a fluted crystal glass, a far cry from the little clay cup he had used at that last meal, with the Twelve around him like frightened children, wondering what was to come. One of you will betray me; lord, will it be me? He shook the memory away and, meeting Max's eyes, saw that they had gone momentarily blank and knew that Max had shared the memory with him. He spoke quickly, impulsively.

"Tell me what you've been doing all these years. Tell all of us. What did you do, what did you see?"

"Colors," Max said slowly. The table was well lit; Calypso had found a silver candelabra ten branches strong and set it between the plates of food. The wallpaper in the dining room, red velvet richly flocked with white, throbbed sinuously at them as the lines of flame chased across it. "Colors. Gray skies, blue seas, the green and brown of the lands of my birth. Golden wheat, growing in fertile fields, the pods turning dusty brown and blowing away from me. So many places, all of them bright, all of them colors."

The Son said nothing, but his eyes had dimmed. A tear forced its way down Max's cheek. "I made my way down to Egypt after they crucified you. Egypt and then to the Lebanon. I walked through the souks there, looking at the vendors with the djellabas—green and red and the purple dye they used, so rich it could break your heart." He shook his head. "So many colors."

"Why do you keep saying that?"

Max turned to face Calypso, who had asked the question with the directness of a child. "Because the colors are what I remember best. It's easier, far easier, to remember only the outer shells; much more difficult, you know, to steel yourself and map the soul. It was hard, you see, hard to look at the faces. They would age, grow old, die, and the people they loved, their children and their mates, would grow old with them. Natural balance. Order. Not me, though. I was stuck, and as long as I was stuck I knew I could never allow myself to love anyone. Not a single living soul; it would have been too painful."

"That was the idea." The words were brutal but the Son's lips were trembling; the pain in Max's face was naked and indecent.

Max turned his own glass in one hand, and stared into the deep red wine. "Yes. I remember a girl in the deserts of Africa, brown as a nut, slender as a reed. Ten years she kept me warm in the tents at night, Ashtoki her name was. Five copper necklaces at her throat, ornamental scars in her cheeks. Sometimes the tribe would all come together for a sacred dance; hunts, you know, or flood season, something to be placated. She, all the women, would paint the scars with red ocher and indigo. Colors."

Calypso's mouth shone with chicken grease. Standing, she wiped her hands carefully on a paper napkin and came to put her arms around Max's shoulders, holding him close to her, laying her cheek against his white hair. "So much sorrow. Tell us more; we have all done something like this, all of us."

Max's hands came up to clutch involuntarily at the soft arms. "What I'm trying to say is that I can't recall; well, Ashtoki is a perfect example. I can't remember her features; I can't remember her personality. I can't remember Ashtoki herself, the woman she was, the soul within. I can only remember the colors of her life. Nothing was real to me anymore; it all ran together, became a canvas or a tapestry."

"That was how you protected yourself against the pain?"

"Yes, Raj. And make no mistake, pain there was and plenty of it." He shifted his gaze to the candlelight. "Oh, I saw things. I saw so much I nearly drowned in it. I went to Rome, such a bizarre place, wealthy families served by undernourished slave children. Formal fights in the arenas for the pleasure of the well-to-do."

"I remember," the Son said softly. His eyes, too, had found the candles; something moved in them, no more than a vagrant memory of half-naked people, each with a roughly outlined fish painted on his bare chest, huddled under flickering torches. "I think I remember."

Max looked up and spoke eagerly; he had never spoken of his life and something, some internal dam, had been breached. "And do you remember when the Hun swept down toward Rome, the fields across Asia Minor dotted with crosses? They may have held the Romans in contempt, but they adopted a few of their nastier habits."

Bodies hanging on crosses, iron nails, the hot sun on slowly blackening skin and the raucous cries of the scavenger birds wheeling overhead . . . "Tell us more," the Son said.

Max emptied his wine down a throat gone suddenly dry. "Gaul and Britain, full of savages and soldiers. There was a woman there, a woman of the Iceni, she got her people together and they cut an entire Roman legion to pieces. In the name of freedom, they said." A spasm of silent painful laughter shook him. "What a joke. It made no difference, of course, in the end; does it ever? After all, mathematics works wonderfully, even when they're backward. There were thirty thousand Romans there, all armed to the teeth, and perhaps fifty thousand naked savages armed with spears and stones. That equation worked itself out nicely. You take my point, I suppose? The people didn't matter, the weapons did. Isn't physics wonderful? I left the islands after that; Christianity was already taking hold of things; it was actually rather nice in those days, a breath of hope."

"Yes, oh yes." More streaks through the remembered gray haze, the Son's name chanted to wondering crowds. Max's voice, harsh and angry, shattered the pretty picture.

"Charlemagne. William. It didn't stay nice for long."

"In my country," Raj said before the Son could speak, "we had a different worship there, yes. Not Christian. Older. It was very cruel sometimes but also better in some ways; we understood nature, you see, nature of the earth and sky and also human nature. Christianity did not. That is balance. But worship always breeds barbarism, and you cannot have a change without someone paying the cost."

"Did it have to be that way?" None of them had heard this passion in Max's voice before; it lashed out, searing them. His anger was almost solid, visible, fists of rage and a frustration nurtured over too long a time. The words spilled out of him in a breathless flood. "Did it? In Africa there were tribes that worshiped fertility, the female principle, and the men suffered there; breeding stock, that's all they were, no rights and no say, dehumanized. The children of Christos here took that and turned it around, fixing it so that the men had the benefit and the women none. But they never changed it; same old story, new names, that's all. It was supposed to get better; isn't that the whole point of change? Why couldn't it have gotten better?"

He hunched across the table toward where the Son sat, with head bowed, the ancient scars on the backs of his hands livid in the uncertain light. "You were the chosen, the supplanter, the hope of something better. And what did you bring them? Death to Jews and Moors in Spain—I swear your mother must have turned in her grave. Wealth in your houses of worship while the poor who had raised you to godhood starved and died in the streets. To the sick and the hurting, promises of an eternal salvation that never came. To women who could barely feed themselves, threats of eternal damnation if they didn't produce children for the church. Bodies stretched and broken on the rack of people whose only crime was that they couldn't reconcile themselves to what your disciples taught. Do you know, I think that was the worst part of my punishment, listening to the descendants of the earliest believers perpetrating violence and stupidity in your name. Why, Christos? You could have stopped it; none of those things were what you taught during your lifetime. I was there, I know, I remember. You never said that women were to be pariahs, that children had no rights as human beings, that the animal world lived only to be slaughtered. How could you let it go on?"

A dreadful silence fell on the small room. They were all staring at him, even as the Twelve had stared at him at that other table, waiting for his words. The words, that other time, had been there: one of you will betray me. Now it was he who was accused of betrayal and he had no words, for he simply did not know the answer. Yet something must be said; Max's question demanded a reply. And as painful as the question was, it was good for him to think about such things; the haze of abstraction was gone, never to return.

"I think," he said finally, "I think that what happened was that I lost my grasp of things. Time erodes, you know, even in the shadowlands, and I was handicapped from the start; no humor, and no understanding of nature, just as Raj said." His voice took on a note of defensiveness. "I told you, I could only see what was going on in bits and pieces. Now I'm beginning to wonder if what I saw, what I heard, was only what my Church intended me to see and hear."

"And what did you see and hear?" Calypso, still holding Max's shoulders like a mother trying to soothe a restless baby, spoke softly.

"Colors." He looked across the table at Max and smiled, a smile like sun breaking over water. "You're right, Max. It's the colors you remember after so much time; the gold of a saint's relic held aloft against gray stone walls, the scarlet of a cardinal's robe. No faces, nothing with any individuality; nothing to separate one from another. Just colors. I heard my name ringing from a billion throats, and the music had a color all its own. Colors."

"Red for blood." Max had begun to shake; reaction was setting in. "I went back to my homeland, you know. Islam had taken hold by then . . ."

"But Islam was only another kind of Christianity," Raj said with sudden authority. "Did you not know this?"

"Of course I knew it. The point is, the followers of Islam didn't." Max laughed, but the laughter was bitter, and held no amusement. "My timing was never what you'd call wonderful; incredible as it may seem, I got back there just in time for the Second Crusade. More of the same, would you believe it? Richard Plantagenet executed hundreds of Islamic prisoners; the plain truth was that he couldn't spare the money to feed them, but he announced in a ringing head tone that he was killing these people in the name of Christ. And Saladin, sending boys no older than ten to their deaths under the hooves of the Christian militia."

The empty laughter rang out again. "Is that ironic, or isn't it? Both on the same side, and they killed each other, never knowing the truth. Colors."

"I loved a man once, a man of the western sea," Calypso sang, and the others twisted in their seats to stare at her; the music in her voice was wild and haunting, impossible to ignore. "And you are right, both of you, all of you. Brown salty skin, blue water, the timbers of his little craft bleaching whiter than bones under the sun of my island. I remember all these things, but the man himself? Was he good or evil, driven, more or less than what I felt him to be? I remember the tones of his life with me. I wish I might remember his name."

"Odysseus," said Max, surprised. "Everyone knows that, little nymph. Odysseus of Ithaca. Another of my kind, you might say; a wanderer."

She gave a little shriek and danced away from him, a firefly in a dirty white dress. "Yes, yes, that was it! After all this time, I have his name again! Oh, Max!"

At the far end of the room, Whimsy lifted his head from his paws to stare at them sleepily. He yawned hugely, his pink tongue lolling, the gray and white tips of his coarse fur looking soft in the moving light.

"What's all the noise about, friends?" he asked amiably. "What's going on? Did I miss something?"

"Trout?"

Gad sat on the river's edge, crouched and waiting. Her summons was soft and imperative and her tail twitched. Above her head the sky had darkened into lambent threat, and the ground by the waterside was already muddy.

"Trout, I need you."

Bubbles, iridescent and small, broke sharply against the surface. "Guardian? Is that you?"

"Yes." My, she thought, but the old one was a thing

of beauty and majesty; he lay like a thick fleshy dagger, as still as she. "Trout? Listen now."

"What is it, gray cat?"

"I think it's starting, and I think it's ending, and I need your eyes. Mine don't seem to be working just now."

The water rippled suddenly, whether with rain or motion Gad could not tell. "Starting. Do you mean the Child?"

Gad spoke rapidly, pulled by urgency. "Julia went into Sparrowdene today. The two children went with her, and the horse pulled the cart. She saw something, heard something, on the way." Gad drew a deep breath; she, too, had sensed the confrontation Julia had witnessed, but she had been unable to make out a single word of it. Gad had never before experienced this exclusion, this feeling of being shut out, and it had seriously disturbed her.

"Well?"

"It was the Son, trout. Coming to slay her, and so preserve himself. She saw him; I saw him. I think the Child intervened, but I can't be certain. I'm sure something happened, something was settled, resolved. Do you know?"

Old Trout said nothing for a long moment. When he did speak, his answer was oblique. "How did she seem, when she came back to her house again?"

"Happy." A huge raindrop landed, plop, precisely between Gad's ears, and she shook her head irritably. "Damn this rain. Happy, calm, serene. First time I've seen her that way, most unlike the Julia I've gotten used to. She reminded me . . ." The thought died as the memory Julia had evoked eluded her. To her surprise, the canny old warrior in the water completed the unspoken thought.

"Priestesses in the firelight; I know. If she was happy, it makes no difference what passed between Son and Child. The issue must have been a happy one."

"I can't get through to Luke." Another source of worry, that; the sudden clogging of her energies had shaken Gad badly. "It might just be the weather, it's harder to see with all this electricity in the air. Luke called me, oh, many hours ago, to say that they were all together; Max had got hold of a car and some charts and they were driving here, they were on the way. But since then, there's been nothing; he hasn't called me and he's not answering. So I don't know where they are right now."

"Not far," Old Trout said lazily. "The Child will wait for them; no need to worry there. As for you . . ."

Gad stiffened; she had asked for his help, after all, and must now listen to his opinion and whatever strictures or unpalatable truths he chose to offer. "Yes?"

"You haven't done this in too long a time, little one. Your senses are clouded, but so are mine; cataclysm has that effect. The Child has us all in hand. Why worry?"

A manger, a shift in the stars as a new one blazed into life, snow blowing across the fields . . . Gad shook her wet head, sending water flying.

"You're right. I'd forgotten. I knew there was some reason I suddenly got to thinking the Child would come tonight. But I wasn't far wrong, was I? It's close, very close. I'm sure of that much, at last. Well, I'm right, aren't I?" Silence. "Trout?"

"There are children coming, you know." The high old voice sounded as close to cheerful as it ever could. "On the road from London, and Cardiff, and Edinburgh, little groups of children walking. They aren't sure where they're going, but they're walking, holding hands, singing. There are nine of them right now, at this very moment, sitting in the middle of a stone circle set like a jewel in the Cornish hills, singing, touching. They're all touching." He rumbled with laughter, and the surface of the stream broke in agitation. "No fools, hey, cat? Good senses of smell, you might say?"

"You old sinner." But Gad had relaxed. Her instincts

still functioned, however badly her internal senses might be clogged with anticipation or immediacy. Julia had been happy; she had heard the Child, the Son, eavesdropped upon their meeting. Something had indeed been resolved, some dark question set to rest, and Julia had ceased to worry. She was ready now, primed in her acceptance; the stress of fecundity had softened to serenity, and the Child, when it came, would be born with all the help its mother could give it. Still . . .

As usual, Trout read her perfectly. "Oh, is *that* what's upsetting you? Really, guardian. You've got Ben there, and the children, too; no one expects you to deliver a human child on your own. When has the wheel ever saddled you with such a burden? Anyway, I've already told you, the Child will wait. It will stay where it is until its entourage is complete. If Max and the others arrive tomorrow, the Child will arrive to greet them; if they are delayed for a week, a month, a year, so too will the Child delay, and no harm to the Mother. She's safe, as are we all; protected, secure. You'll have all the help you need."

The banks were churning now, becoming a sucking bog under the steadily increasing pressure of the rain. Gad, her gray fur plastered to her ribs, ignored it; a small lizard scuttled past her and into a hole in the mud. She watched the tip of its long tail thresh for a moment as it wriggled its way to shelter.

"Well," she said eventually. "If you think all's well."

"Oh, I do. You'll have the others here soon enough, so stop worrying. The two ravens that stayed to guard the wise man, are they still fretting over their friends?" He chuckled again, massively. "Such an adventure for them."

"John is, but of course John would. No problem there, trout. I can keep him calm enough."

"Good. Well, then, if that's all, perhaps you'd better get back out of the rain. Water's not congenial for such as you, is it?"

"Bloody right it's not," Gad said with feeling, but she

spoke to emptiness; the great fish had sunk out of sight and hearing. He would curl up in the silt that thickly covered the stream bed, dreaming the storm away.

Gad, stepping carefully and with fastidious distaste through the sea of mud around her, picked her way back toward Sparrow House.

"You'll catch cold," John told Ben. "Really. You will."

Ben, his radiant smile planted across his face, lifted brush from canvas and turned to look at John. The raven was perched on the parapet of the terrace; his feathers were soaked, and every inch of his small body radiated misery. The rain was a blinding curtain, hiding them from the sky and crushing the power of voice and movement.

"No, I won't. I'm never ill, you know that."

"Well, then, I'll catch cold." As if to bear out this plaintive statement, John suddenly sneezed. The sodden black feathers puffed out with the force of it and then settled again. Ben had the look of a child in a fun house at the fair, its face made crazy by staring into distorting mirrors; one eye was fixed on John while the other kept trying to skew back to his canvas. Matthew, craftily deciding that if John was going to stay out here and keep an eye on the painter he had no need to do so, had long since disappeared into the comfort of the old stables.

"Look, Johnny, why don't you go inside?" Ben asked reasonably. "I'm all right; nothing can happen to me where I am. I often paint out in the rain, and I want to finish this picture while the light's so perfect."

"But there isn't any bleeding light!" This came out as an accusing wail. "The whole sky's going to crack like a cannon in a minute, thunder and lightning and I don't know what else besides, and you're staying out here just asking to be struck and turned into a potato crisp! Come on, Ben," the raven said beseechingly, "show sense, have pity."

Ben opened his mouth to reply, but broke off as the

glass doors behind him swung open. Dilly came out, her eyes wide and smiling, her hands floury.

"Oooooh," she breathed, "what are you painting?"

"Now don't you go encouraging him," John began, but was ignored. Ben stepped aside to give Dilly a better view.

"It's the sky," she said uncertainly. "At least—is it the sky? Seems to me . . ."

"Clouds." Ben laughed. "All the clouds in the sky, all of them dressed in their summer clothes. Colors."

Dilly reached out to touch the edge of the canvas with a tentative finger. "But it's more than just clouds, Ben. I see things that aren't clouds. Isn't that a—what is that?"

John, with an effort that made nonsense of his wet feathers, fluttered off the parapet and landed on Ben's shoulder; although he would never admit it, he held Ben's genius in some awe. The three of them stared at the painting, and the bright oils took on vibrancy and glitter as the rain fell around them.

Clouds, yes, the summer sky shot with storm; the painting was a giant jigsaw puzzle, each piece outlined by scarlet or purple or dull gold. Ben had not painted individual clouds, or even masses of them. Rather, he seemed to have seen a hundred small sections in his mind's eye, locking them together with borders of shade and form.

And Dilly was quite right, there was something else in the painting, a dim shape, a trick of the eye, an enigma that swam out of the storm of paint.

"A child," Dilly said. "Sort of."

"Oh," Ben said, surprised and pleased at this conundrum. "A child, you said? I didn't mean to paint one. Where?" He peered at his work; there it was, an amorphous shape with tiny projections that were hands and feet, something that looked like a small body, a large luminous head and the whole thing curled into a tight ball. A blotch of paint, something that might have been the curling edge of rain or a small flat eye or both, stared out at them.

"Oh," Ben said again. "Peculiar. I didn't realize that was there."

"Hadn't we better bring it inside? We don't want the rain spoiling it." Dilly caught the frantic nod of approval from John, and added hastily, "Anyway, I've got a duck cooking, I mustn't let it burn, and Maddy's in there alone. Come on, Ben, let's go in. It looks finished to me, and I'll help you carry it."

Upstairs in her warm room, Julia stood at the window and stared down at their bent and unknowing heads. She was moving slowly tonight, and her hands seemed to have fallen into a permanent position across her stomach. The house was redolent of the smell of roast duck; Matthew, surprisingly, had brought one down that afternoon and dragged it back for Dilly to cook, a gift, he said, for Julia. The smell of food slowly cooking, so mysterious and comforting, drifted up the stairs, and a faint tantalizing haze of it lay across Julia's bedroom like smoke.

She stood at her window, hands across her belly and eyes on her companions three floors below. She was in a strange mood, very strange, something she could not have described even to herself. It was more than a state of mind; her body, too, had succumbed to oddity. All of her muscles seemed to have tautened, put themselves into a state of awareness. Her breathing, too, was coming more slowly than it usually did; she thought she could hear every motion of every individual sinew of lung and throat as they performed their allotted tasks. It made Julia think of old movies, submarines prowling in deep water, bouncing shapes off their sonar. Blip, blip, she thought, but the energy of laughter was beyond her. There was a kind of passivity to all this, a sense of dislocation and yet of purpose, something completely out of her experience. She could not explain it, or object to it; she could only wait for it to make itself clear.

"The sun on your face," she said softly, to no one,

but was that the truth? Certainly she had a sense of someone listening intently, its attention caught, its agreement total. "The rain in your hair."

Something tightened in her belly, and her slow breathing momentarily shortened. Her eyes widened with surprise, but before she could react it was gone and she had slipped back into the cavern of detached calm. Pictures, mere impressions of faces and places, flickered in and out of this strange lightness; a large hairy dog with a pink tongue asleep on a rug, a band of children holding hands and singing as they skipped down a wet and empty highway, a pair of hands, hauntingly familiar, touching thin dark arms that wrapped around their owner as if in protection.

"Go where you wish. Learn what you can." She spoke to the papered walls and the electric atmosphere, her eyes fixed on the group clustered on the terrace. As she watched, Ben made a sweeping gesture with one arm, and took his canvas—what mystery had he painted this time?—from behind. Dilly, a small acolyte, held the drawing room doors open for him as he edged through them; even from this altitude, Julia could see how careful he was being not to smear the wet paint. Dilly followed him inside, and the terrace was empty but for the bird and the wooden easel.

The raven (from this distance it looked like John) waited only for the doors to swing shut behind them. Then he took to the air with clumsy haste, and Julia watched him as he made for the stables with indecent speed.

"Max," she said softly, and cocked her head, listening for an impossible reply, a sign that someone heard. "Max." Another picture, as unclear and alien as the others—this time of a dark head bowed to the flickering tips of many candles. It was as strange and incomprehensible as the others had been, but she felt no compulsion to make sense of it. Some part of her had come to understand that she saw these things through eyes not her own, that however she might be involved they really had little to do with her. A gift, she thought distantly, or an accident; it hardly mattered. To question them, to push, would have been graceless at best and useless in any case.

The smell of cooking was stronger now, and the stimulus breached her fog of abstraction. She realized that she was ravenously hungry; was that garden peas in butter she could smell, hot fruit pie with its sensual perfume, and why was her nose so sensitive all of a sudden? Never mind; just another facet of this strange night, this strange life, this strange world. Go down and eat, and ask no questions.

Colors, colors, more pictures. blended this time. A dancing flame of a young woman with eyes like Max's, holding the wing of a fowl in one hand and wiping grease from her mouth with the other. A long thin hand, male, with a curious gold ring on one finger; the hand lay restfully on a scarred wooden table. What, who, did it matter? Above her, Angelica Kaufman's privileged beauties watched in knowing sympathy.

"Oh, to hell with it," she said out loud, and with her hands cupped under her belly in a timeless gesture of protection and support, she turned toward the source of the tempting smells.

She had reached the door, had actually set her hand on the brass knob, when her muscles contracted in a wrench of violence and pain that nearly knocked her over. She reeled, fighting for breath, and as the room turned wildly she felt the heavy vital shock of the Child dropping and the cold trickle of placental fluid running down her legs.

13

All Roads Lead Somewhere

"MAX?" HE STIRRED, moaning a little to himself. Someone was speaking directly into his ear, the voice penetrating through layers of sleep that were so unusually dense tonight; he was dreaming possibly, or possibly not.

"Max."

Cramps, small and sharp and vindictive, ran up his legs and dragged him a bit closer toward consciousness. With the groggy abstraction of the sleeper, he grew aware that he, who always slept flat on his back, had tonight pulled himself into a ball. His legs had been tucked up against his chest, perhaps for hours, and the constricted blood vessels were protesting, punishing him as they expanded with blood that was suddenly free to move again. He flexed his ankles, instinctively trying to stretch away the needling agony in his limbs.

"Max!"

The voice, this time, was imperative, banishing what sleep still lingered. He opened his eyes.

The first thing to hit him was the silence. As he slept,

as they all slept, the storm had blown itself out, leaving a bottomless quiet and a sharp clean smell behind it. Not a cricket sang, not a leaf stirred; the narrow child's bed on which he lay might have been adrift in the vacuum of deep space for all the noise that surrounded it, and his own name spoken in Raj's soft voice boomed impossibly loud.

Raj himself stood, a knife-thin shape towering over Max in the fresh darkness. He caught the glint of bright metal as the Indian lifted his hand, but no, he was hallucinating or dreaming or something, the room was utterly dark and not even gold shines in darkness. And yet the ring was shimmering, pulsing, alive . . .

"What?" Max muttered, and tried to knuckle the mists of sleep from his eyes. "What, Raj?"

"We must go. We must go *now.*" Raj squatted by the bedside, his hands coming to rest on the light blanket; Max, caught by fascination, stared at the ring. There was no mistake. The ring grew brighter as he stared, and the slender serpents twisted and cavorted—good grief, were they moving? No, it couldn't be . . .

"Hurry." The soft high voice ran across the room at him; Calypso, fully dressed, stood in the doorway. And there was the Son behind her, his skin that under this wash of moon was the color of fine old pottery gleaming like the gold of the ring, his face consumed by a strange hunger, an impossible need.

"Please, please." Raj stood once more, and fluttered his hands in an agony of impatience. "No time to dawdle, no, none. We must . . ."

"Oh. Oh!" And now it had come clear to Max as well, the knowledge behind their heavy urgency, the pearly shape slowly rotating so that its head now pointed downward, the trembling and roaring as the still body of fluid it swam in was disturbed, something breaching the sac and the fluid draining away to nothing. "Oh lord, oh no, not yet, it's too soon, too soon. What time it is, anyway? And where in hell are my clothes, I can't find my—"

"It is half past three, or very nearly. I think this has been building for some hours, and we are late. The Child will await us, I think. But the longer we tarry here, the longer Julia's suffering. Here. Hurry." Raj handed Max a sock, a shoe, a pair of trousers.

Outside the window, the night was split by a wild croaking; the ravens, lashed by impatience, were circling the house. Max wrenched his shirt over his head and pulled the keys to the Volvo from his pants pocket.

"All right," he said, and even to his own ears his voice was strange, too loud, too high, the baritone turned by the alchemy of events to a tenor, and underlined by a dreadful expectancy. "Come along."

He pulled the car out onto the motorway at a dangerous speed, bouncing Whimsy into a muted protest as the heavy tires skidded in the standing pools of rainwater. Above them, the ravens spread their wings to catch an updraft and shot forward until they had been nearly swallowed by the darkness, racing ahead of the Volvo.

The green sign that said TAUNTON was no more than half a mile behind them when they spotted the first children, walking toward the north.

They were a ragged group, a dozen strong and not one of them older than ten, and they were singing; the voices were uneven and delightful, a high-pitched choir with angelic overtones. They held hands, never even glancing at the car, and in his window seat beside Max the Son looked at them and heard their soaring joy. Warm tears filled his eyes and spilled down his cheeks.

"*Benedictus,*" he said quietly, "*Benedictus domini.* Too soon or not, it's coming."

"Yes." The urgency was intolerable, a wasp buzzing angrily in Max's ear, growing thicker with every passing moment. Regardless of the slick and dangerous road, he pushed the stick into its highest gear and stamped his foot down on the accelerator as far as it would go, wishing for a vagrant moment that, in choosing a chariot, he had opted for speed rather than reliability.

But the Volvo surprised him; after an initial shudder at this unexpected treatment, it seemed to flex its muscles and shrug in agreement. The engine gave a single shattering roar and the big car leaped forward at a hundred miles an hour. The green hills, growing more distinct as the day grew closer, flashed by; the road curved westward. Bridgewater. Warminster. A swing to the north once again; the turnoff for Frome, and a split for the London road. He kept one wary eye on the amount of petrol left in the tank, another on the dashboard clock. Half past four. If he had to stop . . .

In the back seat, Calypso gave a sigh of pleasure. She spun the handle of her window, letting the night in, and stuck her head out to catch the wind in her hair. Raj, whose temperament and training in meditation made high speed for any reason an anathema to him, had been sitting in miserable silence for nearly an hour. He turned his head to regard her now with a mixture of awe and surprise. She caught his gaze and pulled her head back inside.

"I am enjoying this very much," she said apologetically. "To move like the birds, or the great cats of the savanna, I mean. Never have I done this, for to sail is to depend on the wind. If it is willing, your sails fill and you move well, but never like this; if it gives no mercy, you may be becalmed for days, weeks, a long time. This," and she swept her hands skyward, "is different. It moves of itself, very fast; see, we go faster than even the ravens."

"More children," Max said, and the others turned to stare; there were five of them this time, hardly more than babies. Calypso, yearning toward their song, watched them grow larger, then smaller; they finally disappeared in a kaleidoscope of overalls and pale waving hands as the car flashed by. In the distance, they could just make out the graceful lines of a cathedral spire. The small high voices, haunting the coming morning with song, trailed the car for a few moments and were gone.

"How long, how long?" The Son was watching the eastern sky, where the ravens flew; the black birds were gradually developing silhouettes against broadening streaks of light. "Dawn's coming."

"An hour or so. I don't know. Don't distract me." But the road ahead held more than promise, it held phantom shapes. Julia on her back, her great bare stomach a mountain range on a golden quilt. A man whose hands looked newly scrubbed pressing gently here, there, a sudden sharp cry from the woman on the bed as her whole body tensed and then relaxed. Sweat gleaming on her brow. Red hair, sticky with exertion, streaming across a sodden pillow. Two little girls, one on the floor, the other sitting on the edge of the bed, holding Julia's hand. Dim shapes that seemed outside the picture, a horse, a sheep, graceful marble stairs curving into a green lawn. Outside the room, birds that were twin to the ones above his own head perched uneasily on the window ledge.

And a gray cat at the foot of the bed, her long body alert and aware in every muscle, her yellow eyes gleaming like beacons.

"How soon, Ben?"

"Haven't a clue. I've never done this before, you know, not with a person. Lambs, once or twice, and puppies." Ben was apologetic, and Julia managed a feeble smile. Really, Gad thought, she was coping very well, considering pain and fever and pure apprehension. Gad, of them all, was an old hand at birth. But she had always borne her kittens with perfect ease, and privately considered the travails human mothers went through to be a bad joke on the part of nature; surely, twelve hours of pain was excessive?

Julia tensed, relaxed, let her breath out. She had bitten deep into her lower lip, and her face was flushed. She turned her head on the pillow with a jerky, spasmodic motion, and looked beseechingly at Gad.

"Nowhere near ready yet," the cat told her quietly,

answering that look. "I make it every ten minutes." A thought flashed through her mind, and she shared it with Julia; perhaps trouble shared was, after all, trouble eased. "I'm pregnant myself, did you know? Traditionally, I have my litter the same day this happens; I've always timed it that way. I didn't realize it was coming so early, so this lot will be just another litter of plain kittens." Ah, well; she'd had a good night's mating out of it, anyway.

Julia's chuckle turned into a whimper of pain, and the bones of her thin face suddenly stretched the skin. "Gad. You swear that Max is coming?"

"He's on his way." She had been unable to get through to him; something, perhaps the very urgency of her need, had blocked her. But if she could not communicate with him, she could see him perfectly. The pictures were the clearest she had yet received. The blue car was traveling at an incredible speed, road signs and children and empty cities flashing by in a blur. "In an hour, maybe less. Not to worry; there's plenty of time."

Light footsteps sounded on the parquet floors outside the bedroom, and Dilly poked her head in. "I've brought up some apple juice, and hot buns. Anyone?"

"Yes, please." Of anything else that she had felt during the long slow hours of increasingly dreadful pain, Julia would remember the constant thirst as the worst of it. She had already drained a quart of bottled water and would have consumed even more, had Gad let her. But Gad had wryly pointed out that getting up and strolling into the bathroom would create some problems, and Gad certainly knew what she was talking about. "Dilly?"

"Here." Julia, lifting her head and closing her eyes against another thrust of pain, groped for the glass with gratitude. This was not the way she had envisioned these hours, so many months of planning, imagining, waiting. A sterile room, nurses with their starched caps and blue and white uniforms, machines to monitor heartbeat and breathing and heaven only knew what else, the squeak of sensible rubber-soled shoes at her bedside, the murmur and hum of a busy hospital. Instead . . .

"Drink." The liquid trickled down her throat. She swallowed it gratefully, wishing she had asked questions about dealing with labor while there were still people alive to ask, wondering if all female creatures in this situation had moments of hating what they carried, resenting it for the pain it caused, seeing the invisible child as a parasite, a leech, caring for nothing but itself.

"Well, of course we do." Gad came to curl up beside her, and gently licked her face; the rough tongue was alive and reassuring, far better than a proper rag dipped in cool water could ever be. "Humans get it the worst before it's born, you know, and that's hardly surprising when you consider the anatomy and complexity involved here. Nine bloody months, good grief, what a travesty, and then hours of pain before the little bleeder decides it's ready. Cats, most other creatures really, get it more after the babies are born; hours spent lying on your side, half the time you're out in the wild and you have to do your own hunting and you can't. Days and days without food, but you have to feed the kittens, they're always hungry."

"Hungry." Julia relaxed a little. The pain had receded a bit, and Gad's bitterness was somehow soothing; it gave her a sense of communion, of travails shared.

The cat shuddered reminiscently. "Squeaking in your ear, four or five of them if you're lucky. Once or twice I've had *eight*. And all the time they're flexing their claws against you, and believe me, Julia my love, those claws are sharp. And if danger threatens, you can't just leave, oh no. You have to stand and fight. If there was just the one baby you might be able to get yourself up a tree, but with four or five, no. At least you people usually only have one."

"But you don't go through this." Julia waved one limp arm; the gesture encompassed the previous seven hours, the huge stain on the rug, the pain that seemed to mount with constant malevolence, the flood of fever that had taken her in a harsh grip some time before midnight and refused to relinquish its hold. "Yours is quick, isn't it?"

"Quicker than this mess, yes. I'll give it that." Why so long for humans, anyway? It was a question that had often exercised Gad's mind. Was it, in fact, because a human baby is such a complexity? Was it because so much more went into their genetic makeup? Original sin, good grief? And did it really matter, anyway?

"Gar," Maddy said from the floor, "Gar."

The cat, surprised, looked down. Maddy was sitting upright, vaguely gesturing at the window; Gad had swung herself around before her ears had properly registered the sudden commotion outside.

A flapping of wings, croaks. Something dropped out of the indigo sky and landed on the window ledge. Where two ravens had sat there were now three.

While the drama was being acted out in the big bedroom, the two birds had sat silent and watchful. Neither bird had ever seen a human child being born; indeed, being males, even their exposure to egg laying was minimal. Not knowing what to say or how to react in a situation alien to them, John and Matthew had opted for the role of uneasy observers. They did not speak, even to each other; John, watching Ben, was aware of an occasional flicker of pride in his pet that surprised him.

They said nothing, yet their concentration on the scene before them was total. So absorbed were they, in fact, that until Luke alighted between them on the broad ledge they were unaware of his proximity. Matthew, in particular, was startled into nearly losing his grip.

"Luke!"

"Morning, mates." Luke hunched and settled. "Fine day for flying. How's tricks?"

"What?" John turned to gaze at his friend. "What are you doing here? Where's Mark?"

"Still guiding the others. No, don't get your knickers in a twist; they're nearly at Chippenham, or were when

I left them. Give them another twenty minutes, half-hour at the most, and they'll be here. We just thought one of us had better stay to show them the roads—that map Max got isn't too clear on the country lanes around here." He craned his neck toward the room. "Julia all right, then?"

"As well as can be expected." As if in protest of this reading, Julia gasped, her knuckles knotting as she gripped the edge of the quilt; Luke, his eyes popping, turned in bewilderment to John, but the other shook his head and Luke was silent. Gad, who had been making for the window, immediately turned back to the bed where Ben was bending over, his hand on Julia's brow.

"Julia," he was saying urgently. "Julia?"

"A bad one. Closer together now." The voice was paper thin, and her pupils had expanded until her eyes looked completely black. "My god. If I'd known . . ."

The light. Where is the light?

"Oh god." They had all heard it, words bouncing off walls, off skulls, off the lining of thought and will that is in the world outside. Julia was trembling. "Oh no."

Simply a matter of finding the light at the end of the tunnel. A little joke, no more than that.

"Ouch, damn, blast." They saw the wave of pain hit her and then recede; four minutes apart, Gad thought, and stretched her neck desperately toward the window. Come on, people, hurry, please, things are moving, it isn't fair. "Not yet," she said wildly, in her mind, "they aren't here yet, stay where you are, you mustn't . . ."

Tell them to hurry. Gravity works very well, and I'm being pulled. Can't wait forever. Not much longer.

In the sky to the south, a small black dot rose high against the breaking sunrise. It moved rapidly toward them, taking on shape and clarity, a rough suggestion of shape becoming wings, head, body. It came closer at high speed.

Julia, unaware of anything but the wracking spasms that shook her entire body, had at last given in to tears; she was crying steadily, a mixture of joy and resentment and hurt, the tears running off her flattened cheekbones, soaking the pillow beneath her head. As if in ironic counterpoint to the slow wrenching sobs, they all heard the approaching hum of a car's engine.

Voices, voices.

The Child could hear them all perfectly. More than that, it felt the texture and shape of them; each was alive, each held a life-colored nugget of something different, something useful, something valuable, something to help or hinder it as it left the broken waters of the womb behind.

The Guardian, desperate and pleading, wanting it to stay within its pulsing cavern until the time was right . . .

and the Mother, that lovely and tender spirit, bruised and crushed under the weight of a new life, weeping as the Child would weep when it was hungry or needed comfort, struggling, moving in her complex supine ballet, wanting only that this pain be done and over with . . .

and the Father, an entity both visceral and cerebral, a living picture: flaming with tension, his lips compressed, his eyes narrowed, pointing at the Child like an arrow but not quite yet where he needed to be . . .

and the Adversary who was an adversary no longer, beautiful and placid, wrestling with memories of his own birth in deepest winter in a decrepit barn so far from here, a new star in the western sky or was it the eastern and somewhere there were silver voices raised in song . . .

and the Grandfather, that ancient teacher, lying deep in his bed of mud and running water, waiting and calm . . .

and children, so many children, holding hands, each of them a little flag of joyous self-possession, their voices ringing out to whoever or whatever might be listening . . .

and the Three, bearing gifts, one close by with the gift of vision, two together, bearing living gold and an old clay jar full of healing . . .

and the Shadow, the Comfort, old Simon with his horns

curling away from his strong broad head, planted in his meadow outside . . .

and from somewhere an incomprehensible image, long sleek metal ships moving slowly across the ocean floor . . .

and of course the Child itself, listening idly to its own voice, its attention elsewhere.

Blip, blip.

The light I can see the light

"No, get back, not yet, wait just a few moments more, please, I can hear the car" and that was Gad.

Muscles wrapped around me I'm being pushed the game is almost over now I've been in here long enough

"Twist your head a little you're hurting too much drop your arms to your sides are you trying to rip the poor woman in half it's like swimming just pretend you're swimming use those feet come along" and that was Old Trout.

Fluid, dance, what are these things that move behind me, they're pushing me toward the light, something's banging, what is that noise is it me what

"A car door" and that was someone the Child couldn't quite place, a girl child, a light patter of footsteps as small feet raced across a carpeted floor, the steps growing both louder and fainter as they moved from carpet to wood. "Here up here we're all waiting for you it's coming we can see the top of its head!"

My head is stuck no it isn't I can see but the light is blinding me, too bright, someone dim the lights

"Max" and that was the Mother's voice, torn to shreds with pain and anger and disbelief and delight. "It's coming I can oh god help me someone please . . ."

"Some liar's game," the Father said and the bed shook with the weight of him as he went to work. "Sun's just about up now, of course it would get itself born at sunrise, we should have known."

I can move my head, here is the world, almost free

"It's all right now, everything's fine, there's the head—oh, look, it's got lots of hair, soft red hair like yours, lovely, push, Julia, push harder, it's almost out, it's almost free'' and that was the Father's voice again, was it the Father's voice, could that harsh line of accumulated grudges really sound so gentle, yes it could. "Here, help me."

Air, I can breathe, what, it's cold, noise

"It's a girl," someone said, a female voice, she of the Three who carried the precious balm on her shoulder, and as the Child drew in lungfuls of the first morning and began to wail lustily, a pair of soft arms laid it against an even softer breast and covered it as the rosebud mouth found a single nipple and began to feed. "Very pretty, a little girl like a small pale flower. Now we must cut the cord, and clean it."

"No harder than plucking a chicken," the Father said, and he had taken Julia's free hand and was holding it hard and his voice was light and teasing as it had never once been in two thousand years.

"A girl," the Mother said, and her voice was worn to a rasp. "A girl. Max, is it you, is it really you, I wanted to kill you, strangle you, but I don't now. Why don't I want to strangle you anymore?"

"Never mind," he said soothingly, "never mind. You can strangle me later, if you'd like. It might even have some result now. I can die now if I want to, that's right, isn't it?" His laughter rang out, startling the birds at the window, reaching the lawn below where Simon and Whiskey were trying to assure a large woolly sheepdog that he ought to relax a bit, no need for his talents with only one sheep.

Dying who said anything about dying no dying now

"A girl," said the Guardian, stretching out a paw to touch the large downy head with infinite gentleness. "It's been a long time since you people had one of those atop the wheel. A very long time. I should have guessed."

"Pretty," said Ben, smiling, and at the window his own guardians smiled with him as well as birds can smile. "I want to make a picture of her. Is that all right?"

"Benedictus," said the Adversary, on his knees beside the bed. Whatever lusts or memories or needs had hag-ridden him were gone now; he smiled at the Child, his face holding nothing but a tranquil joy. *"Benedictus domini."*

"Excuse me," said the last of the Three, the one who was pulling the golden ring off his finger and laying it on the small table near Julia's head. The snakes were motionless now, their power stilled or perhaps simply transmuted into something else. On the floor, the older of the two little girls was examining a clay jar, shaking it, trying to guess what it held. "I am sure that your Latin is better than mine, yes, but should that not be *domina*?"

Epilogue

"YOU'RE GOING? WHAT do you mean, you're going? Going where, what are you talking about?"

Julia set her book—a tattered mystery novel—face down on the grass, and turned to stare up at the two men. On the lawn a few feet away, the little girl was playing with a raven; the cloudy blue eyes possessed by all infants had long since altered, by the weird and subtle chemistry of growth, to a gray as stormy as Calypso's sea, and the thick red down had become a feathery mop of deep auburn curls. She was fourteen months old now, just beginning to walk, and her face was smeared with chocolate. From the heat-hazed distance, down by the stream where Old Trout lay, they could hear the distorted echo of Calypso, singing.

"Well." Max stood looking down at his small daughter, his black eyes impossible to read. "I wanted . . . that is, we wanted . . ."

"Spit it out, spit it out." John, hopping back from the pinch of the Child's plump fingers, looked up; he nearly tripped over a large atlas, the publisher's imprint covered by a metallic sticker that said Kindred's Book of Exeter, Ltd., and gave an irritable croak. "What's the story, then? You blokes restless? Just a wee little touch of the old wanderlust, maybe?"

Max began to speak slowly, as if he were trying to clarify something to himself as well as to Julia. "I thought, you see, that when the Child was born, that was it, the end, finis. I was supposed to stay alive until a certain time came and a certain chain of events had been achieved. No longer than that. But I was wrong, as it turns out." He smiled sideways at the Son, who stood beside him, and made a small pun. "Dead wrong."

Julia, bewildered, opened her mouth for speech. The Son interrupted her.

"I saw it when I first spoke with Her. She told me that I'd been robbed of my life, that it was due to me; She told me there was to be no more dying, that lives would go far longer now. So I have time, time to see things that were kept from me, denied me. And that isn't only truth for me, you see. It's truth for Max, too."

"I go, but you remain." Julia, who had no wish to understand, understood nevertheless. She felt her heart turn over. "Except that's backward now, isn't it? You go, but I remain. You're restless."

"Very." Really, Max looked like a small boy standing there; he kept shifting his weight from foot to foot and his eyes, refusing to be held, kept sliding guiltily away from hers. "Seventy more years, maybe even more, but with a difference this time. I'll age now, I can love now, I'll die eventually. But not yet. So . . ."

"Restless." There was a weight of unshed tears in Julia's heart, but she nodded, smiling; on the grass the Child had grown quiet, watching them out of her wide gray eyes. "Both of you. Restless."

"Yes." The Son spoke eagerly. "There was so much I never got to see, and now I can, I have the time to see it, to travel, to look at the world I ruled but never really saw." He suddenly became aware of the pain in her face, and his voice faltered. "Julia . . ."

Go. You'll come back again, and we'll be waiting.

"Thank you." Max bent to tousle his daughter's hair; she smiled, a closed-mouth smile that showed no teeth, and reached out to touch the brilliantly colored atlas her father had brought, along with the maps he had needed to find her, from Exeter. "I can guide him, Julia; there isn't a corner of this world I don't know or haven't seen. And anyway, I'd like to go. After two thousand years of movement, sitting on my hands comes hard."

"Well." There would be loss, yes, but there would be vision too. She would see them, Max and the man who now called himself Josh, as they passed over the wide lawns, stopping off to bid farewell to Dilly, making sure that the stream-driven generator they had built to power her oven would function without them. She would pick up their shadows as they made their way through Sparrowdene, past the leaded windows of Congreve's to the small Georgian cottages where groups of children now lived. The foam of the sea would fall gently across her skin, she would taste the salt along with them, as they woke Calypso's small craft from its year-long rest at Plymouth and set it to the southern lands.

And they would come back; the Child had promised.

"A few years." Max bent and kissed her nose. "Only a few years, and we'll be back; Josh wants to see Rome, and America, and the deserts of Africa. We'll be back before you really notice we're gone."

"Liar." Julia smiled, but her eyes were hazed with tears. "Well, go on then, what are you waiting for? Pack up some food if you'd like; Gad brought us some fish and I've smoked it, so it'll keep awhile. Good thing to take with you. Have you said goodbye to the others?"

"No. But we will. Julia?"

Eyes that were tunnels into time . . . "What?"

"Stay young for me." And then they were going, walking across the green to the waiting road, lifting their hands to wave at the horse and the sheep who grazed together in peace, stopping to pat the dog, stilling a moment as Gad's voice reached them from wherever she hunted, free of those last four mewling kittens at last.

Come back, Julia thought, come back someday, and as if in reply their voices reached her, thin, already distant, Josh's wheedling and cajoling.

"Come on, Max, you've kept me dangling long enough. Don't you know any jokes? You must have learned some jokes in two thousand years, and where I was they were, well, discouraged. Jokes? Please, Max?"

"I know one," came the rich baritone, consciously amused and wicked, and as they swung through the gates to the world Julia's face crinkled in tears and laughter. "A good one, about a carpenter's son and a toy maker named Gepetto . . ."

to gaze at the horse and the sheep who grazed together in peace, stopping to pat the dog, smiling a moment as God's voice patched them from wherever she moved, free of those last four meowling kittens at last.

"Come back, Jesus! Come back someday," and as if in reply their voices reached her, dim, already distant, Josh's wheedling and cajoling.

"Come on, Josh, you've kept me dangling long enough. Don't you know any jokes? You must have learned some jokes in two thousand years, and where I was they were, well, discouraged. Jokes? Please, Man?"

"I know one," came the rich baritone, conspicuously amused and wicked, and as they swung through the gates to the world Jenna's face crinkled in tears and laughter. "A good one, about a carpenter's son and a toy maker named Geppetto . . ."

ABOUT THE AUTHOR

Deborah Grabien has previously published a mystery, *Eyes in the Fire*, and a historical novel, *The Fire Queen*. She divides her time between her home in San Francisco and her father's native England.